PATRIOTS: VOL..
SONS OF LIBERTY

DANIEL REED—Firstborn son of a wealthy Virginia family, he has come to Boston to continue his education in the law. But his plans soon fall hostage to history as he follows the siren call of freedom for the British colonies.

ROXANNE DARRAGH—A fiery-haired, hot-tempered young woman, she is sometimes led by her devotion to liberty to take foolish risks. She has sworn that no other affection will replace her dedication to her cause, but the dashing Daniel Reed may give her reason to renounce her vow.

ELLIOT MARKHAM—The son of a successful Boston businessman and staunch supporter of King George III, he feels trapped by the high expectations of his family. He is torn between the ideals of his cousin Daniel and the loyalist leanings of the young woman he loves, and soon he must make his choice.

QUINCY REED—Daniel's impulsive fourteen-year-old brother, he embraces with reckless enthusiasm everything life has to offer—including joining the growing rebellion against the Crown. One day his adventures may cut his young life short.

MURDOCH BUCHANAN—A rough frontiersman accustomed to living at the edge of civilization in the Ohio River valley, he returns to Boston in time to join in the patriots' cause. A man who has learned to fight with any weapon, from tomahawk to flintlock, bare knuckles to knives, he will become a close friend to Daniel . . . and a valuable ally.

PATRIOTS
Volume I

SONS
OF
LIBERTY

Adam Rutledge

BCI Producers of **The First Americans,**
The Holts and **The Frontier Trilogy: Westward!**

Book Creations Inc., Canaan, NY • Lyle Kenyon Engel, Founder

SONS OF LIBERTY

*A Bantam Domain Book / published by arrangement with
Book Creations, Inc.*

Bantam edition / July 1992

*Produced by Book Creations, Inc.
Lyle Kenyon Engel, Founder*

*DOMAIN and the portrayal of a boxed "d" are trademarks of
Bantam Books, a division of
Bantam Doubleday Dell Publishing Group, Inc.*

ISBN 0-553-29199-8

Published simultaneously in the United States and Canada

*Bantam Books are published by Bantam Books, a division of Bantam
Doubleday Dell Publishing Group, Inc. Its trademark, consisting of the
words "Bantam Books" and the portrayal of a rooster, is Registered in
U.S. Patent and Trademark Office and in other countries. Marca
Registrada. Bantam Books, 666 Fifth Avenue, New York, New York
10103.*

PRINTED IN THE UNITED STATES OF AMERICA

OPM   0 9 8 7 6 5 4 3 2 1

SONS
OF
LIBERTY

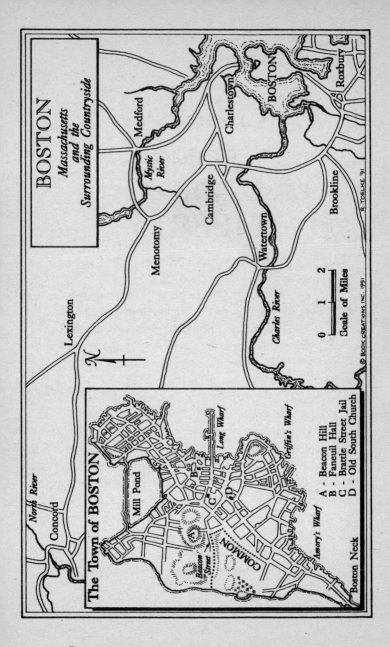

Chapter One

T he young man on the big bay horse was thirsty. He had been riding since early morning and, anxious to get to his destination, had not stopped for food or drink. Now as he spotted a tavern up ahead at a little crossroads, a grin broke out across his tanned face. Surely it would not hurt to stop for a quick mug of ale on a hot day.

In this summer of 1773, Daniel Reed was twenty years old, and much of that twenty years had been spent on the plantation of his parents, Geoffrey and Pamela Reed. It had not been idle time. Daniel had hunted and fished and spent every possible moment outdoors. His skin had acquired a healthy brown sheen, and the sun had also lightened his curly, naturally dark brown hair. Even relaxing in the saddle of the horse he had ridden from Virginia, he appeared unusually tall, lean, and muscular. He wore high-topped boots, dark brown whipcord pants, a lightweight linen shirt, and a black tricorn hat canted to the back of his head.

His brown eyes were intelligent. Despite his outdoor activities, his academic education had not been neglected. He had been to the best academy in Virginia and then to Yale College in the colony of Connecticut, and he had excelled in his studies at both places. He had done well enough that his parents had decided he should continue his schooling near Boston.

A long-barreled flintlock musket, powder horn, and shot pouch were slung on one side of the saddle. Another bag filled with food and other supplies hung from the opposite side. To some people, a journey on horseback from Virginia to Massachusetts might be a daunting prospect. Daniel, however, had thoroughly enjoyed the trip, even dawdling along the way to do some hunting.

As he reined the bay to a halt in front of the tavern, he heard loud voices coming from within the building. Several horses were tied up at the front rail. This was farming country, and no doubt the tavern served as a gathering place for the people who lived hereabouts. Daniel was not surprised to find it doing a brisk business, even at this time of day.

He walked in and went directly across the room to the long bar behind which the white-aproned proprietor held court. The man was saying to several patrons lined up at the bar, "The British were begging for trouble, if you ask me. That damned Dudington put a lot o' good men in jail."

"A lot of smugglers, you mean," countered one of the men. "Common criminals, that's what they are."

"For bringing in tea that ain't taxed half to death?" the bartender asked. "That's no crime as far as I'm concerned."

Another man spoke up. "Those Rhode Islanders went too far when they burned the *Gaspee*, though. Wanton destruction's not going to solve anything."

Daniel leaned on the bar and, as he listened to the discussion, tried to catch the eye of the proprietor. The men's voices were loud and angry on both sides of the argument. Daniel frowned in concentration and finally remembered the incident about which they were talking. The year before, one of the British ships assigned to patrol the coast off Rhode Island had gone aground, and several boatloads of colonists, angry with the Crown's policies on the importing of tea, had rowed out to the vessel, taken it over from its crew, and set it on fire. The British authorities had been furious over the matter, but they had never been able to track down the men responsible. Daniel had read about it in the Virginia newspapers, as well as having heard his father and other men discuss it.

But all that had happened over a year earlier. Why were these Massachusetts men still arguing about it?

He finally got the attention of the bartender and asked, "Could I have a mug of ale, please?"

The man sauntered down the bar, leaned his big palms on the hardwood, and gave Daniel a dubious stare. "Be ye a patriot or a Tory?" he demanded.

Daniel blinked, taken aback by the question. "I . . . I don't suppose I know," he finally replied.

Men from both sides of the discussion seized on that. They gathered around him, hammering sharp questions at him, demanding to know his allegiances. He yearned to shout out that all he really wanted was to get to Boston.

"Forget about the ale," he told the bartender, turning and trying to push his way out of the knot of men that had formed around him. "I'll just water my horse and be gone."

"Not so quick, lad." A hard hand fell on his shoulder, stopping him. "Ye haven't answered our questions. Nobody's neutral in this anymore. Yer either a patriot or a damned loyalist!"

"Damned loyalist, is it?" snapped one of the men. "Better that than a treasonous, treacherous rebel!"

"Ye'd best take that back, Finn!"

"I'll do no such. And I'll not kowtow to the likes of you, either!"

Nervously licking his lips, Daniel watched both sides surge toward each other, with him in the middle. "Excuse me . . ." he began.

Then the punches started to fly.

Daniel ducked under them, intending to head for the floor and get out of this ludicrous predicament any way he could. On the way down, though, someone shoved him hard, and he lost his balance. He fell heavily, and someone stepped on him. Above him, the argument had degenerated into a brawl. Men shouted curses and grunted in pain as blows fell.

Rolling over desperately, Daniel got clear of the melee and sprang to his feet. Everyone else in the place seemed to have forgotten about him. They were too busy swinging fists and trying to smash mugs over one another's heads. Regretting that he had ever stopped, Daniel scrambled for his hat, which had come off during the confusion, brushed himself off, and headed for the door.

Outside, he watered the bay at the trough, swung up into the saddle, and decided he was willing to stay thirsty until he got to Boston.

It was amazing, he thought as he sent the horse cantering down the road, that men would come to blows over something that had happened somewhere else over a year earlier. They had to hold strong views about the situation if they were willing to fight about it now.

He would have to think about that, he told himself, but later. Right now, he had the last leg of his journey to complete. With any luck he would be in Boston before the day was over.

Daniel felt excitement surge through him as he drew rein and brought his horse to a stop on a hill overlooking the city of Boston, its blue harbor to the east and the Charles River to the west. He had been to this bustling Atlantic coast city before, but the sight of it never failed to thrill him.

"Bound for town, are ye?"

Daniel turned to locate the source of the question. An old man in a floppy hat was at the reins of a mule-drawn wagon loaded with produce from one of the area's outlying farms. As he passed slowly he grinned at Daniel, revealing a large gap in his front teeth.

"That's right," Daniel said. "I'm going to Boston."

The old man gave him a little wave and moved on. Daniel stayed where he was, wanting to enjoy the sensation of looking out over the city for a few more minutes.

Arrangements had been made for Daniel to stay with his aunt and uncle during the summer, before finding a place of his own in the fall when he entered Harvard to read for the law. He was eager to see his cousin Elliot again. Putting his horse into a trot, he headed down the hill toward the Shawmut peninsula.

The road led to Boston Neck, a narrow spit of land where the Charles and the harbor just about met. On the other side of Boston Neck, past the public gallows, the peninsula widened rapidly, its confines filled by the sprawling community. Daniel followed Orange Street for several blocks, then cut over to Common Street, which ran along the east side of Boston Common. Traffic was heavy. He made his way among carriages, wagons, men on horseback like himself, and many pedestrians. On this sunny day the large, open, parklike green was busy. Couples strolled hand in hand on the soft grass; children trailed by barking dogs ran and played; old-timers, enjoying the youngsters' antics, sat under the double row of trees that bounded the common.

Under other circumstances, Daniel might have considered stopping for a few moments. Benjamin and Polly Markham, his uncle and aunt, knew he was coming, but considering the distance between Virginia and Massachusetts, it had been impossible to predict to the day when he would arrive. However, he felt sure his relatives would not be sitting around waiting for him. If he knew his mother's brother, Uncle Benjamin would be hard at work as usual, furthering the interests of the shipping company in which he was a partner.

Though no one would object if he stayed to enjoy the common for a while, Daniel pushed on, unwilling to delay his arrival any longer. The road cut across the northeast corner of the common and then ran straight through the fashionable residential district of Beacon Hill, where the first house in Boston had been built a hundred and fifty years earlier by William Blackstone, a settler from Charlestown, across the river to the north. The pace was more sedate here, with fewer people on the streets.

The Markham family owned a large house on one of Beacon Hill's cobblestone lanes. To someone accustomed to the open spaces of Virginia, the houses in Boston seemed to be crammed too close together, but Daniel knew that he would soon get used to the crowded living conditions of the city. With water surrounding it on both sides, he thought, Boston had grown about as much as it ever could.

He rode up the hill and drew rein in front of the elegant

three-story home owned by his aunt and uncle. It was con-
structed of red brick and sat behind a flagstone sidewalk. As
he swung down from his saddle and fastened the horse's
reins to a wrought-iron pole that supported an oil lamp, the
front door of the house burst open and a young man came
running out.

"Daniel!" he called. "Is that you?"

"It's been less than a year since you saw me in Virginia,
Elliot," Daniel replied with a grin, turning to greet his
cousin. "You ought to recognize me."

Elliot Markham came to a stop in front of Daniel.
"Yes, I think I do recall that ugly countenance," he gibed.
Suddenly, he grabbed Daniel's hand and pumped it up and
down in an enthusiastic handshake. "How are you, cousin?"

"Slightly saddlesore but fine." Smiling broadly and still
shaking Elliot's hand, Daniel threw his other arm around his
cousin and thumped him heartily on the back. "What about
you?"

"Never better, now that you're here."

Elliot Markham was a year younger than Daniel, an
inch shorter, and had blue eyes to go with his blond hair and
fair skin. He was also hopeless when it came to woodcraft,
Daniel remembered from Elliot's visits to the Reed plantation. They had gone hunting together often but rarely
bagged anything—since hunting with Elliot was like tramp-
ing through the woods with a squad of militia. He made
enough noise for twelve men—more, if they were
Virginians.

But Daniel supposed he was just as much out of place
here in the city. There was no denying that Elliot was more
worldly and sophisticated, even though he was a year
younger. Daniel did not consider himself a bumpkin, and he
was certainly not an embarrassment in a social setting . . . but

he had his cousin to thank for refining his manners to meet the stringent standards of Boston. He had learned a great deal from Elliot.

"Come on inside," Elliot said, linking arms with Daniel to steer him toward the door. "I'm sure Mother and Father will be very glad to see you. We didn't know when you'd get here, but I've been keeping my eyes open for you. I just happened to be passing by the front window when I saw you ride up."

The door was still open. Elliot took Daniel through it into the foyer. The walls were papered in a rich brocade pattern, and to one side sat a small table with elaborately carved legs. Covering it was a linen cloth, and an oil lamp with a crystal mantle was set in the middle. On the opposite wall were hung two paintings, both landscapes of pastoral English scenes. At least Daniel had always supposed they were English; he had never been to England and possessed no desire to go there. The colonies were plenty big enough for him.

The parlor opened to the left of the foyer, and a hallway led straight ahead. Elliot started down this corridor, saying, "Father's in his study. He has some of his associates with him, but I'm sure he won't mind being interrupted. He said to let him know as soon as you got here."

Before they reached the heavy oak door of his uncle's study, Daniel heard Benjamin Markham's booming voice. He could not make out all the words in the tirade, but he caught "damnable insurrectionists," "high treason against the Crown," and "put a stop to it any way we have to!"

Elliot grinned and said, "You'll have to excuse Father. There was another meeting at Faneuil Hall last night, and when he heard about it, he got incensed, as usual."

Daniel shook his head. "Meeting? What sort of meeting?"

"Oh, the usual arguing about the king's taxes. People get together and talk about how awful the levies are, but it's just a bunch of hot air, in my opinion. I mean, you can't really do anything about what the king decrees, can you?"

"I suppose not. There was a mighty brawl at a tavern I visited on my trip north about the same sort of thing, though," Daniel said with a shrug. Down in Virginia, there had been ill feelings about some of the Crown's policies, but Daniel had never taken a great deal of interest in the discussions.

"At any rate, Father thinks there shouldn't be any talk against the king, and he despises Samuel Adams and that bunch," Elliot went on casually. "I just thought I should warn you, in case you've developed any so-called insurrectionist leanings."

Daniel laughed shortly. "Not likely. I have other things on my mind these days, such as going to Harvard College this fall."

"It's going to be good to have you around," Elliot said, his grin widening. "Come on. Let's beard the lion in its den, shall we?" He knocked quickly, then opened the door of the study and swept his arm around, gesturing for Daniel to precede him.

Daniel stepped into the gloomy room, which was paneled with dark wood and had thick curtains over its single window. When he had visited as a boy, he had never liked his uncle's study, except for the bookcases full of Benjamin Markham's intriguing leather-bound volumes. The books had always held a great attraction for Daniel, and he had managed to read quite a few of them during his stays.

Now the air was full of pipe smoke, and the room was

as shadowy as he remembered. Daniel could tell by
Benjamin Markham's stance in the center of the room that he
had been pacing back and forth in front of his desk. He
clutched an old briar pipe in his blunt fingers. Still straight
and sturdily built in middle age, Benjamin had a strong jaw,
piercing blue eyes, and a fringe of gray hair around a bald
pate. He wore a black coat and breeches and a gray vest that
were elegant and expensive despite their simplicity.

"Sorry to interrupt, Father," said Elliot, entering the
room behind Daniel, "but look who's here."

"Hello, Daniel," Benjamin said cordially but without an
excess of warmth. He stepped forward to greet his nephew.
"How was your journey?"

"Just fine, Uncle Benjamin," Daniel replied as he
shook the hand the older man thrust toward him.

"Well, it's good to see you. Your aunt and I have been
looking forward to your visit." Benjamin gestured toward a
trio of occupied armchairs arranged in a half circle in front
of the desk. "Are you acquainted with these gentlemen?"

"Only Mr. Cummings, sir." Daniel nodded to one of the
men, a thin, balding individual with rather pinched features.
Daniel knew Theophilus Cummings was Benjamin
Markham's business partner. The other two men were
undoubtedly associates of theirs.

Benjamin confirmed that guess by saying, "This is Mr.
Satterwaite and Mr. Johnson, two of our finest local merchants. Gentlemen, my nephew Daniel Reed."

The two men nodded to Daniel, and one of them—
Satterwaite, Daniel thought—asked, "Where are you from,
lad? Your accent marks you as a southerner."

"My family settled in Virginia, sir," Daniel said.

The man nodded and might have been about to say
something else, but Benjamin spoke up first. "We've just

been discussing the intolerable behavior of that rabble down at Faneuil Hall. Are you aware of the situation, Daniel?"

"Vaguely, sir."

"And your opinion?" Benjamin snapped.

Daniel had to shrug. "I'm not sure I have one."

"You don't have an opinion?" Cummings said in a sour voice that matched his expression. "Those people are talking about rebellion! Surely you have an opinion on that, young man."

"Well, I'm not in favor of violence," Daniel ventured.

"That's what they're going to get," Benjamin said. "If this constant badgering of the authorities continues, mark my words, there'll be trouble again, just like back in seventy."

Daniel knew what his uncle was talking about. Three years earlier, he had been planning to visit Elliot in Boston during the summer, but that spring, the so-called Boston Massacre had taken place, resulting in the deaths of several colonists during a melee with British troops. Tensions had remained high during that summer, and Daniel's parents had decided that a trip to Boston would not be wise. Instead, Elliot's mother and father had sent him to Virginia that year.

"I certainly hope it doesn't come to that," Daniel offered. "There's been enough fighting."

"There'll be more. Goddamned rebels—"

Elliot closed his hand over Daniel's arm and broke in on his father's vitriolic comments by saying, "I'll show you your room, Daniel. I'm sure you must be tired after your journey."

"Yes, I am, a bit." Daniel nodded to Benjamin. "It's good to see you again, Uncle. Thank you for allowing me to visit."

"Always glad to have you," Benjamin said gruffly. He

puffed on his pipe for a moment as Elliot took Daniel out into the hall. When Elliot was closing the door, Benjamin resumed, "The king ought to send more troops . . ."

The angry statement was cut off as the door clicked shut. Elliot led Daniel to the wide staircase at the right of the foyer. "I'm sorry," he said quietly. "I really thought Father might stop talking politics long enough to give you a proper welcome. Instead he just tried to draw you into the argument."

Daniel waved off the apology. "That's all right," he assured his cousin. "I'm flattered they thought enough of me to ask my opinion. I was a bit embarrassed that I'm not more well versed in the controversy, though."

"Who can keep up with it? If you ask me, the whole thing is overblown."

"Well, I don't know," Daniel said slowly as they climbed the stairs. "It's an interesting situation. This conflict between England and the colonies has been growing for quite a while. I'm afraid your father may be right. There could be more trouble."

Elliot glanced over at him. "And which side will you be on, cousin?"

Daniel had to pause at the second-floor landing and shake his head. "I honestly don't know. I haven't thought about it that much. As I said, I've had other things on my mind."

As they went down the hallway, Daniel found himself frowning. Perhaps he should have devoted more thought to the growing antagonism between England and the colonies. Somehow, down in Virginia on the plantation where he had grown up, all the troubles had seemed so far away. Daniel's parents were more concerned with making a home and a living for themselves and their children than they were with political intricacies, and Daniel supposed that attitude had rubbed off on him to a certain extent.

"Well, I haven't thought a lot about it either," Elliot said, "but I'm sure my father is right. The people who are complaining are just stirring up trouble for everyone. I mean, my God, what would they have us do? Revolt against the king? It's absurd. It's high treason, just as my father says."

Something about Elliot's statements did not quite ring true to Daniel's ears, but he supposed that was because Elliot was only repeating what he had heard his father say many times. That could make the words sound false, even though Elliot might agree wholeheartedly with the position he was taking. All Daniel knew was that he did not want to press the matter.

The door to one of the bedrooms opened, and a stout woman with graying brown hair stepped out. She stopped short at the sight of Daniel, and a smile brightened her pleasantly handsome face. "Daniel!" she exclaimed. "You're here! I just opened the window in your room to let it air out a bit."

Daniel stepped forward and leaned over to brush a kiss across the woman's cheek. "Hello, Aunt Polly," he said.

"Did you just get here?"

"A few minutes ago," Elliot supplied the answer. "I've already taken him in to say hello to Father and get his political indoctrination." He grinned.

"I hope Benjamin and his friends didn't make you uncomfortable, Daniel," Polly Markham said. "They do go on about all this trouble with the government."

"It was fine," Daniel assured her. "I was interested in what they had to say."

"You may get tired of hearing about it before you

leave us," Polly said, rolling her eyes. "All day and every evening it's the same thing—insurrectionists and rabble-rousers. I'd much rather talk about pleasant things . . . like your mother and father. How are they?"

"Both of them are quite well, thank you. They send their love, of course."

"And little Quincy?"

Daniel had to smile at hearing his younger brother described as little. Quincy had shot up in the last year, since turning fourteen, and he was almost as tall as Daniel. "He's doing very well, Aunt Polly. You'll be seeing him in a few weeks when the rest of the family comes up for a visit."

"Of course. I haven't forgotten. It's going to be so good to see everyone again." Polly stepped aside. "Well, you go on in. I'll have one of the servants bring in your things."

"There's just one bag tied to the saddle. And my rifle, of course. But if you could have someone bring that in and take my horse around to the stable . . . ?"

"Certainly." Polly smiled at him again, dimples appearing in her plump cheeks. "It's good to have you here with us, Daniel. I hope you'll enjoy your visit."

"I'm sure I will."

And with everything that is going on in Boston right now, Daniel mused, *it may indeed turn out to be a very interesting summer.*

Chapter Two

For a few days, Daniel took it easy, resting after his long trip from Virginia. Then his active, inquisitive nature took over, and he and Elliot spent several days seeing the sights of Boston.

Which, not to Daniel's surprise, included several taverns. After all, Elliot pointed out, they were young men of the world now, and deserved some worldly amusement.

As the only child of Benjamin Markham, Elliot would one day be expected to take over his share of the business established by his father and Theophilus Cummings. Strictly speaking, Elliot was now employed by Markham & Cummings Shipping in order to learn what would be expected of him. Like Daniel, Elliot had graduated from a preparatory academy, the prestigious Boston Latin School, but he had not gone on to college. His academic education was at an end. From now on, he would deal more in practical matters.

At least, that was the way it was supposed to be. During his first two weeks in Boston, Daniel saw little sign that Elliot was applying himself to this program. The young men occasionally dropped in at the offices of Markham & Cummings, but only so that Elliot could borrow some coins from his father, who usually frowned sternly but passed over the money. That was the closest Elliot came to attending to his job.

Still, it was none of his business, Daniel told himself. It was Benjamin's responsibility to take his son in hand if he wished to. Besides, these evenings of drinking ale and carousing with serving wenches would end soon enough when Geoffrey and Pamela Reed arrived from Virginia for their visit, along with their younger son, Quincy.

Late one afternoon, as the two young men were relaxing over tankards of ale at the Salutation Tavern, a short, round-faced, gray-haired man puffing on a white clay pipe strolled past their table. The stranger paused, stared down at them for a long moment, then gave a disgusted "Harrumph!" He stalked off and went through a door into a back room.

"Who was that?" Daniel asked, frowning in surprise at the way the man had acted.

"That, my friend, was Samuel Adams," Elliot told him. "The next thing to Satan himself, to hear my esteemed father speak of him. More than once, I've heard Father declare that a noose around the neck of Sam Adams would put an end to all the troubles plaguing the colonies."

"But why was he so disapproving of us? We're not doing anything but sitting here enjoying ourselves."

"Ah, but we should be doing more than that. We should be joining the Committee of Safety and protesting the Crown's policies." Elliot drained the last of his ale and thumped the empty tankard down on the table. "Stirring things up seems to be Samuel Adams's life's work, and anyone who is not with him is against him."

"That's not a very friendly attitude."

Elliot shrugged. "I don't believe Adams is particularly interested in winning friends, only allies." One of the serving girls was passing by, and Elliot suddenly reached out, slid an arm around her waist, and pulled the surprised girl onto his lap. "I, on the other hand," he said to Daniel with a grin, "am much more interested in making friends."

The girl squealed and giggled as Elliot started to nuzzle the back of her neck under the white kerchief tied around her hair.

Daniel just smiled and lifted his tankard. As Elliot said, with all the other things in Boston to capture a young man's fancy, politics was just a waste of time.

A few days later Daniel was sitting in the parlor of his aunt and uncle's house, his feet propped on an ottoman while he leaned back in a wing chair with a volume of Shakespeare's plays. Elliot had gone to spend the afternoon at his father's offices, having finally succumbed to Benjamin's pointed comments about neglecting his duties. Aunt Polly was somewhere in the house, Daniel knew, as were a few servants, but here in the parlor everything was quiet, and he was grateful for the opportunity to catch his breath after the busy days and nights he had spent with Elliot.

The sound of wheels in the street outside made Daniel look up from his book. Through the lacy curtains over the parlor window, he saw a carriage pulling up in front of the house, followed by a light wagon. Hastily, Daniel shut the book and stood up. He went to the window, pushed the curtains aside, and looked more closely at the people disembarking from the carriage. A grin broke out on his face.

Hurrying to the front door, Daniel threw it open and

called, "Mother! Father!" He ran down the flagstone path, then embraced and kissed the attractive blond woman who was holding out her arms to him.

"How are you, Daniel?" she asked, returning the kiss and then holding him at arm's length to look at him.

"I'm fine," he told her. "Didn't you get my letter telling you that I didn't have any trouble on the trip up here?"

"We received the letter, son," said the stocky, impressive-looking man next to the blond woman. "But you know how your mother is. She was worried that you wouldn't tell her if there had been any trouble."

"No trouble up here," he assured his mother. And in one way of looking at it, that was true, Daniel thought. Massachusetts might be having its share of trials and tribulations, but he had nothing to do with it.

Geoffrey Reed shook hands with his son, and then the lanky young man in the carriage could no longer contain himself. Almost as tall as Daniel, with a thatch of light chestnut hair, he grabbed his brother, pummeled him on the back, and asked, "What have you and Elliot been up to? You'll have to tell me all about it. I'll wager all the tavern wenches in Boston know that you're here for a visit!"

"Quincy!" Pamela Reed exclaimed, shocked by her younger son's antics.

"You've got it all wrong, little brother," Daniel told Quincy with a grin. "Elliot and I have been engaged only in cultural pursuits."

Quincy hooted with laughter. "You don't expect me to believe that, do you?"

Geoffrey Reed cut in by saying, "Why don't the three of you go inside? I'll pay the drivers and see to having our bags unloaded."

Daniel led his mother and brother into the house, while

Geoffrey paid off the driver of the carriage and the man at the reins of the wagon, both of whom had hopped down from their vehicles to unload the baggage. The Reeds had come from Virginia by coach, then continued to the Markham house in these hired vehicles.

Inside, Pamela hugged her sister-in-law, Polly. Then the two women began catching up on everything that had happened since their last visit. They sat in the parlor with Geoffrey, who listened politely to the conversation. Daniel led Quincy upstairs.

"Thanks," Quincy said with a heartfelt sigh as they reached the second-floor landing. "I was afraid I'd have to sit down there with Father and be bored by all the gossip about cousins and nieces and nephews. I'm glad you were here this afternoon, Daniel, and not out with Elliot."

"I am, too. How was the trip?"

"Not bad. I was hoping our coach might be set upon by highwaymen, so that I could watch Father dispatch the brigands with his pistols, but the roads seem to be positively safe these days. I suppose everyone is too angry at the British to waste any effort on mere thievery."

All Daniel could do was smile faintly and shake his head at his brother's comments. Quincy had been like this for as long as he could remember, full of life and possessed of enough energy for three youngsters.

"You'll be staying with me again," Daniel said as he opened the door to the room he had been given, "and Mother and Father will be down the hall in their usual room."

Quincy bounced up and down on the bed a couple of times, testing the feather mattress. "I suppose it'll do. Now tell me—what sort of excitement do you and Elliot have planned for my visit?"

"We haven't really planned anything."

"Good! Then you can just take me with you to the taverns. I think I'm old enough now to be properly introduced to the concept of debauchery."

Daniel stared at him for a second before finding his voice. "I think you're mistaken," he said firmly.

"But Mother and Father don't have to know—"

Daniel shook his head. "You're trying to get both of us into trouble, Quincy, and I'm not going to allow it. You'll be going back to Virginia in a few weeks, but I have to stay in Boston. I'm not going to have your antics ruining my reputation first thing."

"Sorry," Quincy mumbled. "I didn't mean to make you angry. I'm just excited about being here with you."

Throwing an arm around his brother's shoulders, Daniel said, "I know that. And we'll have a fine time while you're here, I promise you."

He just hoped that his definition of a fine time came somewhat close to Quincy's.

That evening, the long table in the Markham dining room was almost full. In addition to the Markhams and the Reeds, Benjamin had invited the Cummings family to join them. Theophilus Cummings, his wife, Agatha, and their daughter, Sarah, brought to ten the number of people seated at the rosewood table. Daniel noticed that Sarah had managed to position herself directly across the table from Elliot, and judging from the sly glances and secret smiles they were sharing, the seating arrangement was no accident.

Only a few years earlier, Sarah Cummings had been, in Daniel's opinion, a scrawny, hopelessly immature adolescent. As she was the daughter of his father's business partner, Elliot had been forced to endure her company from time to time, and he had complained bitterly about it to his cousin during Daniel's visits. Sarah had been a nuisance and nothing more.

Obviously that had changed, along with Sarah's appearance. The slender, boyish body had been replaced by the intriguingly curved form of a woman. Angular, freckled features had turned into fair-skinned loveliness. And lank hair the color of sand was now an elaborate arrangement of thick blond curls atop Sarah's head. Daniel had to admit to himself that she was one of the most attractive young women he had ever seen, and he hoped he had been able to conceal his surprise at the change in her when they were reintroduced.

The meal was hearty, consisting of potato soup, roasted mutton, baked beans, greens, and thick slices of bread. Daniel's appetite was good, but it could not approach Quincy's, which amazed Daniel.

A few times during the meal, Benjamin Markham attempted to make some comment about the current troubles, only to have the conversation steered back to more genteel areas by his wife. When the plates were being cleared away by the servants, though, Benjamin would be denied no longer. "If you ladies will excuse us . . ." he growled meaningfully.

"Of course, dear," Polly said sweetly. She stood up along with Pamela Reed, Agatha Cummings, and Sarah. All the gentlemen, even Quincy, sprang to their feet and stood politely while the ladies filed out of the room.

When they were gone, Benjamin snapped his fingers, and the butler went to a sideboard and began pouring glasses of brandy. He carried them to the dining table on a silver tray and placed a glass in front of everyone except Quincy. As his younger son opened his mouth to protest, Geoffrey lifted a finger and said, "Don't bother. It's enough that we didn't make you leave with the ladies."

"It's time the lad began learning some things about this world we live in," Benjamin said, taking out his pipe and tobacco pouch. Geoffrey and Cummings followed suit. Daniel and Elliot contented themselves with sipping their brandy. Daniel felt the gravity of the occasion. To be allowed to share in the men's after-dinner conversation meant a great deal to him.

"What's the news from Virginia, Geoffrey?" Benjamin asked when he had lit his pipe with a taper handed to him by the butler. "Is that firebrand Patrick Henry still trying to incite a revolt?"

"Henry speaks frequently in the House of Burgesses," Geoffrey replied. "I couldn't say whether or not revolution is his intent, though."

"Please, sir," Cummings said. "It's well-known that Henry is nothing but a treasonous rebel. He's just like Sam Adams and all the other rabble-rousers up here, preaching that the colonies should be free and independent."

Quincy, who was seated to Daniel's right, leaned over and asked his brother in a whisper, "Did he say rouser mousers?"

"Rabble-rousers," Daniel said out of the corner of his mouth. "You should know the word, seeing as you exemplify its meaning."

Quincy grinned and then sat back, taking heed of the warning glance his father shot in his direction.

"The Crown should hang every member of that so-called Committee of Safety," Benjamin went on. "That would put a stop to their insolence and a stop to the problems as well."

Geoffrey Reed shook his head. "I can't be as certain of

that as you seem to be, Benjamin. Practically everything that the British have done to put down the unrest has only made it stronger. Remember the Quartering Act and the Writs of Assistance?"

"And what was wrong with sending British troops over here to keep order and giving them the power to search for smugglers and other troublemakers?" Benjamin demanded.

"The people resented them, that's what was wrong."

"The people," echoed Benjamin, smoke from his pipe wreathing his head. "The people have little concept of what they really want or need. That's why we have a king."

"Some would say George is England's king . . . not ours."

"Well, they'd be wrong!" Benjamin slapped his palm down on the table. "For God's sake, Geoffrey, you're beginning to sound like Patrick Henry himself."

Daniel felt his jaw tighten. He did not want to see his father and his uncle get into an argument, but he did not think his father should allow Benjamin to run roughshod over him, either.

If Geoffrey was offended by his brother-in-law's blunt talk, he showed no sign of it. He merely smiled and said, "Perhaps I'm just playing the devil's advocate. But you have to admit, Benjamin, the British have brought much of this trouble on themselves with one blunder after another."

"That's another thing," Benjamin snapped, pointing the stem of his pipe at Geoffrey. "You speak of the British? Well, what are *we* if not British? We're subjects of the king, just like any other Englishmen!"

"But we're *not* like any other Englishmen," Geoffrey insisted. "Our loyalty may still be to king and crown, but you were born here in the colonies, Benjamin, and so was I. Our children were born here. Doesn't that make us different, even though we may still be English, too?"

"Not to me, it doesn't," Benjamin said.

"Nor to me," Cummings put in.

Geoffrey leaned back in his chair and sipped his brandy. "Well, then, gentlemen, we have a difference of opinion. It's hardly the first, and I daresay it won't be the last. But as civilized men, we can still be friends, eh?"

"Of course," grumbled Benjamin. Cummings just sniffed and tossed back the rest of his brandy.

This was the first time Daniel had heard his father speak so much about politics, and he found himself thinking about the things Geoffrey had said. It was true, he decided, that there were differences between the British and those who had been born and raised here in the colonies. Why, the British even talked differently, as any fool could plainly hear when speaking with someone who had recently come from England. But were those differences important enough to warrant all the strife and divisiveness that was going on? Daniel could not say.

In an attempt to change the subject, Geoffrey looked at his youngest son and asked, "What are you planning to do while you're here in Boston, Quincy?"

"That depends on what Daniel and Elliot will allow me to do," Quincy replied immediately. "They act as though they haven't done anything but go to tearooms and lectures and chamber music soirees since Daniel's been here, but I don't believe them for a second."

"Believe what you wish," Daniel told him with a smile, "but remember that you're six years younger than I am."

"That's no excuse to neglect your brother, Daniel," Geoffrey said sternly. "I expect you to take Quincy under your wing."

"Of course, Father."

"We'll be happy to show the lad around, Uncle Geoffrey," Elliot added.

Benjamin grunted. "Just don't take him to any of your usual haunts—such as the Red Lion Tavern."

Elliot flushed at the mention of the notorious inn and tried to claim that he did not know what his father was talking about, but Benjamin brushed away his protests.

"I know more about your activities than you think I do, young man," he said. "You'd do well to walk a path closer to the straight and narrow."

Daniel just stared down at the table, well aware that his own father was watching him. He did not care for the turn this conversation had taken. It would have been better if they had continued discussing the problems with the British, he thought.

Quincy rescued all three of the young men by saying, "I'd like to go to Boston Common tomorrow. I imagine it's lovely this time of year."

"Indeed," Benjamin agreed.

"Perhaps we could even take a picnic lunch," Quincy went on, his enthusiasm growing. "What do you say, Daniel? Elliot?"

"Sounds like a good idea to me," Daniel muttered.

"And to me as well," Elliot agreed.

Benjamin nodded. "I'll tell the cook to prepare a basket of food for you. It's fine for young men to get out in the fresh air. An outing will be just the thing the three of you need . . . to keep you out of trouble," he added.

Much to Daniel's relief, the conversation took another turn then, as Geoffrey inquired as to how business was for Markham & Cummings Shipping. Both partners answered at length. They were involved in a discussion of the company's financial dealings when Daniel, Elliot, and Quincy asked if they could be excused. To be invited to join the men after dinner had been an honor, but there was such a thing as too much honor. None of the adults minded when the three young men slipped out of the dining room.

They went to the rear staircase near the kitchen, and as they paused at the bottom of the stairs, Elliot said, "Why don't the two of you go on up? I'll join you shortly."

Daniel had a feeling his cousin was up to something, but he said, "All right, we'll do that. Come on, Quincy."

The brothers started up the stairs while Elliot walked quickly and quietly toward the back door of the house. Daniel paused, craning his neck to look down and see the direction Elliot was taking. "You go on up, Quincy," Daniel said. "I'll be there in a few minutes."

"What's going on, Daniel?" Quincy demanded, a suspicious look on his face.

"Nothing. You just go on up to the room."

Quincy shook his head emphatically. "No, sir. You and Elliot have something sportive planned, and I'm going to find out what it is."

"We made no plans for this evening," Daniel answered truthfully. "I'm just curious—"

"And so am I," Quincy insisted.

Daniel sighed. "All right. I can see I'm not going to get anywhere arguing with you. Come along. But see that you keep quiet."

Quincy nodded eagerly and followed Daniel back down the stairs. Then Daniel walked quietly up the central hallway of the house, taking him to the front foyer and the parlor. He motioned for Quincy to stop before they reached the parlor entrance, then leaned over and listened intently. He heard the voices of his mother, his aunt, and Agatha

Cummings; if Sarah was there, she was not joining in the conversation. With a slight smile, Daniel jerked his thumb toward the rear of the house and led Quincy in that direction again.

When they were well away from the parlor, Quincy asked again, "What's going on?"

"Just come with me," Daniel said. "I think we'll get a little fresh air in the garden."

The yard behind the Markham house was long and narrow, like the house itself. Tall hedges bordered its sides, and the interior was landscaped with mature trees, shrubbery, blooming flower beds, and flagstone walks. Opening and shutting the rear door of the house as quietly as possible, Daniel and Quincy entered the yard.

The garden was quite dark. A little light filtered in from the oil lamps along the street, and the moon and stars also provided a small amount of illumination. The place was shadowy, though, and Daniel and Quincy moved slowly and carefully as they made their way from the house toward the rear of the yard.

A voice made them freeze in their tracks. It murmured, "Oh, Elliot . . ."

Both of them recognized the speaker as Sarah Cummings. Daniel crouched, went to one knee, and caught Quincy's sleeve to tug the lad down with him. They knelt there behind a fringe of bushes as they heard Elliot whisper from the other side of the foliage, "I've missed you terribly, darling."

There was a long silence, during which Daniel was convinced that Elliot and Sarah were sharing a kiss. Part of Daniel felt terribly ashamed to be spying on his cousin, but at the same time, the natural, long-running rivalry between the two young men held him here. He began to think of what he could do to surprise the young lovers. . . .

The rear door of the house opened again, and Theophilus Cummings's strident voice called, "Sarah! Are you out there, Sarah?"

Daniel's head snapped up, and he stiffened at the summons. He heard both Elliot and Sarah gasp on the other side of the bushes, and then Sarah moaned, "Oh, dear Lord, it's my father!"

With the wheels of his keen mind turning rapidly, Daniel suddenly reached out, grasped Quincy's arm again, and jerked the younger boy upright. He hissed, "Come on!" and plunged through the bushes, dragging Quincy with him. They collided with a shocked Elliot and Sarah.

"Who's that?" Elliot snapped angrily.

From the house Cummings asked peevishly, "What's going on out there?"

"It's only me," Daniel said quietly to his cousin. He added urgently, "Follow my lead."

Elliot started to mutter a question, then stopped as Daniel stepped out onto the path again. He still held Quincy's arm with one hand, and with the other hand he now grasped Elliot's arm. Elliot had hold of Sarah, so Daniel's action impelled all of them into the open.

"Mr. Cummings!" Daniel hailed. "Here we are. Elliot and your charming daughter were being so kind as to show Quincy and me around the garden."

"Oh . . ." Sarah breathed, catching on to what Daniel was trying to do. She slipped her arm through Elliot's and attemped to relax and look casual.

The four young people strolled toward the house. As they neared the rear door, Daniel added, "You were right, Elliot. Even in the moonlight, this is a lovely garden."

Enough light shone on Theophilus Cummings as he stood in the doorway for Daniel to see the pinched look on the man's face. Obviously, Cummings was not happy about the fact that his daughter had been walking in a darkened garden with three young males, but at least that was better than her being out there alone with one of them.

"Your mother was worried about you," he snapped at Sarah when the young people stepped up to the door.

"I'm sorry, Father," she murmured contritely. "But Elliot and I were just trying to be hospitable to Daniel and young Quincy."

"Of course, of course. Come along now. We're leaving." Cummings reached out, took Sarah's arm, and steered her none too gently away from the others. He led her down the hall toward the front of the house.

Elliot took a deep breath and let it out in a long sigh. "Good Lord, that was close," he said fervently. "You don't think he suspects, do you?"

"That you were bussing his daughter in the garden?" Daniel chuckled. "I don't think so."

"Good. That was quick thinking on your part, Daniel."

With a shrug, Daniel said, "I just thought Cummings would be less likely to be upset if he thought we were all out together . . . chaperoning one another, as it were."

"Anyway," Quincy added with a grin, "what's wrong with a quick kiss in a garden? That's what pretty girls are for, isn't it?"

"Perhaps you had best not offer opinions on something you know so little about," Daniel told him dryly before turning back to Elliot. "I take it you and Sarah . . . ?"

"We have an understanding," Elliot said. "I think it's taken for granted by my father and probably by Sarah's, too, that she and I will be married someday. Until that time comes, though, we have to be circumspect. You know how Boston is—the old Puritans who founded the place still walk about as ghosts."

"Perhaps," Daniel mused.

Elliot went on, "Now maybe you'll tell me just what you and Quincy were doing out here in the dark? A little spying on your poor cousin, was that it?"

Daniel laughed and slapped Elliot on the back. "If I were you, cousin, I'd just be glad we were there. Otherwise you might have an angry father summoning a minister at this very moment."

"God forbid!" Elliot said with a shudder. "I'm not ready for that!"

Laughing, the three young men went inside.

Chapter Three

The next morning, Daniel was roused out of bed early by Quincy, whose excitement at visiting Boston was too great to allow him to sleep late. Quincy dragged Elliot out of bed as well, and the three young men shared a hearty breakfast of ham, eggs, and wheatcakes. They walked down from Beacon Hill and spent the morning strolling among the many shops of downtown Boston, then returned to the Markham house to pick up the picnic lunch that the cook had prepared for them.

As usual, the common was crowded with people enjoying its green confines as Daniel, Quincy, and Elliot walked down George Street and approached the park. To their right as they entered the common, situated on a small hill, was a good-sized brick building with a rounded roof. A smaller, similar structure stood at the base of the gentle slope. The larger building, Daniel knew, was used as a powder house by the British troops. Its companion was a watchhouse, where a sentry sometimes stood guard. No soldiers were in sight at the moment, however, indicating that either the powder house was not currently in use, or tensions had eased a bit in the city so that a constant guard was not deemed necessary. The latter possibility seemed unlikely to Daniel, and he wondered idly if the British forces had moved their munitions elsewhere, perhaps to a secret location.

Elliot was carrying the picnic basket. He pointed out a large open area that was unoccupied and asked, "How about over there?"

Daniel nodded. "Looks fine to me. There's even a bit of shade from that tree."

The sun was warm, not unpleasantly so but enough that some shade was welcome. Later in the summer, Daniel knew, the sultry heat would become intolerable here in the city. At the moment, however, the weather was still quite nice.

When they reached the spot Elliot had picked out, he opened the basket and took a cloth from it, which he handed to Daniel and Quincy. "Spread that out on the ground for the food," he instructed them.

Trust a Bostonian to do things elegantly, Daniel thought with a wry grin. In Virginia, eating outdoors would not involve an expensive silk cloth. In Daniel's experience, meals such as this would usually entail a campfire, a cooking spit made from branches, and a recently snared rabbit or a freshly caught fish.

Instead, Elliot took from the basket a baked hen, a loaf of bread, some jam, and a pot of beans. A small jug of wine had also been packed in with the food. The three young men sat down around the cloth and dug in, enjoying the picnic.

"You still haven't fully explained what the two of you were doing out in the garden last night," Elliot commented after a few moments.

"Why, we were just looking out for your best interests, weren't we, Quincy?" Daniel said innocently.

"I'm sure. Spying on me is more like it." Elliot grinned. "But I don't really care. I make no secret of the fact that I'm in love with Sarah."

Quincy spoke up. "She certainly is pretty."

"And she's well aware of that fact, too," Elliot said. "Not that she's vain, mind you."

"Of course not," Daniel said, even though vain was exactly the word he would have chosen to describe Sarah Cummings.

"I was just thinking about it, though," mused Quincy. "If you marry Sarah, that means old Mr. Cummings will be your father-in-law. Won't he?"

Elliot grimaced slightly. "There is that to consider, I'll grant you. Sarah's mother is all right, but Theophilus is a bit intimidating. Still, my father owns a larger share of the firm than he does, so there's not a great deal he can say about the match. Father will support any decision I care to make."

Daniel frowned a little. He hoped Elliot was not overestimating the lengths his father would go to help him. It had struck Daniel on several occasions that Uncle Benjamin was rapidly running out of patience with Elliot's indolent attitude.

Elliot had never been one to spend a great deal of time listening to advice, however, as Daniel well knew. He put that worry out of his mind for the time being and concentrated instead on the drumstick in his hand. He gnawed off another bite of the perfectly cooked meat and then reached for the jug of wine.

A hand swooped down and picked up the jug before Daniel could touch it. "'Ere, wot's this?" a rough voice asked.

Daniel glanced up and saw three men standing over

them. One of the men was holding the jug, and he lifted it to his mouth for a long swallow. When he lowered it, he wiped the back of his hand across his mouth and leered. "This is too good for a litter o' pups. We'd best take it off their 'ands, mates." The other two men joined him in coarse laughter.

They wore shoes with run-down heels, breeches, patched linsey-woolsey shirts, and battered caps. Daniel pegged them as workers from the docks that lined Boston Harbor. What they were doing at midday here at the common, on the other side of town, he could not have said.

A glance over at Elliot showed Daniel that his cousin's face was taut with anger. Pushing himself to his feet, Elliot said, "Excuse me, gentlemen, but that's our wine. I'll have it back, please."

"'I'll 'ave it back, please,'" mocked one of the men. "Ain't you the fancy 'un?"

Daniel and Quincy both stood up, and Daniel hurriedly put a hand on Elliot's arm. "Take it easy, Elliot," he cautioned.

The man holding the jug placed the fingers of his other hand against the front of Elliot's shirt and shoved. "Yeah, take it easy, mate," he sneered.

Daniel tightened his grip on Elliot's arm and said, "Take the wine if you want it. We're not looking for trouble."

"Well maybe we are," the third man growled. "Lost our jobs, we did, 'cos business is down at the wharves on account of the 'ell bein' raised by you bloody colonials. It ain't enough t' treat us to a jug o' wine. Ye owe us more than that!"

"We don't owe you a damned thing," Elliot said coldly. "Now give me back that wine, or I'll summon the constabulary!"

The face of the man holding the jug darkened with rage. "Ye want the wine, do ye? Well, I'll give it to ye!"

And as Daniel shouted a warning, the man swung the jug at Elliot's head with all the force of his brawny body behind the swing.

Elliot saw the blow coming in time to jerk free of Daniel's grip and leap to one side. The jug missed his head, and the unspent force of the blow pulled the man off-balance. Elliot crashed into him, knocking him backward. The man outweighed Elliot, but in his awkward position, he could not keep his feet. He fell back heavily.

Landing atop the man as the jug went tumbling away, Elliot smashed two quick punches to his opponent's face. He would have done even more damage if another of the men had not grabbed his coat collar and flung him aside with a roar of anger. The third man kicked Elliot in the side as the young Bostonian sprawled to the ground.

Daniel hesitated only long enough to snap, "Stay out of this, Quincy!" Then he leapt forward, grabbed the shoulder of the man who had just kicked Elliot, and spun him around. A hard, perfectly timed right fist caught the man's jaw.

Before Daniel could throw another punch, arms grabbed him from behind. "I've got 'im!" a voice shouted in his ear. "Teach 'im a lesson!"

Daniel saw both men advancing toward him as the third one held him tightly. Beyond them, Elliot was curled up on the ground, holding his midsection and gasping for breath. Daniel looked around wildly for help, but although the fight had drawn the attention of some people in the common, no one seemed to be running to his aid.

Quincy changed that. The lad let out a howl and landed on the back of the man holding Daniel. Looping his left arm around the man's neck, Quincy held on with all his strength while he reached around and pounded his other hand into the man's face. With a harsh curse, the man released Daniel and clawed at the new tormentor, who seemed to be attached to his back like a leech.

Daniel stumbled forward, ducked a punch, and grappled with one of the men. He was up against a foe with superior weight, reach, and strength, Daniel realized, and his only chance was to use the one advantage he might have—speed. He hammered a flurry of blows to the man's belly and then leapt back out of reach, letting his opponent expend some energy with a pair of wild, sweeping punches that hit nothing but air.

Unfortunately, as long as Elliot was out of the fight, the odds were uneven. Daniel's second foe hit him from the side and knocked him down. Daniel landed hard on the grass, his vision swimming, but he had the presence of mind to get a leg up as one of the men dove at him. The man crashed against Daniel's boot, the heel driving into his stomach. Daniel's leg bent at the knee, but then he straightened it, forcefully throwing the man aside. His blurry vision cleared a bit just as the other man tried to kick him in the head. Twisting desperately away from the blow, Daniel managed to grab his attacker's ankle and tug on it as hard as he could. The man was upended and fell with a grunt of pain.

Daniel rolled over and scrambled to his feet. He saw that the third man had finally thrown Quincy off his back. The man had a hold on Quincy's shirt and was slapping him, the hard blows rocking Quincy's head back and forth.

With a shout of rage, Daniel clubbed his hands together and crashed them down on the back of the man's neck. The man's head jerked up, and he stiffened, then folded like a house of cards, crumpling to the ground, unconscious.

Both of the other men hit Daniel from behind, bearing

him to the ground. Their crushing weight landed on top of him as his face was driven into the dirt and grass. Choking on the taste, he tried to wriggle free, but to no avail. A knee was driven hard into his kidneys and made him gasp in pain.

"Get off him, you bastards!"

Daniel heard Elliot's shout only vaguely, but he felt the burden on his back suddenly lighten, enough so that he was able to twist to the side and drive an elbow up at the leering face of the man looming over him. It connected with a satisfying jolt that sent shivers of pain to Daniel's shoulder. Still, the pain was worth it, because the man who had been holding him down fell to one side, moaning and clutching a broken jaw.

Daniel rolled onto his back and lifted himself on his elbows. He saw Elliot wrestling with the final member of the trio of troublemakers. The man was getting the best of the struggle, his fingers wrapped around Elliot's throat. Elliot's face was brick red as he struggled to draw breath and punched futilely at the face of the man strangling him.

Before Daniel could make it to his feet to go to his cousin's assistance, a shot rang out, its echo rolling across the common. The circle of onlookers that had formed around the struggle suddenly parted, and four men clad in black boots, white trousers, bright red coats, and black hats stalked through the opening. Each held a Brown Bess musket with a bayonet attached to the barrel. Powder smoke still wisped from the muzzle of one man's musket. Another of the British soldiers placed the sharp tip of his bayonet against the neck of the man holding Elliot and said sharply, "Release that man!"

The burly dockworker uncurled his fingers from Elliot's throat. He got up carefully, following the commands of the redcoat. "Didn't mean no harm, guv'nor," he said in a surly voice. "Just 'avin' a bit of a tussle."

"Oh? It looked more as if you and your friends were try-ing to kill these lads." The soldier glanced around at the bodies sprawled on the ground and smiled grimly. "Although it appears to me that the lads were getting the best of you."

Daniel and Quincy helped Elliot to his feet. Elliot was pale and shaken, and his voice was hoarse, but he was com-posed as he said, "I'm sorry for the disturbance, Sergeant. These men—" He waved a hand at the laborers, only one of whom was still conscious. "—stole our wine and assaulted us. My cousins and I were only protecting ourselves."

"And who might you boys be?"

"I'm Elliot Markham, of Markham and Cummings Shipping. These are my cousins from Virginia, Daniel and Quincy Reed. We were just trying to have a peaceful picnic—"

"Well, young Master Markham, I suggest that you and your cousins gather up what's left of your picnic and vacate the area. We'll turn this lot over to the constable and let him deal with them."

Elliot frowned. "But it's not fair we should have to leave. We've done nothing wrong."

"Perhaps not, lad." The British sergeant, whose face was nearly as red as his coat, lowered his voice as he went on, "But some people in this crowd can look at your clothes and tell that the three of you are well-to-do. It may not sit right with them when we haul your opponents off to jail. Some of them see these red coats and get angry no matter what we do."

"He's right, Elliot," Daniel said, keeping his own voice pitched low. "We'd better go on before this turns into a riot."

"I suppose you have a point," Elliot admitted with a sigh. "Come on." He began gathering up the scattered debris left over from the picnic lunch.

They ignored the muttering of the crowd as they left the common. While there were undoubtedly many people who were sympathetic to them, there were also those who would take the side of the dockworkers.

"Well, our picnic was ruined," Elliot said as they walked up Beacon Hill.

"There will be other picnics," Daniel told him. "I'm not worried about it. Are you, Quincy?"

Quincy shook his head. "I just wish I'd gotten in a few more blows before those redcoats broke up the fight."

Daniel studied his brother's rumpled, grass-stained clothes and the bruises already forming on Quincy's face. He knew that Elliot and he looked equally battered.

"If you regret that the trouble came to an end too soon," Daniel said, "just wait until Father hears about this. Then, I daresay, there'll be more trouble than even you could want, Quincy!"

Daniel's prophecy turned out to be all too true.

"Brawling with a trio of wharf rats as though you were nothing but street hoodlums yourselves!" Geoffrey Reed thundered as he stalked back and forth in Benjamin Markham's study. Benjamin was more calm on the surface, but the fingers of one of his hands drummed in a maddening rhythm on the desk behind which he sat.

Daniel, Elliot, and Quincy stood in front of the desk, their eyes downcast as Geoffrey continued to lambaste them. The constable had paid a visit to the Markham house that afternoon to inform both men of the altercation on the common. No charges were being pressed against the young men, of course, and the three dockworkers who had started the fight had already been fined and sentenced to three nights in jail. In the eyes of Geoffrey and Benjamin, however, that scarcely improved the situation.

"You may not realize it," Benjamin said when Geoffrey paused for breath, "but Boston is still a small town in many ways. We have a reputation to uphold, Elliot. Young men of your social circle do *not* settle disagreements with their fists. You've never heard of your friend Avery Wallingford being involved in such behavior, have you?"

"That's not fair, Father," Elliot protested. "Avery Wallingford is afraid of his own shadow."

Benjamin's mouth tightened angrily.

"Anyway," Elliot rushed on, "it was hardly our fault. We were just defending ourselves from those ruffians. Isn't that right, Daniel?"

"One of them *did* throw the first punch," Daniel agreed. "After that, we were too busy to think about what was right or proper."

Geoffrey glared at him. "So you involved your brother in a fight in which he might have been seriously injured."

"Daniel told me to stay out of it," Quincy said. "But I didn't have any choice, Father. If I hadn't jumped that rapscallion, he and his friends would have beaten Daniel to within an inch of his life!"

"Well, perhaps the situation was not quite that desperate . . . " Daniel said.

And yet he knew that it had been. The British dockworkers had been angry, vengeful, and out for colonial blood. If things had gone differently, he and Quincy and Elliot might have been killed.

Geoffrey sighed. "Well, it's over and done with, and nothing else can be done about it now. I have to admit it's not as if you had been in a tavern or somewhere like that and gotten into a brawl. Respectable young men should be able to

visit Boston Common without being accosted and forced to
defend themselves."

Daniel could tell from his father's tone of voice that his
initial anger was dissipating. Geoffrey Reed could be hotheaded, but he was also a fair-minded man, and reason usually won out once his temper had run its course.

"We'll be here for another two weeks," Geoffrey went
on. "See that you don't get in trouble during that time."

Benjamin added, "I'm holding you responsible, Elliot.
After all, Daniel and Quincy are your guests."

All three young men muttered their agreement.

Geoffrey waved a hand at them. "Go on upstairs and get
cleaned up. Luckily, the constable spoke to Benjamin and myself out of the hearing of your mothers. There's no need for
them to know about this debacle yet—although those bruises
on your faces will make concealment unlikely for long."

"Thanks, Father," Daniel said quickly. He had been
equally worried about his mother's reaction to the news.
Although he never recalled Pamela Reed's raising her voice,
one look from her could strike just as much terror in the
hearts of her sons as any of their father's blusterings. It was
all right with him to postpone that moment as long as possible.

Without wasting any time, Daniel, Quincy, and Elliot
went upstairs to wash their faces and change clothes, re-
placing their dirty, grass-stained garments for fresh ones.
Quincy wadded his soiled clothes into a ball and tossed them
into a corner of the room before Daniel told him to pick
them up again.

Elliot entered their room a moment later without knocking. He shut the door, leaned against the wall, and crossed his
arms over his chest. "Well, I don't know about you lads," he
said, "but in my opinion, we got off lightly. I think my father

wanted to take me out and have me flogged." He shook his head. "And we were the injured parties! It still seems unfair to me."

"Your father just doesn't want anything to hurt the good name of the Markham family," Daniel said as he laced up a clean shirt.

"So we should have let those men thrash us, just to preserve a façade of gentility?"

"I didn't say that," Daniel replied, grinning as he remembered how it had felt when his enemy's jawbone had cracked under the blow from his elbow. *I really am a barbarian at heart,* he thought. *Maybe one of my ancestors was a wild Celtic chieftain. . . .*

"I still wish those redcoats hadn't shown up when they did," Quincy complained. "I was just getting started."

"And I was getting killed," Elliot pointed out. "Or have you forgotten that scoundrel had his hands wrapped around my throat? I swear, the sky was going red and black when that soldier finally got him off me."

Quincy clapped his cousin on the shoulder. "If he had killed you, Elliot, Daniel and I would have avenged your death. You can be sure of that."

"That's a great comfort," Elliot said with a wry chuckle. The sound of a bell floated up the stairs, audible even through the closed door of the room. Elliot sighed and went on, "That'll be dinner. Our mothers are sure to notice some of these marks on us. What say, men? Are you ready to go down and face the gallows of maternal wrath?"

"Lead on, cousin," Daniel said, grinning and throwing an arm around Elliot's shoulders. Quincy did the same on the other side. "Lead on."

Chapter Four

For several days, Daniel, Quincy, and Elliot suffered the cold, silent anger of their respective mothers for their part in the brawl, but that was soon forgotten, vanishing even before the bruises that were the primary legacy of the battle. Daniel and Elliot still had their hands full keeping Quincy out of trouble—the lad had a positive genius for harebrained schemes, such as rowing across the Charles and setting off fireworks atop Breed's Hill—but overall, the Reeds' sojourn was turning into a quiet, peaceful one.

Daniel should have known not to expect that to go on.

The evening before Geoffrey, Pamela, and Quincy were to leave for Virginia, Benjamin and Polly Markham gave a dinner in their honor, inviting friends and business associates from all over the Boston area. As he went downstairs that evening, Daniel tugged in annoyance at the tight collar and silk cravat surrounding his neck. His waistcoat and breeches were trimmed in matching blue embroidery and were the same white as his stockings. He was having trouble with tassels used to close his fashionable cut-away coat. If there was anything more uncomfortable than such a getup, Daniel did not know what it was.

Elliot followed right behind him down the stairs. More accustomed to affairs such as this, Elliot did not seem to mind in the least dressing up in his best suit.

The high-ceilinged parlor was quite crowded as Daniel and Elliot entered. They made their way through the press of people, most of whom Daniel did not know. Several men greeted Elliot, as did a few young women. Elliot had eyes only for Sarah Cummings, though, and he and Daniel located her standing with her father and mother, listening politely but without a great deal of attention as Theophilus Cummings expounded at length on the deplorable situation in the colonies.

"Not that I think things will ever come to open rebellion," Cummings was saying. "The damned insurrectionists don't have the stomach for that. All they'll really do is shout and march around and make bloody—please forgive my language, ladies—fools of themselves, but they'll make things more difficult for all the law-abiding citizens in the process."

"I hope you're not underestimating them, Theophilus," said one of Cummings's listeners. "Several times, Sam Adams and James Otis have stopped just short of advocating armed revolt."

"Adams and Otis . . . bah! No one takes them seriously anymore. They're merely shadow men with which to frighten loyalist children who misbehave."

That was one of the most ludicrous statements Daniel had ever heard, and he had to make an effort to restrain himself from contradicting Cummings. He had heard and read a great deal about Samuel Adams, James Otis, and the other men comprising the Committee of Safety, the outgrowth of the old Sons of Liberty association. Most people in Boston, no matter on which side of the issue they stood, seemed to take Adams and Otis seriously.

Elliot moved up beside the lovely blonde and murmured, "Hello, Sarah." His hand stole over to hers, caught it, and gave her fingers a quick squeeze before releasing them. Daniel saw the gesture, but it was so smooth and so quickly done that he doubted if anyone else noticed.

Before Sarah could make any reply to Elliot's greeting, another young man suddenly appeared next to her. He smirked as he passed her and said, "Why, good evening, Elliot. And who's this?" The newcomer's dark eyes fastened on Daniel.

Elliot's jaw tightened at the interruption, but he answered the question in a civil tone. "You remember my cousin Daniel, don't you, Avery?"

"Wild Daniel from the Virginia countryside? Of course! How are you, Daniel? You've changed since I saw you last. You don't look so much like a . . . a woodsman now."

"I left off the bearskin robe and coonskin cap for the summer," Daniel said dryly. "All that fur gets a little warm and itchy, you know, Avery."

"Yes, I'm sure it must," Avery Wallingford said solemnly.

He was a slender young man, slightly taller than Elliot, which put his eyes on the same level as Daniel's. Wearing his expensive silk and satin clothes as if he had been born in them, he was handsome with lean features and sleek dark hair. Daniel had met him in the past. Avery and Elliot had been friends when they were children, but the friendship had faded as they grew older, leaving only a rivalry that was polite on the surface but bitter underneath. Daniel knew that much from hearing Elliot talk about Avery.

The reason for Elliot's dislike became rapidly apparent as Avery switched his attention from Daniel and Elliot to Sarah Cummings. He flirted shamelessly with her, telling her how beautiful she was this evening. Sarah seemed pleased with Avery's never-ending stream of compliments, but Elliot was grinding his teeth in frustration. Daniel knew how he felt. It would have been very soul satisfying to grab Avery's elegantly ruffled collar, march him to the front door, and throw him out into the night. But neither he nor Elliot could do such a thing, Daniel thought glumly. Avery was a guest here tonight, along with his father—who happened to be one of Boston's leading bankers—and he had to be treated with respect.

Theophilus Cummings glanced over his shoulder, noticed that Avery had come up, and drew him into the conversation. "What about you, young Wallingford?" he asked, putting a hand on Avery's shoulder. "What do you think about the activities of these damned traitors?"

"Why, I think they're positively treasonous," Avery responded instantly.

"At last, a young man who shows some good sense," Cummings said with a meaningful glance at Elliot.

"You haven't heard me speaking up to defend Adams and his friends," protested Elliot, knowing full well that Cummings had directed the comment at him.

Cummings smirked. "I haven't heard you denouncing them, either, young man. In times like these, one cannot afford to be indecisive."

Daniel saw the sympathetic look Sarah gave Elliot. It passed quickly, and then she made her lovely face impassive again. Daniel could well imagine that it might be unpleasant for her to side openly with Elliot against her father. Theophilus Cummings would see that it was so.

"It seems to me," Daniel said, stepping into the conversation, "that we cannot condemn someone for speaking his mind."

"Even when those minds are turned toward treason?" Cummings shot back with a frown, obviously not happy that Daniel had seen fit to involve himself.

A hand came down on Daniel's shoulder before he could answer, and he looked over to see his father standing there. "Daniel is still making up his mind about things, Mr. Cummings," Geoffrey Reed said with a polite smile. "That's one reason he's going to Harvard in a few weeks—so that he can learn to think for himself and reach his own decisions. I think he's got a good start on that already."

"As long as those decisions are the correct ones," Cummings said with a sneer.

"They will be. . . . At least, they'll be correct for him."

Daniel smiled at his father, glad that Geoffrey had come to his assistance.

Cummings was not ready to let go. He said, "And what about you, Reed? What do you think of these rebels?"

"There's no rebellion that I know of," Geoffrey replied. "Just some men honestly expressing their opinions. I see nothing wrong with that."

"Well, I see something wrong with your attitude, sir!" Cummings snapped. "It's thinking like yours that encourages all the troublemakers."

Daniel saw his father's lips tighten into a grim line and knew that Cummings was pushing Geoffrey perilously close to losing his temper. Daniel was not sure whether to hope that happened or not. On the one hand, he would hate to see his father involved in an angry argument with Cummings, but on the other, it would be nice to witness the comeuppance Cummings would receive at the hands of Geoffrey Reed.

That was fated not to happen. Benjamin Markham appeared and said hastily, "Dinner will be served soon, gentlemen. Theophilus, I need to talk to you for a few minutes. Some business matters have come up."

"Certainly." Cummings nodded, then allowed Benjamin to steer him away from the group. Avery Wallingford tagged along, eager as always to overhear any conversation possibly regarding money.

Daniel found himself wondering if his uncle really needed to discuss business with Cummings, or if that had only been an excuse to get him away from the group before a full-fledged argument broke out. Always the good host, Benjamin had probably sensed that trouble was in the offing and acted to forestall it.

Standing with his father, Elliot, and Sarah, Daniel turned to Geoffrey and said, "Thanks for coming over. I wasn't sure what I was going to wind up saying to Mr. Cummings."

"Better not to say any more than necessary to a . . . a gentleman like Mr. Cummings," Geoffrey said, with a guilty glance at Sarah for the thoughts that were obviously in his head.

She smiled. "You were about to say a blowhard like my father, weren't you?"

Geoffrey began, "I would never—"

"Don't worry, Mr. Reed. I know what Father is like. I happen to agree with him most of the time, but I realize how overbearing he is." She turned to Elliot. "I especially hate to see him arguing with you."

Elliot shrugged. "I'm used to him by now, Sarah. Don't forget, he and my father have been partners for a long time." He summoned up a grin. "Why, when they formed Markham and Cummings, you were nothing but an annoying little tomboy."

"I was never a tomboy," Sarah said archly, but her blue eyes were twinkling with amusement as she straightened her shoulders, causing the neckline of her cream satin-and-lace gown to reveal slightly more equally creamy bosom.

This crisis, minor though it had been, was now over, Daniel sensed, and he turned his attention to other matters. "Where's Quincy?" he asked his father. "I haven't seen him since I came downstairs."

"He's over there with your mother," Geoffrey said. "The lad seems rather distracted tonight, as if something's bothering him. When I asked him about it, though, he said everything was fine."

Now that his father had mentioned it, Daniel thought that Quincy had seemed rather moody today. He attributed it to the fact that the family was leaving Boston. Quincy had enjoyed his stay here, and he probably did not want to go home.

A few minutes later, the guests were summoned into the dining room by the announcement that dinner was served. Daniel was seated next to Sarah, and he saw from Elliot's envious look that his cousin was jealous of him. If he had been able to do so discreetly, he would have gladly switched places with Elliot. His opinion of Sarah Cummings had risen slightly since he had gotten better acquainted with her, but he had absolutely no romantic interest in her.

Elliot, unfortunately, was seated next to Avery

Wallingford, and Daniel could tell that it was taking an effort on Elliot's part to retain a polite façade in the face of Avery's asinine comments.

Dinner was interminable, despite the high quality of the food. Sarah was on Daniel's left, and on his right was the wife of a Boston businessman, a stout, middle-aged lady who persisted in talking to him as if he were eight years old instead of twenty. Daniel struggled to keep up a conversation with his companions.

Across the long table and several seats to Daniel's right was Quincy. The fourteen-year-old wore a glum expression through most of the meal, but he brightened somewhat when the desserts were brought out. That was Quincy for you, thought Daniel, grinning to himself. Nothing like a cherry tart to improve his mood.

The pie was not the only thing lifting Quincy's spirits, Daniel discovered a few moments later. Quincy had reached a decision and settled a problem that had been bothering him for quite some time. The revelation came as Geoffrey was talking about the family's imminent return trip to Virginia.

"I'm not going back," Quincy suddenly announced.

His voice was loud enough to draw the attention of everyone around the table. As conversations gradually died away and eyes turned to look at Quincy, Geoffrey asked quietly, "What did you say, son?"

"I said I'm not going back to Virginia. That's simple enough, isn't it, Father?"

"Simple enough," Geoffrey repeated. His tone sharpened as he went on, "Simpleminded, in fact. How did you reach this ridiculous decision?" he grated, ignoring his wife's warning touch on his arm.

"I don't see anything ridiculous about it," Quincy said as he put down his fork and glared at his father. "Daniel is staying here in Boston. I don't understand why I can't, too."

"Daniel is going to Harvard— "

"Well, I could go to school here, too." Quincy swung around to face his cousin. "You went to the Boston Latin School, Elliot. Didn't you say it was a fine academy?"

Elliot hesitated, obviously unwilling to be drawn into this argument between father and son. Still, he had to tell the truth. "It's a fine institution, Quincy, and has quite a reputation as such."

"And I could go there, couldn't I?"

Elliot shrugged. "I don't see why not . . . if you can pass the entrance exams."

"The point is, you're too young even to be thinking about such a thing," Geoffrey said heavily. "You can't stay by yourself, and I'm not going to burden Benjamin and Polly with taking care of you."

Benjamin started to protest that of course Polly and he would be glad to have Quincy stay on with them, but Daniel could clearly hear the insincerity in his uncle's voice. Having visitors for a short time was one thing; having those visitors move in permanently was something else entirely.

He had been listening to the discussion in silence so far, but Daniel knew the time had come for him to speak up. "There's another solution, Father," he said. "Before the fall term begins at Harvard, I'm going to be finding quarters of my own. Quincy could share them with me."

"You see," Quincy exclaimed. "I told you it made perfect sense, Father."

Pamela Reed frowned. "I don't know, Geoffrey," she said slowly. "I've already been worried about Daniel's staying here, and adding the responsibility of looking out for Quincy . . ."

"He won't have to look out for me," Quincy insisted. "I can get along just fine."

Daniel doubted that seriously, and he could tell by the skeptical expression on his father's face that Geoffrey shared his opinion. Quincy needed someone to keep his enthusiasm reined in, at least part of the time.

Geoffrey shook his head. "I'm sorry, Quincy. This is neither the time nor the place to discuss this, but since you've forced the issue, I have to say that you'll return with your mother and me to Virginia, and you'll come along without making a fuss. Is that understood?"

His features taut and turning pale, Quincy stared at his father for a long moment, then opened his mouth to make what was certain to be an angry reply that would only prolong the argument and further embarrass the family and guests around the dinner table. Daniel did not want that to happen.

"Wait a minute, Father," he said quickly, forestalling Quincy's protest. "I don't mind looking after Quincy. Not that he'll take much looking after. He's more grown up than you think he is." That was stretching the truth a bit, Daniel thought, but it was necessary under the circumstances.

"You'll have enough to do just getting started at Harvard, son," Geoffrey said. "You don't need any added burdens."

"I wouldn't be a burden," Quincy began hotly.

Geoffrey held up a hand to stop him. Turning his attention back to his older son, Geoffrey regarded Daniel intently. "Are you sure this is something you want to do?" he asked after a moment.

Daniel nodded, although he was not sure at all. "I don't mind." He forced a smile. "In fact, I think it would be a good idea. If Quincy stays with me, I won't have to live by myself."

Frowning in concentration, Geoffrey rubbed his jaw and thought deeply. "I suppose it could work out," he finally mused. He glanced at his wife and asked, "What do you think, Pamela?"

"Well . . . I know how strong willed *all* the men in my family are," she said with a smile. "I suppose we could try the arrangement for a time, and things could always be changed later if need be."

"All right," Geoffrey said decisively. "It's settled. But this is only a provisional agreement, you two lads. If there's any trouble, Quincy, you'll come right back to Virginia."

"Of course, Father. But there won't be any trouble."

Daniel wished he could be as sure of that as Quincy sounded.

With the argument over, the dinner conversation quickly returned to normal. After the meal, the guests adjourned to the parlor. Daniel and Quincy found themselves standing together in a corner of the room.

Quincy could barely contain his excitement. He put a hand on Daniel's shoulder and said, "This is going to be great fun, isn't it, Daniel?"

"Well, it's not going to be the holiday you seem to think it's going to be," Daniel replied. "I intend to work hard on my studies, and you will, too, if you want to remain here in Boston. From what I've heard, the Latin School is quite demanding."

"I can handle it," Quincy insisted. "And I still say it's going to be fun living with you."

"We'll see about that," Daniel said. "We'll just see."

Chapter Five

With so much happening in his own life during the next few weeks, Daniel Reed had little time to miss his parents or think about politics and the worsening situation between England and the American colonies. Once it had been decided that Quincy would stay with him, the first order of business was finding a place to live.

Benjamin Markham helped out with that, locating a small apartment for rent in Cambridge, across the Charles River from Boston. Harvard College was also in Cambridge, within walking distance of the rooms located above a stationer's shop.

The apartment was small, but it had a sitting room with two large windows overlooking a small common and one bedroom for the boys to share. It was comfortably furnished with well-worn overstuffed furniture, a desk, and a long table with four wooden chairs. There was a fireplace in one corner, and the floors were covered with shabby Persian carpets. The stationer's wife would bring the boys their meals from the kitchen downstairs where she cooked for her family.

It would do just fine for Quincy and him, Daniel decided after looking it over. He gave the landlord some coins from the funds left for him by his father, then headed back to the Markham's Beacon Hill residence to prepare for the move.

By the first week in September, the Reed brothers were settled into their new home, Daniel was enrolled at Harvard, and Quincy had been accepted into the Boston Latin School. Quincy had bought a horse so that he could make the ride into Boston proper each day. His mount, along with Daniel's, was stabled in a barn just down the street from the apartment.

As the days passed, Daniel had to admit that so far Quincy had been completely cooperative, cheerfully doing his share of the work and applying himself to his studies without complaint.

The only drawback to the arrangement was that Daniel saw less of Elliot now. Both of them were busy with their own affairs, and their paths seldom crossed. That was why Elliot made a point to invite Daniel and Quincy to dinner at the Markham house at least one night every week.

It was at one of these dinners during October that the subject of friction between England and the colonies again cropped up. Benjamin Markham said harshly, "Those blasted troublemakers have done it again."

Daniel did not have to ask what troublemakers his uncle meant. There was only one group that so incensed Benjamin. But he did ask, "What have they done now?"

"It's the rebels in New York this time," Benjamin

replied. "The fever of treason has spread down there, unfortunately."

"You're talking about the tea situation, aren't you, Father?" Elliot asked.

"I wish you wouldn't argue at the dinner table, Benjamin," Polly put in, but her husband was not about to be swayed from his course.

"No one is arguing, my dear," Benjamin said. "We're just deploring the dreadful circumstances sweeping the colonies." He fixed his gaze on Daniel. "You know about the East India Company, don't you?"

"Of course," Daniel said quickly, not wanting his uncle to think he was completely ignorant.

"Well, a band of rebels down in New York turned back their ships, wouldn't even let them dock, much less unload their cargoes of tea. It was nothing less than a criminal act."

"Some people say the criminal act is the tax on that tea, Father," Elliot commented. "People in England don't have to pay it."

"Bah! Three pence for each pound of tea? Is that worth a revolution?"

"I didn't say they were right," Elliot replied. "I just said that's what people are upset about."

"Well, they're wrong. The Crown knows what it's doing." Benjamin slowly shook his head. "But I hate to think about what may happen when the tea ships reach Boston. With Sam Adams right here to enflame everyone's emotions, there's no telling what may occur."

Now that he thought about it, Daniel had heard quite a bit of talk at Harvard about the Tea Act, which had levied a tax on tea imported to the colonies by the East India Company while making it illegal to buy or sell tea from any other source. Coming on the heels of the Stamp Act and the Sugar Act—similar levies that had been repealed through the efforts of British moderates like William Pitt after impassioned outcries of protest from the colonies—the Tea Act threatened to push the angry colonists over the line into outright rebellion. That concept was difficult for Daniel to grasp. He was a colonist, of course, born and raised here, but he was also an Englishman with a duty to follow the edicts of the Crown. *Wasn't he?*

Sitting here at the Markham dinner table with a frown on his face, he suddenly realized that he could not answer that question.

"A friend of mine from school says that the British will never unload tea here in Boston," Quincy spoke up. "His father is a member of the Committee of Safety, and they won't allow it."

"The Committee of Safety." Benjamin repeated the words as if they left a bad taste in his mouth. "That's nothing but a smoke screen for radicals like Sam Adams, who want anarchy to rule in our streets." His hand came down sharply on the table, making his wife flinch. "This is a land of law, the king's law, by God! And anyone who can't follow it should be driven out!"

"That's going too far, Uncle Benjamin," Quincy protested. "You can't arrest people or drive them away simply because you don't agree with them."

"That's not it at all, young man," Benjamin said stiffly. "It's not a matter of whether or not these men agree with *me*. It's when they disagree with *the Crown* that they become traitors."

That was putting it too strongly, Daniel thought, but he knew the futility of challenging his uncle. Nothing was going to change Benjamin Markham's opinions.

"Well, I still say there's liable to be trouble when the East India ships get here," Quincy said.

Benjamin fixed him with a baleful stare. "At least we agree on that, lad."

Nothing further was said about the problems with the tea tax at the meal, but over the next few weeks, Daniel heard more and more talk about it. Everywhere he went it seemed that people were discussing what should be done when the East India Company ships loaded with tea arrived in Boston Harbor.

He heard a great deal about the subject from Quincy, who was constantly quoting his schoolmate Roger Malvern, whose father was a friend of Samuel Adams. According to, Roger, the group opposed to the Tea Act fully expected the ships to be turned away, just as other vessels loaded with East India tea had been denied entrance to other ports up and down the Atlantic coast.

"When he sees the depth of the opposition to this tax, Governor Hutchinson will surely turn back the ships," Quincy told Daniel one Sunday evening after he had spent the afternoon with Roger at Faneuil Hall, the marketplace in downtown Boston where those opposed to the Crown's policies often held meetings.

Daniel was seated at his desk, busy with quill pen and inkwell as he wrote out an assignment from one of his instructors at Harvard. He was beginning to wonder if it had been a mistake to read for the law. So far, the work load had been heavy and quite difficult. Still, he had confidence in his ability to rise to the challenge.

"What did you say?" he muttered distractedly to Quincy, not taking his eyes off the sheet of foolscap in front of him.

"I said the governor will surely deny the ships the right to land in Boston Harbor."

"I wouldn't count on that," Daniel said with a shake of his head. He finally looked up at Quincy, who was still gnawing on a chicken leg left over from their supper as he sprawled on the sofa. "Governor Hutchinson strikes me as the type to do whatever the king—or the East India Company—tells him to do."

"You mean he's a craven, spineless coward."

Daniel smiled. "Your words, not mine, brother. Maybe the ships will sink before they ever reach Boston and spare us all the confusion their arrival is sure to bring."

"No, they'll get here," Quincy said quietly. "It's ordained. This whole prickly situation is coming to a head, Daniel."

"You sound like Uncle Benjamin when you start predicting the future. Don't forget to say, 'Now mark my words . . .'" Daniel's deep-voiced imitation of his uncle made the young men laugh.

And as they laughed, a cold wind swept in off the Atlantic, its touch felt across Boston and the surrounding area. Soon, that wind would bring with it the ships of the East India Company, with their cargo of potential disaster.

As autumn settled in over Boston, the flames of discontent began to burn brighter in the city, as brightly as the torches in the hands of the men who gathered to protest the British policies. Angry speeches were made, fists were shaken in the air, and crudely lettered signs vowing opposition to the Crown began to appear around Boston. Daniel tried to ignore the distraction and immerse himself in his academic work, but that was difficult to do. Not a day passed that he did not hear someone speaking passionately on one side of the issue or the other.

He was really more worried about Quincy, however. The boy was being caught up in the frenzy of unrest sweeping through the area. Perhaps it was the influence of his friend Roger Malvern or just that Quincy was ripe for anything that stirred up the emotions and promised excitement. All Daniel knew for certain was that it was wise to beg off on the dinner invitations from Elliot; otherwise, Quincy might well have wound up arguing hotly with Uncle Benjamin.

The center of the controversy had become the merchants for whom the shipments of tea from the East India Company were intended. Only a few men, selected by the Crown, would be allowed to sell the tea, and that was another bone of contention to the colonists. These merchants— Joshua Winslow, Richard Clarke, Benjamin Faneuil, and the two sons of Massachusetts's Governor Hutchinson himself—were urged to refuse the tea. The public pressure showed few signs of success, however. To most of these businessmen, the question was one of money, not politics.

The morning of November third brought a new development. Upon arising and going out of their homes, the citizens of Boston found that during the night someone had tacked up copies of a handbill all over town. In no uncertain language, the handbill read:

To the Freemen of this and neighboring towns.
GENTLEMEN,—You are desired to meet at Liberty Tree, this day, at twelve o'clock at noon; and then and there to hear the persons to whom the tea shipped by the East India Company is consigned, make a public resignation of their office as consignors upon oath; and

*also swear that they will re-ship any teas that may be
consigned to them by said company by the first vessel
sailing for London.*

When Daniel returned to his apartment that afternoon, he found Quincy waiting for him, and almost before
Daniel had set down the pack in which he carried his books,
Quincy thrust a paper into his hands. "Read that," Quincy
said excitedly. "It was all over Boston this morning! I got
that copy from Roger."

Daniel lowered himself wearily into a chair. If Roger
Malvern was the source of this document, he expected it to
be inflammatory, and it certainly was. He scanned the words
once, then read them over more carefully and looked up at
Quincy. "Did you hear what happened at this meeting?"

"Better than that," Quincy said. "I saw it!"

Despite his tiredness, Daniel sprang to his feet. Quincy
had the look of someone who realized he had said too
much. Daniel demanded, "What do you mean, you saw it?
Weren't you in school?"

Quincy shrugged. "Roger and I decided we should go
see what happened. This is more important than any stuffy
old classes, Daniel! This is going to determine how we in the
colonies live the rest of our lives."

"I think you're placing too much significance on one
rally." Daniel sighed. "At any rate, tell me what you saw."

"None of the merchants showed up, so Samuel Adams
gave a speech—"

"That certainly comes as a surprise," Daniel said
dryly.

"As I was saying," Quincy went on, "Samuel Adams
gave a speech about the Tea Act. Then Dr. Benjamin Church
spoke and got everyone so excited that they marched over to

Richard Clarke's store to demand that he refuse the East India tea."

"And did Clarke agree?"

Quincy shook his head. "He most certainly did not. So the crowd wrecked the place!"

"Good Lord! You mean there was a riot?" Daniel grasped Quincy's shoulders. "And you were right in the middle of it?"

With a twist of his body, Quincy pulled loose from Daniel's grasp. "Of course not. Roger and I watched from a block away. But I suppose you would have to call what happened a riot. Clarke summoned the British troops to restore order, but by the time they got there, all the patriots were gone."

"Patriots . . ." Daniel murmured. That was one way of describing the coterie of malcontents who followed Samuel Adams. His uncle Benjamin would prefer words like *rabble* and *traitors*. "Did it ever occur to you that Samuel Adams knew what the response of the merchants would be to that handbill?" Daniel asked.

"What do you mean?" Quincy said sharply and suspiciously. "Are you saying that Adams *planned* the riot?"

"I'm saying it's a possibility. Samuel Adams is no fool, Quincy. He had to be aware of how Clarke and the others would react. Good grief, two of those businessmen are Governor Hutchinson's own sons!"

"Well . . . maybe," Quincy admitted grudgingly. "I suppose it's possible Adams hoped things would turn out as they did. But the important thing is that the populace is so aroused now they'll never allow the British tea to land here!"

"I'm not going to waste my breath arguing with you," Daniel said firmly. For one thing, he added silently to himself, he still was not sure whether he agreed or disagreed with the position taken by the patriots. "All I'm going to say is that if you ever leave school again for any reason other than a legitimate one, I'll put you on the first coach back to Virginia. Father would tan both our hides if he found out what you did today."

Sheepishly, Quincy looked down at the floor. "I suppose you're right. It's just that everything that's going on is so rousing—"

"Try getting excited by your schoolwork, instead."

"Sure, Daniel."

Despite Quincy's effort to sound sincere, Daniel had his doubts. Maybe nothing would happen when the East India tea arrived, he thought. Then this whole mess would blow over, and he and Quincy could settle down to the business of furthering their educations.

Yes, Daniel decided optimistically, all the fuss would soon blow over. . . .

The East India Company ship the *Dartmouth* sailed into Boston Harbor on November twenty-eighth, carrying as her cargo one hundred and fourteen crates of tea from the Orient. It docked at Long Wharf, the principal pier jutting out into the harbor from the east side of the city. While the ship was still being made fast, men armed with muskets and flintlock pistols appeared on the dock, lining the area where the *Dartmouth* was berthed.

The captain of the ship exchanged an uneasy glance with his first mate at the sight of the grim-faced men on the dock. No challenges were issued on either side; no demands were made. But it was rapidly decided that the prudent response might be to allow the crates of tea to sit right where they were, in the cargo hold, for the time being.

If the captain expected British troops—or a delegation from Governor Hutchinson—to show up and allow his cargo to be unloaded in safety, he was disappointed. The governor sent unofficial word that he was going to stay out of this awkward situation as long as possible, leaving any decisions that had to be made up to the captain. After a nervous night and a long day of angry meetings and rallies, the shouts from which were clearly audible to the men on the *Dartmouth*, the captain determined that the best course of action would be to get the devil out while he still had the chance.

He was under strict orders from his superiors at the East India Company, however, and could not abandon the job that had been given him. So he did the next best thing.

Quietly, under cover of darkness, the *Dartmouth* left Long Wharf and moved quietly down the harbor and around the South Battery to the smaller Griffin's Wharf. Several days later, when the *Dartmouth*'s sister ships, the *Eleanor* and the *Beaver*, arrived, they were also directed to Griffin's Wharf.

The British sailors might have hoped that they would be less noticable at their new location, but they were mistaken. The feeling of tension grew stronger every day, and when Governor Hutchinson finally decided the time had come for him to take action, his announcement that the ships would not be allowed to leave until the tea had been unloaded only fanned the flames of insurrection.

Flames that now were burning brightly in the breast of Quincy Reed. . . .

Chapter Six

Daniel just didn't understand, Quincy told himself as he rode toward the Latin School on the morning of December sixteenth. The stalemate in the harbor had been going on for two weeks now, with no signs that it would end any time soon. In fact, Governor Hutchinson had stiffened his stance in the last few days, ordering two gunships to guard the harbor entrance just to make sure the East India ships did not leave until their cargo had been unloaded.

And with all that going on, Daniel seemed to think Quincy should spend his days studying Latin and mathematics and the natural sciences.

Quincy tugged down his tricorn hat and squared his shoulders in his woolen coat. It was a cold, blustery morning, and a chilly mist had begun to fall. The weather had little effect on the busy streets, however, and he had to weave in and out among wagons, carriages, and men on horseback. As he approached the imposing edifice of the Latin School, he saw his friend Roger Malvern waiting at the gate in the fence that surrounded the building.

In contrast to the tall, slender Quincy, Roger was short and stocky, with a florid face and a shock of straw-colored hair. His rotund form reminded Quincy of a much younger Samuel Adams, although Quincy had never mentioned that to Roger. The fifteen-year-old Roger shared more than that with Adams; he had the same fiery zeal for independence.

"Have you heard?" Roger asked excitedly as Quincy reined in and swung down from the saddle.

"Heard what?"

"There's a meeting at the Old South Church. It should be starting right now."

"What sort of meeting?" Quincy asked, although he was fairly certain he knew the answer.

"Samuel Adams has sent one final request to Governor Hutchinson, asking him to change his mind and allow the tea to be sent back to England. If the governor refuses . . ." Roger's face broke into a grin of anticipation. "Well, all I can tell you is that he'll wish he had."

Instantly, an eager thrill raced through Quincy, warming him despite the cold air. "You've heard your father talking to Adams again," he guessed. "The Committee of Safety has something planned, don't they?"

Roger shook his head. "I can't say any more. But I'm going to that meeting at the church. I want to be there when the word comes from the governor."

"I'm going, too," Quincy said without hesitation. He cast a glance at the somber walls of the school building and felt a twinge of guilt. Daniel was attending classes at

Harvard, comfortable in the knowledge that Quincy would be at his own school, where he was supposed to be.

But Quincy had convinced himself that Daniel had no idea how important this was. This could be the final confrontation that forced the colonists into outright rebellion. If that occurred, Quincy wanted to be able to say he was there when it started.

"Are you sure?" Roger asked. "We take a chance on being expelled every time we leave school like this."

"Of course I'm sure," Quincy replied with a laugh. "What's more important, a lot of stuffy old classes—or history in the making?"

Roger slapped him on the back. "I can't argue with that. Let me get my horse."

The Old South Church was on Boylston Street, and a few minutes later the two boys, their hearts pounding with anticipation, were riding toward it. As they approached the church, Quincy saw that a steady stream of people was headed for the same destination. In fact, the cobblestone streets were so congested that Quincy and Roger had to pull their horses to a halt, dismount, and tie the animals to a post in front of a public house. "We'll have to go the rest of the way on foot," Quincy told his companion, and Roger nodded.

Already they could hear the uproar coming from the vicinity of the church, several blocks away. As they drew closer, they heard someone making a speech and recognized the voice as that of Samuel Adams. After nearly every sentence, Adams was interrupted by cheers from the crowd, which had already grown to such a size that it had spilled out of the meetinghouse and was blocking the street outside.

"There must be two thousand people here!" exclaimed Roger as his gaze swept over the crowd.

"More than that," Quincy said. "I've never seen anything like this."

They moved toward the front of the throng, making their way slowly and carefully through the press of people. Most of the ones gathered here were men, but a few women stood in the crowd as well. And all of them, men and women alike, seemed to be angry. Angry at the arrogance of King George, his Parliament, the East India Company, and Governor Hutchinson. Angry enough, Quincy thought, to finally do something about their grievances.

"Where's your father?" Quincy asked Roger, lifting his voice so that he could be heard above the tumult filling the street in front of the meetinghouse.

Roger shook his head. "I don't know. But I'm sure he's here somewhere."

"Will he be upset if he sees us and realizes we're not at school?"

"I don't think so," Roger replied with a grin, wiping away the cold mist that had collected on his forehead. "He knows how important this is."

Quincy wished that Daniel could grasp that, too. Schoolwork paled in comparison with the events going on all around them these days. And it was not just a young man's thirst for adventure that motivated his feelings, Quincy told himself. He was genuinely convinced that the British authorities were wrong and had to be shown the error of their ways—even if it meant a revolution.

When Samuel Adams was through with his speech, he went back inside the church, but he was replaced on the makeshift podium by James Otis. The lawyer was followed by John Adams, cousin of Samuel Adams, the silversmith

Paul Revere, and Dr. Joseph Warren, all of whom made impassioned speeches on behalf of the patriot cause. As swept up as the crowd was by the noble orations, however, the sense of restlessness in the air grew steadily. These people had come here to find out how Governor Hutchinson was going to react to what was probably his final chance to make peace, and speeches were not going to satisfy that curiosity.

Quincy and Roger listened to everything the men had to say; after all, these were the original Sons of Liberty, who had started the movement for freedom many years earlier. But as the hour drew on toward noon and a cold rain began to fall, Quincy felt his attention waning.

"I don't think Hutchinson is even going to answer," he told Roger.

"The governor *has* to answer. Look at this crowd." Roger swept his hand at the mass of humanity filling the street and the church. The crowd had grown, had more than doubled in size, in fact, in the time that Quincy and Roger had been here. At least five thousand people now crowded into this corner of Boston. Roger went on, "Hutchinson can't ignore this demonstration. He simply can't."

Quincy wished he shared his friend's confidence.

They ate lunch at a nearby public house, standing in line for over an hour as they waited for a bowl of stew and a chunk of bread. If nothing else, the massive meeting had been good for business. The food was not particularly appetizing, but it gave them the strength to return to the church and take up the vigil once more. The leaders, it was said, had vowed to remain there until an answer was received from the governor, no matter how long it took.

Quincy and Roger were united in their determination to wait for an answer, too.

As the afternoon wore on, though, that determination began to weaken, at least in Quincy. The rain had stopped earlier, but the air was still raw, damp, and unpleasant. As he and Roger walked around in front of the church, he stamped his booted feet in an effort to warm them.

Most of the crowd members were milling around. The speeches had ended, and there was nothing to do but wait. Some men formed smaller groups and discussed the situation; others passed around bottles and played cards. As Quincy and Roger ambled from group to group, Quincy tried to put his finger on the feeling that now permeated the meeting. It was not exactly like a funeral, but it was no celebration, either. It felt more like waiting while a doctor worked frantically on a loved one who was not expected to live, Quincy decided. He had never been in a situation like that, but he could imagine how it would feel. The men gathered here wanted some news, any news—but at the same time, they feared that news would be bad when it finally came.

As they wandered around the crowd, Quincy spotted several men with large canvas bags. The bags were tightly closed, and Quincy wondered what was inside them. He frowned a bit, sensing that the men would not have brought these bundles to the meeting if their contents were not important.

What if there were guns inside those bags? Quincy asked himself. What if the plan called for passing out guns and attacking the British forces if the governor's reply was not what the people wanted to hear?

Since his arrival in Boston, Quincy had been flirting with the notion of armed rebellion, but now, on a day when it seemed to be a greater possibility than ever before, he suddenly felt some doubt. It was one thing to cheer a speech or wave a torch in the air or tack up a handbill. It was quite another to take a gun in your hand, point it toward another human being, and pull the trigger, especially when the target would probably be shooting back at you. Quincy's stomach clenched as these thoughts went through his head. He tried to tell himself the reaction was to the poor fare he had consumed at lunch, but deep inside he knew differently.

The crowd continued to grow until by evening a good seven thousand people had gathered. Quincy had never before seen this many people at one time, in one place. It was an awe-inspiring spectacle. Taken one by one, they might be a cold, aggravated, impatient bunch. But when they were all together, they possessed a power and determination that made Quincy proud to be one of their number.

His stomach told him it had been a long time since the meager midday meal, but he did not want to eat again. Roger agreed when Quincy brought up the subject. "I'm staying right here," the older boy said. "The message could come anytime now, and I don't want to miss it after waiting all day."

Quincy could understand that sentiment. He had other worries, though. "Daniel will be home by now," he muttered. "He'll wonder where I am."

"Will he come looking for you?" asked Roger.

Quincy shrugged. "I don't know. It's possible."

"Well, if he rides into Boston, I'm sure he'll notice this gathering," Roger said with a grin. "I don't see how anyone could miss it. But he'll never find us among all these people."

"I hope not." Quincy sighed. "Anyway, he probably

won't come. He'll just think that I stopped by my cousin's house and stayed there for supper . . . I hope."

Darkness settled over the city, and torches were lit in front of the church, so many torches that a glow almost as bright as day spread over the whitewashed plank walls of the sanctuary. Someone tried to start the crowd singing a hymn, but the feeble attempt met with failure. Conversations died away, and there was a grim silence. Only the muffled sound of gloved hands being clapped and booted feet being stamped on the cobblestones to keep warm could be heard as everyone waited for what was now assumed to be bad news. Good news would surely have come earlier.

Quincy and Roger were near the door of the church, and standing beside them was a burly man with one of the canvas bags Quincy had noticed earlier. Although tempted to inquire what was inside the bag, Quincy suppressed the impulse. The bleak, angry look on the man's face told him it would be wiser to keep quiet.

Suddenly there was a commotion on the far side of the crowd. People began shouting and stirring, and the crowd parted to allow several men through. Quincy stretched up as tall as he could in order to see them. Beside him, Roger was doing the same thing, but the lad was too short.

"Who is it?" Roger asked excitedly. "Can you see them, Quincy?"

"Three men," Quincy replied. "One of them very tall and thin, with a prominent nose."

"That will be Francis Rotch," Roger exclaimed. "He and two other men were the ones dispatched to Governor Hutchinson with Samuel Adams's letter. The reply has come at last!"

That cry was being taken up by the rest of the crowd. Samuel Adams, John Adams, James Otis, and the other leaders of the movement appeared in the doorway of the church. The three newcomers strode up to them, and they all disappeared inside the building without saying a word. The shouts in the street died away again, and the people were left waiting, tense with anticipation.

It seemed to Quincy that all seven thousand people were holding their breath as Samuel Adams once more trudged out of the church. As a speaker, Adams had several disadvantages. His stature and posture were unimpressive; his voice thin and reedy, seemingly so weak that it could not reach ten yards, let alone to every ear that was so anxiously awaiting his announcement. But everyone heard the words he spoke.

"This meeting can do nothing more to save the country," Samuel Adams said, sadly shaking his head.

The crowd stood there in stunned silence. For every person who had been convinced that Governor Hutchinson would be obstinate, another hoped the governor would be reasonable. That was not to be, though, and as the full import of Samuel Adams's words sunk in, a wave of emotion swept through the crowd, and a great shout went up. In the sound were mingled anger and sorrow—and excitement and anticipation.

That shout came from Quincy Reed's throat, as well as from thousands of others. He thrust a clenched fist in the air and shook it, completely caught up in the dramatic moment. The time for doubts, for questions, was past. Now all that was left was the inevitable reaction to this slap in the face from the British.

The burly man standing nearby loosened the drawstring on the canvas bag he held. "Got enough here for a dozen men," he called. "Gather 'round and get ready, boys!"

His pulse hammering in his head, Quincy turned to face

the man, fully expecting to see him pull some pistols from the bag. Instead, the light from a nearby torch revealed a buckskin shirt decorated with fringe and beads.

"What in the world?" Quincy muttered.

Roger was clearly not surprised at this development. He caught hold of Quincy's arm and tugged him forward. "Come on," he said urgently. "I want to be part of this."

Whatever it was, Quincy did, too. As the crowd surged around the man with the bag, Quincy and Roger were in its forefront, and Quincy accepted without question the shirt and pants thrust into his hands. The pants were made of fringed buckskin that matched the shirt.

"We're going to be Indians," Roger told him, pulling on the buckskin tunic over his shirt. "Hurry up and get dressed."

Quincy did as he was told, awkwardly donning the buckskins over his own garments. Another man appeared in front of him with a tin of lampblack, and he began to daub the stuff on Quincy's face. "Wait!" Quincy exclaimed, jerking back. "What's that for?"

"Don't want to be recognized, do you, lad?"

"No, I suppose not," Quincy admitted as the man continued his task. This was not proceeding at all as he had expected. He had no idea what the men now dressed as Indians were planning to do, but it was bound to be exciting. Quincy felt a thrill run through him. Whatever happened, he was going to be part of it.

When he looked around, he saw that perhaps fifty men, including Roger and himself, were being disguised as savages. Tomahawks were passed around, and Quincy found himself in possession of one, along with a band of cloth with an eagle's feather attached to it. He bound the cloth around his head so that the feather stuck up into the air. He lifted the tomahawk and grinned. It was not a crude weapon with a flint head tied with strips of gut to a wooden handle. Instead it was a small ax with a blade of steel. Not too authentic, perhaps, but in the dark it would look as real as the rest of his costume.

Quincy glanced at the church and saw that Samuel Adams had disappeared. He had probably gone inside with the other leaders of the revolutionary movement. For the sake of appearances, they would have to distance themselves from whatever was about to happen, leaving the impression that tonight's activities were a spontaneous demonstration of the people's anger at Governor Hutchinson's decision. Obviously, though, from what Quincy had seen, some members of the crowd had been expecting the answer they had gotten, and they had been prepared to act.

The throngs parted again, allowing the buckskin-clad men to stride through. "To Griffin's Wharf!" one man shouted, brandishing a tomahawk over his head. Others took up the cry, and in a matter of moments, shouts of "To Griffin's Wharf!" filled the air. The mock Indians, with Quincy and Roger in the center of the group, broke into a run.

Now Quincy understood what they were going to do. The British would not allow the tea to be returned to England, so it would be unloaded tonight—into the waters of Boston Harbor.

Trailed and urged on by thousands of eager Bostonians, the costumed group ran through the streets, whooping and shouting and waving their tomahawks. Surrounded by the clamor, Quincy found it hard to think. It was much easier to let his emotions take control, to carry him along with the tide of angry humanity. He cried out as fiercely and savagely as any of his companions as he raced toward the harbor.

Their pace increased as they came within sight of the wharf where the three British ships were docked. Most of the crew members of the *Dartmouth,* the *Eleanor,* and the *Beaver* were ashore, passing their time in the nearby grog shops and brothels, but a few men had remained on board each vessel. These men came to the railings of the ships, drawn by the uproar of the approaching mob.

The "Indians" split into three groups as they reached the wharf, each group going to the gangplank leading up to a ship. As the bunch Quincy and Roger were in started to clamber up the *Dartmouth*'s gangplank, a mate appeared at the head of the walkway and demanded in a loud voice, " 'Ere now, what's all this? What are you men doin' 'ere?"

The leader of the group thrust his tomahawk in the air. "We've come to have a little tea party!" he shouted into the silence that had fallen following the seaman's question. "Now get out of the way, or you'll go into the harbor along with the tea!" With that, he let out another whoop and charged onto the ship. The other men were right behind him.

The British sailor ducked back quickly, unwilling to try to stop these enraged men just to protect the East India Company's tea. The "Indians" swarmed over the ship, and hatches leading into the cargo hold were jerked up. Men in buckskins dropped down into the hold and began passing up the crates of tea. The scene was being repeated on the *Eleanor* and the *Beaver.*

Quincy was still on deck, and as a crate of tea was dropped in front of Roger and him, they followed the example of their fellows and began chopping the top of it with their tomahawks. When they had smashed it open, they tucked the tomahawks in their belts, picked up the crate, and carried it to the railing on the far side of the deck. Upending the crate, they dumped the tea, sending it swirling into the waters of the harbor, tossing the empty crate in after it.

The tea party continued on all three ships, and in an astonishingly short time the job was completed. Eighteen thousand pounds of tea were dumped into Boston Harbor, emptying the cargo holds of the ships. With each chest of tea that had vanished into the dark, murky water, loud cheers had gone up from the spectators on shore.

Working with Roger, Quincy had disposed of several crates of the stuff, and he felt mildly disappointed when there was no more. Some of the men danced around like the Indians they were pretending to be, but there was no real attempt to fool anyone. The British seamen on duty knew quite well that under the buckskins and lampblack and eagle feathers were colonists. The disguises would make it difficult if not impossible to determine the real identities of the raiders, however.

"Come on," Roger said to Quincy, jerking his head toward the gangplank. "We'd better get out of here now that it's done!"

Quincy ignored him and waved his tomahawk at a small group of sailors standing nearby. "Next time you'll go into the harbor with your damned British tea!" he threatened.

Roger took hold of his arm and steered him firmly toward the dock. For a moment Quincy thought about trying to pull free. Then he realized that Roger was right. So far the sailors had not put up a fight, and no one had been harmed. A glance at the wharf told him that the crowd which had followed them from the Old South Church was dispersing rapidly. This night's work was indeed over, and to push matters any further might result in a bloody riot.

"I'm coming," he muttered. He and Roger scampered

down the gangplank with the other buckskin-garbed men, and given their exhilaration, it was lucky no one tumbled off the narrow walkway. Everyone reached the dock safely, however, and a man standing there told them, "Scatter, lads. You did a fine job. The bloody British will think twice before they send us any more of their damned tea!"

Waving their tomahawks over their heads, Quincy and Roger trotted triumphantly into the darkness that fell as the torches carried by the crowd were extinguished. Quincy's blood was racing; he had never been so stimulated in his life. He and Roger were laughing hilariously as they made their way back to where they had left their horses. Along the way, they tossed the tomahawks into an alley, then stripped off the buckskins and threw them away, too. Except for the lamp-black on their faces, no one would be able to connect them with the raid on the British ships.

"We're going to be famous, my friend," Roger exulted. "No one will ever forget what we did tonight."

Quincy suddenly sobered. Roger was right, he thought. The night's events would be the talk of the town tomorrow.

And when Daniel found out that he had been right in the middle of it . . .

Time enough to worry about that later, Quincy told himself. Right now he could be happy, knowing that tonight he had helped strike a blow against British tyranny. After the Boston Tea Party—nice ring to that, he thought—things would never be the same again.

Chapter Seven

Daniel was trying very hard to concentrate on the volume open on the desk in front of him, but it was difficult. What he wanted to do was leap up, pace wildly back and forth, and discover what in blazes had happened to his brother. He had already spent several hours in just that manner, in fact.

He had considered saddling his horse and riding into Boston from Cambridge, but if he did that, he risked being gone from the apartment should someone bring a message concerning Quincy. For that matter, Quincy himself could show up, and then he would worry if Daniel were absent. The best thing to do, Daniel had decided, was just to be patient and wait, as difficult as that was. To get his mind off the problem, he was trying to force his thoughts onto his schoolwork.

The sound of footsteps pounding up the stairs from the ground floor made his head jerk up. The door burst open and Quincy came in, an animated grin on his face. He stopped short when he saw how taut and grim Daniel's features were.

"Would it do any good to inquire as to where you've been the past five hours?" Daniel asked.

Quincy looked at him for a moment, then closed the door. He shrugged and said, "I've been in Boston."

"You know I can go into town tomorrow and ask Uncle Benjamin and Aunt Polly about that."

"I didn't say I was with them." Quincy moved a couple of steps closer.

Daniel put his hands flat on the desk and pushed himself to his feet. "I can see that," he said, staring at the streaks of black on Quincy's face. It looked as though he had smeared lampblack on his face and then tried to rub it off, not completely successfully. His clothes were rumpled as well. Daniel went on, "Just what the devil have you been up to?"

"If you must know," Quincy said, "I paid a little visit to Griffin's Wharf this evening, along with a few friends."

Daniel stiffened. Griffin's Wharf was where the three ships from England loaded with East India Company tea were berthed. They had been the center of controversy for weeks now.

"What have you done?" Daniel asked in a shaky voice that was little more than a whisper. "What have you gotten mixed up in now, Quincy?"

"Freedom!" Quincy said fervently. "That's what I'm mixed up in, as you put it, Daniel. We showed the bloody British they can't impose their damnable taxes on free men!"

"My God," Daniel breathed. "You've been listening to Samuel Adams and those other firebrands, haven't you?"

"There was a meeting at the Old South Church today.

We were waiting to see what Hutchinson's response would be to one last request to send the tea back to England. He refused, of course."

"You went to this meeting instead of attending your classes?"

Quincy shrugged. "I knew it was more important."

Daniel felt the anger inside him surging to the surface. He did not even attempt to hold it back. "Blast it, Quincy, I told you what would happen if you defied me again! I told you I'd send you right back to Virginia—"

"You're not my father!" Quincy yelled, striding forward to confront his older brother. "You can't give me orders!"

"Mother and Father trusted me to supervise your behavior—"

"I don't need anybody to supervise me," Quincy interrupted again. "I'm almost fifteen years old. That's old enough to make my own decisions."

"About some things, yes," Daniel agreed. "But regardless of your age, you're obviously not grown up enough to be trusted!"

Quincy leaned forward, resting his knuckles on the table across which Daniel was glowering at him. "I had to be there," he insisted. "Daniel, please understand. It was much more important than school."

"That decision isn't for you to make!"

"Well, I'll never be much of a man if I don't learn how to make my own decisions, will I?"

Daniel took a deep breath. "All right, just tell me what happened," he forced himself to say quietly.

At first grudgingly, then in a voice that began to ring with pride at what he had been a part of, Quincy told him about the day-long vigil at the church and the speeches given by Samuel Adams, James Otis, and the others. He described the reaction that had swept through the crowd at the unsatisfactory response from Governor Hutchinson and the way some of the patriots had garbed themselves in Indian clothing to pay a visit to the British ships.

"You don't have to worry, Daniel," Quincy assured his brother when he had finished the tale. "No one could have recognized me, not in that savage's getup with lampblack on my face."

"I thought that was lampblack," Daniel muttered, trying to let everything Quincy had told him sink into his stunned brain. "You actually went on those ships and dumped the tea overboard?"

Quincy grinned. "Every last bit of it. Quite a tea party, eh?"

To his surprise, Daniel found himself smiling a little in return. "I'll wager those British sailors were pretty shocked."

"Oh, they were, but they didn't try to stop us. There was no fighting, no bloodshed. It was a political protest, Daniel, nothing more."

"The Crown will see it as something more, I promise you." Daniel's demeanor became more solemn as the seriousness of the situation struck him. "There'll be trouble because of this."

Quincy shook his head. "I don't care. There'll be a great deal more trouble if the British don't wake up and give us what we want."

"And that is?"

"Freedom!"

"You've become an insurrectionist, then." Daniel's voice was heavy with worry.

"I'd rather be called a patriot. A few concessions from the Crown won't be enough, not now. It's time we were truly free."

Daniel sighed and sank back into his chair, suddenly unutterably weary. "Uncle Benjamin would say you're a traitor if he heard you talking like that."

"Well, you've just heard me." Quincy leaned forward, an intense expression on his young face. "What do you say, Daniel? Am I a traitor—or a patriot?"

The question struck Daniel with the force of a hammer blow. For months he had been considering the issue of the colonists' unrest as an intellectual dilemma, pondering the evidence on both sides. Now Quincy was throwing it in his face and demanding an answer based on what was in his heart rather than his head. Daniel looked up at his brother and gave the only reply he could.

"You're a patriot," he said softly.

"I knew it!" Quincy exclaimed, his smudged face breaking into another grin. "I knew you couldn't be as muddleheaded as Uncle Benjamin, Daniel! You agree with us, then?"

Daniel got to his feet once more. "I agree that the British have pushed things too far, and you and your friends have pushed back. Like it or not, there's going to be trouble over this, and I'm afraid there won't be any turning back on either side."

"Not on ours, I assure you!"

"So it seems that the best thing to do . . . the only thing to do . . . is to carry through with what's been started." Daniel fixed Quincy with a stern glance. "That does not mean that I think you should be getting in the middle of such things."

Quincy's jaw dropped in surprise. "But Daniel, I have to!"

"No, you don't. You're only just fifteen years old. Leave the fate of the world to your elders and get on about your schooling. No more missing school, no more running off to meetings with your friend Roger." Daniel was all too aware that he had issued an ultimatum like this once before, evidently with little effect on Quincy's behavior. There was nothing he could do but try again, unless he wanted to send Quincy home to Virginia and admit to his parents that he had failed to keep the youngster in line. That option was too galling to accept, at least for the time being.

"I can't promise that, Daniel," Quincy said. "I have to do what I think is right."

"As do I." Daniel came around the desk, faced Quincy, and put a hand on his shoulder. "I'm going to go into Boston tomorrow and buy a ticket for passage on the post coach back to Virginia. If you fail to heed what I've asked you to do, Quincy, you'll use that ticket. I can promise you that."

Quincy looked as if he wanted to jerk free from Daniel's grip, but he did not attempt to do so. Instead he just glowered at his older brother in silence.

"Listen," Daniel said. "I may agree with the colonists' cause, but that doesn't mean I want to see you putting yourself in danger, Quincy. And there could have been danger tonight." He paused, then went on, "What if those British sailors had fought back?"

"We'd have shown them the error of their ways," Quincy snapped.

"How? By caving in their skulls with those axes, just as you did the tea chests?"

Quincy blinked, then frowned a little.

"And when you tried that, some of the sailors would have pulled their pistols and gotten off a shot or two before the mob murdered them," Daniel said. "Some of your friends might have been killed. *You* might have been killed."

The lines on Quincy's forehead deepened. "I didn't think about that," he muttered.

"Mobs don't stop to think," Daniel told him. "If you're going to fight the British, you've got to keep a cool head."

My God, what am I doing talking like this? Daniel asked himself. *Fighting the British? Keeping a cool head—so you don't get it blown off by a musket ball?* What was happening to the world? He had come to Boston to complete his education, not to become embroiled in some sort of revolution.

But there was not going to be any staying out of it, he sensed. Sooner or later, everyone in the colonies—man, woman, and child—would be called upon to make a decision.

Quincy had made his, and so, Daniel supposed, had he.

Daniel drew his brother closer and clapped him on the back as he embraced him. "I just want you to be careful," he said quietly. "I don't want you to get hurt."

"But that's what we may have to risk," Quincy said. "If we're to achieve our goals, we may all have to chance being hurt."

"I'm afraid you're right." Daniel rested his hands on Quincy's shoulders. "But not now. Let's wait and see what happens. In the meantime, I want you attending classes."

Quincy smiled and nodded. "All right. I can see there's no arguing with you. You're as stubborn as Father."

Daniel smiled and said, "It's a trait that seems to run in the Reed family."

If Daniel Reed and some other inhabitants of Boston and the surrounding area secretly hoped that the furor caused by the Boston Tea Party would die away, they were soon disappointed. Word of the event spread rapidly throughout the colonies and to England, as fast as a ship bearing a letter from Governor Hutchinson could reach London. The debate in Parliament during the winter of seventy-three and seventy-four was hot enough to offset the usual chill gripping the city.

Referring to the patriots in Boston as a nest of locusts, some politicians called for them to be exterminated. Others, most notably Edmund Burke, counseled patience and advised that the Tea Act, which had caused so much of the resentment, be rescinded. Burke's advice was overwhelmed by an outpouring of anger from his fellow officials, however, culminating in the spring of 1774 in the passage of what the British entitled the Coercive Acts.

To the citizens of Boston, though, they were known as the Intolerable Acts, and that was exactly what they were—intolerable, clearly designed to punish Boston for its effrontery.

The first edict shut down the port, forbidding any ship from entering or leaving the harbor. The second threw out the charter under which the Massachusetts colony had been formed and made town meetings illegal. The third protected all British officials from prosecution by the local courts of the colony, and to enforce these, the fourth of the Intolerable Acts called for the quartering of more British troops in the city of Boston itself. Governor Thomas Hutchinson, considered by the Crown to be too ineffective in his dealings with the colonists, was replaced and a new man put in charge.

The new governor of Massachusetts was General Thomas Gage, the commander in chief of all the British forces in North America. A tough, capable soldier, Gage was unwilling to knuckle under to anyone—least of all a disorderly rabble composed of farmers and merchants.

It was clear that where the Boston Tea Party was concerned, the British government was not going to forgive and forget . . .

* * *

Daniel had been watching the situation closely, hoping that nothing further would arise where Quincy could get himself into trouble. It was obvious, though, as news of the Intolerable Acts reached Boston, followed shortly by General Gage himself, that things were only going to get worse.

One afternoon, when Daniel arrived home from Harvard, he found a piece of paper on the floor just inside the door. Frowning, he picked up the folded, sealed paper, tore it open, unfolded it, and scanned the words inside, written in a neat, precise hand with a minimum of ink smudges. Suddenly, he smiled. Such precision was exactly what he would expect from a schoolmaster like his old friend Nathan Hale.

The note was an invitation to meet Hale, along with two more of Daniel's close friends and classmates from Yale, Benjamin Tallmadge and Robert Townsend, for a glass of ale the next afternoon, Saturday, at a local tavern called the Hare and Hounds Inn. If he could not join them, Hale's note continued, they would get back in touch with him later.

"I'll be there, Nathan," Daniel said aloud as he refolded the piece of paper. With everything that had been going on for the past few months, it would be nice simply to reminisce with three old friends.

When Quincy came in from school a little later, Daniel told him, "I have some business to take care of tomorrow. Why don't you ride in to Uncle Benjamin's, and I'll join you there later?"

Quincy made a face. "Uncle Benjamin is a loyalist. I

don't know if I can stand listening to his opinions. And he's never one to keep them to himself."

"That's true enough." Daniel grinned. "I think you can manage for a little while, though, if only for the sake of Elliot and Aunt Polly. The last time I talked to Elliot, he was upset because you and I don't go there for dinner anymore."

"Well, you can't blame us for that. Uncle Benjamin isn't our father, and we shouldn't have to listen to his muddlebrained views."

"But he is our uncle," Daniel reminded Quincy, "and he's entitled to our respect, whether we agree with him or not."

Quincy shrugged and said, "Maybe. But why can't I go with you, wherever it is you're going?"

Daniel shook his head. "I'm just going to meet some friends from Yale. I'm sure it would be quite boring for you, Quincy."

"All right," Quincy agreed grudgingly. "I'll ride into town tomorrow morning."

"And I'll come later tomorrow afternoon. Thanks, Quincy."

"This had better not become a habit," warned Quincy jokingly.

"I'm sure it won't. I don't know what these lads are doing nowadays, but I'm sure they're busy with their own lives."

Daniel did know that Nathan Hale was teaching school in a small Connecticut town, while Robert Townsend had planned to be a merchant and open a store of some type. The fiery, intelligent Benjamin Tallmadge was the superintendent of a high school in Wethersfield, Connecticut. Daniel was sure he would enjoy catching up with all the activities of his friends when he saw them the next day.

As he entered the Hare and Hounds Inn on Saturday afternoon, he saw that Hale, Tallmadge, and Townsend were already there, seated in a booth toward the rear of the room. They spotted him and lifted mugs of ale in greeting. "Daniel Reed!" called out Nathan Hale. "Back here!"

Grinning, Daniel went over to join them. On the way, he signaled to the publican to bring him a drink.

Tallmadge and Townsend were on one side of the booth, Hale on the other. Daniel slid onto the bench next to Hale and said, "Hello, lads. What brings you to Cambridge?"

"You, of course," Nathan Hale said. "We wanted to see you again, Daniel. It's been a long time."

"Only a year," Daniel pointed out.

Hale shrugged, and Tallmadge said, "A year can seem like an eternity at times, especially when the world is full of trouble."

The tavern keeper brought a large pewter mug filled with ale to the table and set it in front of Daniel. As Daniel reached into his pocket for a coin to pay the man, Townsend motioned for him to keep his money and flipped a coin to the tavern keeper, who bit it, grinned, and shuffled away.

Daniel took a sip of the ale, leaned forward, and looked around at his friends. "What have you three been up to since I saw you last?" he asked. "I know you were planning on teaching school, Nathan. . . ."

"And that's just what I've been doing." Hale, a dark-haired, handsome young man, gave an infectious grin and went on, "It's been quite rewarding. Not financially, of course, but I enjoy working with the youngsters. However, it's not what you would call exciting."

"Nor is keeping a store," Townsend said. He was short and stocky, with curly hair and dark eyes that sparkled with intelligence. He went on, "But it seems to be what I'm best suited for."

"How about you, Benjamin?" Daniel asked, turning his gaze to the third young man.

Tallmadge was taller and leaner than Townsend, but he had the same sort of curly hair and keen eyes. He shrugged and said, "I have left my job behind and am casting about for my lot in life. I don't think I'll have to worry about it much longer, though."

"Oh?" said Daniel. "You're about to embark on something?"

"We all are," Tallmadge said. "Everyone in the colonies is going to be busy soon . . . fighting the damned British."

The young man's voice dropped on the last words, so that he would not be overheard at neighboring tables. Daniel frowned. He had hoped this reunion would not turn into a political discussion. He would much rather talk about the good times he had shared with the three young men during their days at Yale.

"And of course we know what you've been doing, Daniel," Nathan Hale said quickly, casting a glance at Tallmadge as if to chide him for bringing up the subject of the friction between the colonies and the mother country. "You're enrolled at Harvard. What would old Elihu Yale say if he knew one of his own had gone over to the enemy?"

"I daresay he'd wish me luck," Daniel replied. "When he founded the school, I don't think he intended for any sort of rivalry to spring up between it and Harvard."

"Well, it has, and you can't deny it," Townsend said.

"Perhaps," Daniel admitted.

"Yale, Harvard, what difference does it make?"

Tallmadge snapped. "Soon we are all going to have to put aside our petty jealousies and unite against the real enemy— the British."

Nathan Hale sighed. "You're determined to talk about it, aren't you, Benjamin?"

"Well, that's why we're here, isn't it?"

Daniel's frown deepened. "What do you mean, that's why we're here? I thought we were getting together just to have a drink and talk about old times."

"The old times are gone," Townsend said with a sigh. "And I fear Benjamin is right. Soon everything is going to change."

Hale took a healthy swallow of the ale in his mug and said, "I had hoped we could enjoy a bit of conversation before we got down to business, Daniel, but it doesn't appear that's possible now. The three of us got together and asked you to meet us here for a reason."

Daniel gave a grim nod. "I understand that now. But just what is the reason?"

"It's quite simple," Tallmadge said, leaning forward to peer intently across the table at Daniel. "We— the three of us—have decided to devote our lives to the cause of liberty. Because you are our friend, Daniel, we're asking you to join us."

Daniel sat back, assimilating what Tallmadge had just said. It was true enough that at Yale the four of them had done practically everything together, and it made sense now that these three would want him to join their latest endeavor. But he was not sure he was ready to do that.

Keeping his voice pitched low, as they had done, he said, "You say you're going to devote your lives to the cause of liberty. What exactly do you mean by that?"

"We mean that we'll do everything we can to see that

the yoke of the British is taken off the neck of Americans!" Tallmadge responded. "By force if necessary."

"But there's no war, no rebellion."

"There will be." Tallmadge sounded utterly convinced of that pessimistic viewpoint.

"What we're trying to say, Daniel," Townsend put in, "is that whatever happens in the future, we've made up our minds which side we'll be on."

Nathan Hale nodded. "We'd like to know that you're with us, Daniel."

To give himself a moment, Daniel drained the rest of his ale. Then he said, "I have to admit, with the way the British government is cracking down on Boston, there's bound to be more trouble."

"And next time it won't be anything as trivial as pitching some tea into the harbor," Tallmadge said.

"You're right. Still, is there anything wrong with hoping that a peaceful solution can be found?"

"Peace is impossible," Nathan Hale said, "unless England changes her ways. Do you really think that will happen, Daniel?"

With a shake of his head, Daniel looked down at the table. "No, I don't believe it's very likely," he said quietly.

"It's bloody impossible," Tallmadge said. "The Crown will never change."

Abruptly, Daniel pushed himself to his feet. "I'll think about what you've said," he promised.

"Wait a minute," Hale said quickly. "You're leaving?"

"I had hoped this would be a pleasant reunion of old friends," Daniel replied heavily. "But I see now that's not possible. As you said, everything's changed."

Tallmadge's hand shot across the table and gripped

Daniel's arm tightly. "You won't betray us?" he asked harshly.

Daniel merely looked at him for a long moment and then asked, "What do *you* think?"

Tallmadge's fingers dropped away from Daniel's arm, and he shook his head as he looked down at the table. "God, I'm ashamed of myself." He lifted his eyes to Daniel again. "I'm sorry, old man. Regardless of the circumstances and the trouble in the world these days, I had no right to ask a question like that."

"It's all right," Daniel told him gently. He looked around the table at all three of them and went on, "As I said, I'll think about what we've discussed here today. Perhaps next time I see you, I can give you an answer."

"I hope so," Nathan Hale said. "We'll be in touch, Daniel."

With a solemn nod, Daniel turned and walked out of the tavern. As he traveled back toward the apartment, he kept seeing the faces of his friends in his mind. He had seen their intensity, their dedication, their passion for the cause they had adopted as their own. He felt the stirrings of that same passion deep within his own breast.

Benjamin Tallmadge had been right. Soon it would be time for everyone to choose sides in the coming battle.

Revolution, Daniel realized in that moment, was inevitable.

Chapter Eight

W here the devil is my pipe?" Benjamin Markham thundered as he stalked into the parlor of his Beacon Hill home.

Elliot looked up from the pamphlet he was reading and pointed. "Right there on the mantelpiece, Father, where you left it," he said.

"Don't be sarcastic with me, young man," Benjamin muttered as he stalked across the room to retrieve his clay pipe. He glanced at Elliot and went on, "What's that you're reading?"

"Just a new essay by Patrick Henry," Elliot said offhandedly, without thinking.

"What?" Benjamin stepped quickly to Elliot's chair and snatched the pamphlet out of his hands. A snap of his wrist sent it flying into the fireplace, a gesture which would have been considerably more dramatic had a fire been burning at the time. As it was, the pamphlet landed in a pile of ashes and sent a small cloud puffing into the air.

"Father!" Elliot exclaimed. "You had no right to do that!"

"I had every right," Benjamin said coldly. "I won't have any son of mine reading such traitorous trash. 'If this be treason,' indeed!"

Elliot sighed. "I was just trying to stay informed, Father. A man has to know what's going on in the world around him if he's to make rational decisions, doesn't he?"

"Informed? I'll keep you informed, lad. Anything you need to know, I'll tell you. And I'm telling you that I don't want to see such obscene material in my house again, do you understand?"

"Of course, Father. I understand." Elliot sank back in his chair, knowing how futile it was to argue with Benjamin Markham.

Benjamin gave a snort and a nod and left the room, taking with him the pipe he had been looking for when he came in.

Frowning, Elliot peered at the fireplace and considered retrieving the pamphlet but quickly gave up the idea. Not only would he get soot all over his hands, but he had only been reading the pamphlet to pass some idle time. He was glad his father had not asked him where he had gotten the Henry essay. If Benjamin had asked, Elliot would not have known what to tell him. Admitting that the pamphlet had come from Quincy Reed would only have caused more trouble.

Elliot had not been surprised when his young cousin gave him the pamphlet. From comments Quincy had been making since the previous winter, Elliot had a pretty good idea that the lad's sympathies lay with the insurrectionists. As for Daniel . . . well, Elliot was not sure. It had always been difficult for him to know what his cousin was really thinking and feeling. Daniel was a private person and kept many of his thoughts to himself; nevertheless, Elliot suspected that Daniel, too, was leaning toward the cause of liberation from the British.

Elliot was not going to say anything about this to his father. Admitting that Daniel and Quincy might be what Benjamin considered traitors would cause more trouble in the family, and Elliot did not want that. He had enough problems of his own right now.

He stood up, went to the parlor window, and looked out at the sunshine of a warm late spring day. Almost a year had passed since Daniel Reed had come to pay a visit to the Markham family and then find a place to live while he went to Harvard. A great deal had changed in that year, Elliot reflected. Not a week went by without another call from someone for the colonies to be free from England's rule. The tension in the city was enormous, especially since the Tea Party and the passage of the Intolerable Acts. Naturally, the closing of the port had had a great deal of effect on the Markham & Cummings Shipping line. For a few months, trade had been shut down entirely, and ships had floated idly at the wharves of the city.

In recent weeks, though, General Gage had unofficially relaxed that policy somewhat, and certain ship owners were now able to get their vessels in and out of the harbor as long as they did not call a great deal of attention to themselves in the process. Since both partners in Markham & Cummings were staunch loyalists, their ships were among those now allowed to pass.

Elliot had been keeping a close eye on the situation, finding that his interest was growing despite his avowed nonchalance about the business world. There was only so much time one could spend squiring around a beautiful young lady, he had discovered, even a girl as lovely as Sarah Cummings.

As if his thoughts had summoned her, a carriage pulled up in front of the Markham house, and Sarah alighted from it, helped down by her father, who had stepped out of the vehicle first. Elliot had not been expecting them, but it was not unusual for Theophilus Cummings to stop by to discuss business matters with his partner. Elliot hurried to open the door for them.

"Good afternoon, Mr. Cummings," he said as he swung the door open before Cummings could use the brass knocker. "Hello, Sarah."

"Elliot," Cummings said curtly. "I should think that you would be at the office today, my boy. This is a working day, after all."

"I, ah, I was just on my way there," Elliot replied quickly. In point of fact, he had not been near the Markham & Cummings offices for several days now.

Cummings waved off Elliot's comment. "Doesn't matter," he said in a surly voice. "With the way things are these days, we could get by with half the number of clerks. We don't need you down there getting in the way, too." With that, he stalked past Elliot and threw another question over his shoulder. "Where's your father?"

"I believe he went to his study. I can get him for you—"

"Never mind, I'll find him."

Cummings disappeared down the hallway, and Elliot turned to Sarah, who gave him an arch smile. "And I believe that leaves you to entertain me," she said, slipping off her lightweight wrap.

"A task I'll gladly take on," Elliot replied with a slight leer of his own. He shut the door, glanced over his shoulder, and saw that he and Sarah were alone in the foyer. Taking advantage of the opportunity, he drew the lovely blonde into his arms and kissed her.

As always when they were alone, Sarah allowed the wanton side of her personality to come out. Cool and reserved in public, in private she could be a bit of a hellcat, as Elliot well knew. Her lips were warm and tasted of a moist sweetness that drove him half mad. His arms slipped around her waist and drew her against him as her arms twined about his neck, and her hand softly traced the outline of one of his ears. He felt the soft thrust of her breasts through the delicate blue fabric of her dress. He would have liked to run his fingers through the elaborate arrangement of blond curls, on which perched a hat with a tall feather stuck on it that matched her dress, but if he mussed her hair it would be obvious to anyone who saw her what they had been doing. Although he had been linked romantically with her for quite some time, and it was assumed that eventually they would marry, they had to be at least a little circumspect in their actions.

Which meant that he could not sweep her up in his arms, carry her upstairs to his bedroom, and make love to her, even though that was exactly what both of them wanted desperately at this moment.

Taking her lips away from his, Sarah whispered, "We had better go into the parlor before someone sees us."

Elliot nodded, loath to let her go but knowing that she was right. He took his arms from around her but caught hold of one of her hands. "Come on," he said.

When they were both settled down on the comfortable sofa, Sarah said, "Father is very upset. He thinks General Gage isn't being reasonable enough about letting loyalist ships in and out of the harbor."

Elliot shook his head. "I don't see how he can complain. So little trade is going on anyway, he should be happy that the Markham and Cummings line has any part of it."

"Oh, I know that, but you know Father. He's rarely satisfied."

Elliot was well aware of that facet of Theophilus Cummings's personality, all right. It was one Cummings shared with Benjamin Markham. Perhaps that lack of satisfaction was what had made them successful businessmen, mused Elliot. And perhaps that was why business had never held any great appeal for him; until recently, he had been quite satisfied with his life.

If only this conflict between the colonies and England had not sprung up to trouble his mind . . .

"What are you thinking?" Sarah asked, seeing the look on his face.

Elliot shook his head. "Oh, nothing important." He smiled at her. "I'd much rather think about how beautiful you look today."

"Thank you, kind sir. You may allow your mind to dwell on that subject as often as you please." Sarah hesitated, then went on, "However, it might be a good idea if you went into the office occasionally, no matter what my father says. I know he'd be happy if you showed a little more initiative."

"I do my work," Elliot said with a shrug, smarting a little at her reprimand, no matter how gently it had been delivered.

"Do you really?" asked Sarah. "What work have you done today?"

Elliot blinked rapidly, surprised at the turn this conversation had suddenly taken. At first, Sarah had seemed perfectly content to kiss him and flirt seductively with him, but she seemed to have something else on her mind now.

"If you must know," he told her, "I've been reading a pamphlet by Patrick Henry."

Sarah's blue eyes widened. "But . . . but he's an insurrectionist!" she finally exclaimed.

"It's not a disease like the Black Plague that I can catch from reading one of the man's essays."

"It's worse than a disease!"

Elliot stood up and began pacing back and forth in front of the sofa. "What's happened to you, Sarah?" he asked. "You used to hold no political opinions that I was aware of. Why are you so aghast that I've been reading one of Henry's pamphlets?"

"You don't understand, Elliot. I . . . I don't care what the politicians say or do. I suppose I support my father's position on the matter, just as you should support your father's opinions."

He stared at her, once again shocked. "Are you saying that I should just accept whatever way of thinking my father prefers and leave it at that? You're saying I should have no thoughts of my own?"

"That is precisely what I'm saying," Sarah told him primly. "Someday, you'll follow in your father's footsteps and take over the business, and you don't need anything to distract you from that."

"My God," Elliot said, realization dawning on him. "You're saying that I should be a loyalist for business reasons?"

"Of course." She looked up at him ingenuously. "What other reasons could there be?"

For a long moment, Elliot met her gaze, and then abruptly he threw back his head and began to laugh. "Is there nothing in that beautiful head of yours save finances?" he asked. "Do you ever give any thought to the future, to the concepts of freedom and justice?"

She caught her breath, stung by his harsh words. "I've given a great deal of thought to the future, Elliot," she snapped. "And I know what's important to me. I want a comfortable future. I want to marry a successful, financially secure man. I've always thought that man would be you . . . until now."

"And what does *that* mean?"

Sarah closed her eyes and lifted her hands to her temples. "Oh, Elliot, why must we argue? You have to stop thinking about all this silly trouble with England and remember what's really important—you and I and our life together."

"That's what I want," Elliot said huskily, stepping closer to her and resting his hands on her shoulders.

"And I do, too." She opened her eyes and looked up at him. "But it may not be possible unless you stop filling your mind with such treasonous material. If . . . if you were to be won over to that despicable crowd of rebels, I . . . I would have to look elsewhere for my future."

"And where might that be?"

"Well . . . Avery Wallingford has always been quite attentive to me, ever since we were all children, and his father is a banker, you know. A Tory banker on very solid terms with the government."

Elliot felt a great wellspring of anger rising within him. So this was all just a ploy to make him jealous of Avery, he thought. Sarah probably believed that he had been taking her for granted lately, and it was true enough that he had been rather preoccupied in recent weeks. All she really wanted to do was to shake him up a bit, to make sure of his love for her. And he did love her. He felt his anger ebbing away.

Tightening his grip on her shoulders, he pulled Sarah to her feet and gazed down intently into her eyes. "You can forget all about Avery Wallingford," he said firmly. "I love you, and I won't let you down, Sarah."

"Oh, Elliot," she murmured. "I knew you'd understand. I'm so glad you're not angry with me."

"How could I ever be angry with you?" he whispered. Then his lips came down on hers again, and the sensations that flooded through him from the kiss washed away any thoughts about his cousins and the insurrectionist movement. All that mattered was the warm, vital young woman in his arms at this instant. . . .

Footsteps in the hall made them spring apart, and by the time Benjamin Markham and Theophilus Cummings entered the parlor a moment later, Sarah was back on the sofa and Elliot was ensconced in an armchair, and they were chatting politely about an upcoming party.

But neither of them would forget what had happened here today. They had come to an understanding, and Elliot, for one, was glad.

Now, if only he could keep those doubts from creeping back into his mind . . .

With examinations coming up, the last thing he needed to be doing was worrying about anything but his schoolwork, Daniel reminded himself. But as he shoved away the book he had been trying to study, he had to admit that his mind was definitely on other things these days.

Ever since his meeting with Nathan Hale, Benjamin Tallmadge, and Robert Townsend, he had been thinking about the things that were said that day. If revolution was coming—and Daniel now had no doubt that it was—then everyone would indeed have to make a choice. There would be no such thing as neutrality. Each man would have to decide whether he was going to support the rebels or the British.

Daniel knew he could never take the side of the British in this matter. He was a colonist through and through. His life and his loyalties were all on this side of the Atlantic, and he was convinced that the British were morally wrong in trying to impose their will so unfairly on the colonies.

And yet he believed in the rule of law. Once a rebellion started, there would be no more law, only bloodshed and death until one side was too battered to go on. The colonists had no guarantee that they would win such a war. In fact, the odds were heavily against them. How could a ragtag band of settlers stand up against the might of the British Empire?

Daniel sighed. He had pondered these questions over and over, and he was no closer to finding answers for them now than he had been when he first came to Boston.

Quincy's behavior was not helping matters, either. On the surface, the lad was cooperating with Daniel's wishes, apparently attending his classes, and staying away from Roger Malvern and any other hotheaded agitators. Still, there had been some mysterious absences lately, instances that Quincy had passed off as nothing. Daniel had to wonder if he was actually attending some of the insurrectionists' meetings during those times. It was difficult if not impossible to make a fifteen-year-old boy account for every moment of every day.

Daniel closed his book. Once again, he was going to have to give up studying for the evening. It seemed that every time he tried to concentrate on something these days, his mind strayed.

A rap on the door made him look up in surprise. He had not heard anyone coming up the stairs. Besides, he and Quincy seldom had visitors. This one, whoever it was, had to have a light step.

Daniel got up from the desk, went to the door, and swung it open. He was not prepared for what he saw.

"Is this the Reed apartment?" asked the girl who was standing there in the hallway.

Daniel blinked and for a few seconds did not answer. Then he managed to nod and say, "Yes, it is."

"I'm looking for Quincy Reed. Is he here?"

That surprised Daniel even more. Why would a lovely young woman be looking for Quincy?

And there was no denying that she was lovely, Daniel thought. She was a bit younger than he, perhaps twenty but more likely eighteen or nineteen. Daniel had to look down only a little to meet her bright green eyes. She had a slender but well-curved figure to go with her height. Her red tresses were long and thick, tumbling down her back in a mass of curls. She wore a brown dress that hugged the thrust of her breasts appealingly. There was nothing cheap or tartish about her, though, despite her beauty. A smattering of light freckles across her nose and cheeks gave the impression of childlike innocence that contrasted sharply with the bold look in her eyes. All in all, she was one of the most attractive women Daniel Reed had ever seen.

"Quincy?" she reminded him. "Is he here?"

"Ah, no." Daniel shook his head. "He should be back soon, though. He's gone down to the market."

The redhead grimaced, and even that she managed to do prettily. "I was hoping to see him. . . ."

"Why don't you wait for him?" Daniel said quickly. "I'm sure he'll be back in no time." Now that this young woman was here, he did not want her to leave until he found out what was going on. He had suspected that Quincy was up to something lately, but he had never expected anything like this.

She caught her full lower lip between even white teeth and worried it for a moment, then asked with a frown, "Are you sure it would be all right?"

"It'll be just fine," Daniel assured her. He stepped back and bowed slightly as he waved her in. "Welcome to our humble home."

The girl came in, still looking nervous. Daniel shut the door and went on, "Please, have a seat."

She shook her head. "That's all right, thank you. I'll stand."

She did more than stand. She began to stride back and forth, in fact, as Daniel returned to his desk. "I'm Daniel Reed, Quincy's brother," he said. "Can I get you anything?"

"No, thank you." The girl paused in her pacing. "I've heard Quincy speak about you, many times. I . . . I'm Roxanne—Roxanne Darragh."

The name meant absolutely nothing to Daniel, but he nodded and said, "Oh."

"I know you're a student at Harvard," she said, gesturing at the book on the desk. "Please, don't let me take you away from your work."

Daniel shook his head. "I was just preparing for an examination."

"I'm sure it's very important. Please go ahead."

Not wanting to argue with her, Daniel sat down and opened the book again while Roxanne resumed her pacing. She was obviously very upset about something, and although he tried to focus his gaze on the book, his eyes kept glancing up at her, seemingly of their own accord.

After a few minutes, Daniel said again, "Quincy should be back soon."

Roxanne just nodded and kept walking.

Well, he wasn't going to find out anything without asking, he told himself, so he said, "How did you and Quincy meet?"

"We . . . ran into each other here and there."

"Then you're from Boston?"

"Yes," she nodded.

"You know that Quincy is only fifteen years old, don't you?"

"Of course I do." She stopped pacing again and swung to face him. "What does that have to do with—Oh!" A blush spread over her features as she realized what Daniel was getting at. She said quickly, "It's not like that at all, Mr. Reed."

"Daniel."

"Very well, then, Daniel. I'm afraid you've gotten the wrong idea somehow—"

Footsteps and a cheery whistle outside the doorway announced Quincy's arrival and made Roxanne break off her statement. The door opened, and Quincy stepped into the room, carrying a fresh loaf of bread he had just bought at the bakery down the street. He stopped short, eyes widening in surprise, as he saw who was waiting for him.

"Roxanne!" he exclaimed after a second. "What are you doing here?"

"That's no way to greet a guest, Quincy," Daniel said. He got up from the desk and hurried over to take the bag from his brother.

"It's all right," Roxanne said, moving closer to Quincy. "If I could speak to you in private . . ."

"The committee must have sent you." Quincy sounded impressed.

Daniel had been about to put the bread on the table where he and Quincy ate their meals, but he stopped and turned around sharply as Quincy's words sunk in. "The committee?" he echoed. "What committee?"

"Quincy!" hissed Roxanne, looking even more nervous now. "You shouldn't have said anything about that."

Wearing a shamefaced expression, Quincy dropped his gaze to the floor and mumbled, "Sorry, Roxanne. It just slipped out. Anyway, we don't have to worry about Daniel—"

"We have to worry about everyone!" Roxanne said, her voice crackling with anger. "Secrecy is the only way any of us can hope to survive the troubles that are coming."

Daniel looked at his brother and the redheaded visitor, and he felt anger and worry blending into a queasy mixture in his belly. "What's all this about a committee, Quincy?" he demanded. "Are you talking about the Committee of Safety?"

Since the Boston Tea Party, the Committee of Safety had become even more secretive than before, and the members of its inner circle were known only to one another and a trusted few. Public meetings having been banned by one of the Intolerable Acts, they were now forced to meet in secret, but it was likely that would be their plan anyway. It had become dangerous to be too ardent a patriot.

Quincy had a defiant expression on his face as he glanced up at Daniel. "It's my own business," he said. "I'm old enough—"

"Spare me that argument," Daniel snapped. "I've heard it before, and it's no more true now than it was then."

Uneasily, Roxanne began, "I think I'd better go. . . ."

"No, you don't have to," Quincy said, putting out a hand to stop her as she took a hesitant step toward the door. "As I started to say, Daniel can be trusted—even though he is a little stiff necked!"

With an effort, Daniel restrained his anger and said, "You and Miss Darragh are mixed up with the Committee of Safety, aren't you?"

"Yes, we are," Quincy replied, ignoring the warning look Roxanne shot at him. "I've been serving as a courier, passing along messages for some of the men who were with us at the Tea Party."

Daniel looked at Roxanne. "And you?"

"I don't have to answer your questions, sir," she said with a toss of her red hair. Anger flared in her green eyes. "I don't like being interrogated like some sort of criminal."

"You are a criminal—in the eyes of the British. At least you are if you've been helping the Committee of Safety start a revolution."

"You don't sound to me like a man who can be trusted, Daniel Reed," Roxanne said. "I think I had better get out of here."

Suddenly, Daniel did not want her to go. His anger subsided and was replaced by an impending sense of loss. It was amazing how much different the room looked with Roxanne in it, he thought. What had been a drab little chamber was now full of color and life.

"Wait," he said.

Once again, she stopped after taking a step toward the door.

"I'm sorry," Daniel went on. "This whole affair has taken me by surprise. I didn't mean to jump to any conclusions or sound like I was judging you, either one of you. Just . . . tell me what this is all about."

Roxanne took a deep breath, and Daniel could almost see her coming to a decision. "All right," she said. "Since you already know what Quincy and I have been doing, I don't suppose it will hurt anything to give you the details. You can only betray us once."

"I'd never betray you, Miss Darragh," Daniel said, and he meant it.

Roxanne turned to Quincy and asked, "Where were you tonight? Didn't you know you were supposed to meet me at Harrison's wagonyard and carry a message on to the next man in the chain?"

Quincy frowned. "That's tomorrow night, isn't it?"

"No, it was tonight. You must have gotten confused when you were given your instructions."

Quincy slapped his forehead. "Oh, no! I'm sorry, Roxanne . . . I honestly thought . . . What did you do?"

"The only thing I could. When you never showed up, I sought out your contact and passed along the message myself."

"Was there any trouble?"

Roxanne shook her head. "None."

"Thank God for that. I'm truly sorry, Roxanne." Quincy sounded miserable with guilt as he made his apology. "I can promise you, it'll never happen again."

"It had better not." She glanced at Daniel. "There. Are you satisfied? Now you know exactly what my connection is with your brother, and you know what we've been doing."

"And you can trust me with that knowledge," Daniel told her earnestly.

"You see, I told you Daniel is all right," Quincy said. "He's on our side. He just worries about me."

"With good cause." Daniel frowned at Quincy. "You should have taken me into your confidence before now."

"What would you have done if I had? Forbidden me to get involved any further?"

Daniel shrugged. "Maybe. You're awfully young to be mixed up in something like this, Quincy."

"But you see, that's why no one suspects me," Quincy said excitedly. "People look at me and think I'm just a boy, so they don't pay much attention to me."

"Quincy's right, Daniel," Roxanne put in. "He's one of our best couriers . . . just as I am."

Daniel looked at her and said, "It's hard to believe you don't attract a great deal of attention . . . Roxanne."

Once again she flushed, her fair skin turning pink at the implied compliment. "I have to go," she said.

"Roxanne, wait!" exclaimed Quincy. "What's my next assignment?"

"You'll be gotten in touch with, don't worry." She paused at the doorway and turned her head, her gaze fixing on Daniel. "You probably think I was incautious myself in coming here this evening."

"You had to find out what happened to Quincy, why he missed his rendezvous with you," Daniel said with a shrug. "I suppose I should thank you for being concerned with my brother's well-being."

"That was a part of it. But I wanted to meet you, Daniel Reed," she admitted. "I've heard a great deal about you."

Daniel eyed his brother suspiciously, but Quincy just shook his head.

"Not from Quincy," Roxanne continued, "although he has mentioned you quite often. I was speaking instead of your friend Nathan Hale. He thinks very highly of you."

"And I of him," Daniel said, not surprised that Nathan Hale was involved with the same group of patriots as Roxanne and Quincy. Boston was the hotbed of the revolutionary movement right now, and as an ardent supporter of the patriot cause, it was natural that Nathan Hale would be drawn to the area. Daniel had already known that Hale was visiting in the vicinity, along with Tallmadge and Townsend.

"He also believes that your contacts with the Tory faction through the Markham family could prove invaluable to our cause. The more we know about the intentions of the British—"

"You mean you want me to spy?" The exclamation was startled out of Daniel.

"We'd never ask you to do anything that might bring harm to your relatives," Roxanne said quickly.

Daniel frowned, deep in thought. "I don't understand this," he finally said. "First you act as if you're afraid I'm hand in glove with General Gage and will jump at the chance to betray you, and now, not a half hour later, you're asking me to spy for you. That doesn't make sense, Roxanne."

"It does if the real purpose of my coming here tonight was to find out what kind of person you are," she said with a slight smile.

"You mean I didn't really miss a rendezvous?" Quincy asked.

"Yes, you did," Roxanne replied sternly. "That was certainly true. And I did want to make sure nothing had happened to you. But it was also an excuse to talk to your brother." She turned back to Daniel. "What about it? Are you with us?"

"Just like that?"

"Just like that."

Again Daniel felt pushed into a corner, just as he had when asked that question by Nathan Hale. He resented being badgered to think and act a certain way—although he was beginning to lean strongly in favor of the patriot cause—and he also had to take into account the undeniable attraction he felt for this beautiful young woman called Roxanne. He could not tell if she felt any personal interest in him other than wanting to recruit him for her cause; she was too skilled at hiding her emotions for him to really be able to read her, he sensed.

But one thing was certain. If he agreed to her proposition, he would probably be seeing a lot more of her. If he refused, she might well walk out of the apartment and out of his life.

"All right," he said. "I'll do it."

Quincy, who had been watching him with eager anticipation, let out a whoop of excitement. "I knew you'd see things the right way sooner or later!" he told his older brother.

"Mind you, I'm not making any promises about the results," Daniel went on. "I've never played spy before. I'm not sure I can do your cause any good at all."

"It's your cause now, too," Roxanne reminded him with a smile. "And I have a feeling you'll be a good agent in its service, Daniel. Now, I really do have to go. I'll be back in touch with both of you."

With a nod, she went out. "Good night, Roxanne," Quincy called softly after her. Then he shut the door and turned to Daniel. "Isn't this fantastic? You and me, patriots working together in the cause of liberty!"

"We'll see," said Daniel, thinking all the while, *I hope we don't die together in the cause of liberty.* . . .

Chapter Nine

"I don't mind telling you, I'm nervous about this," Daniel said as he helped Roxanne down from the buggy she had picked him up in.

"Don't worry," Roxanne told him. "Everything will be fine. You can't expect the committee to approve of your joining our ranks until they've seen you and talked to you themselves."

Daniel sighed and tethered the horse to a post by the sidewalk. "I suppose not. But I hope one of those British raids you mentioned doesn't take place. I'm in no mood to go diving through windows and racing through alleys with a bunch of redcoats after me."

Roxanne laughed and slipped an arm through his as they walked down the street. "Don't worry," she said. "The British have no idea where this meeting will take place."

Well aware of the warmth of her flesh where their arms were touching, Daniel swallowed the lump in his throat and kept his pace steady as he walked along beside her. This was to be a whole night of firsts, he thought. He would meet the members of the Committee of Safety for the first time, he would be inducted into their service, and he had already felt the touch of Roxanne Darragh. At the moment, he could not have said which of these things was the most important.

A little over a week had passed since Roxanne had come to the Reed brothers' apartment looking for Quincy. Of course, she had been looking for Daniel, too, as she had admitted later. The committee had to have a high opinion of Roxanne, Daniel had decided, if they would trust her judgment in a matter as crucial as finding someone to spy on the Tories for them.

He still felt uncomfortable about using his relationship to the Markham family in such a manner. Uncle Benjamin was a bit of a blowhard, of course, and he was an unabashed loyalist, supportive of the British in their efforts to put an end to any thought of liberty for the colonies. But Aunt Polly had always treated him very well, almost as if he were her own son. And then there was Elliot, who was . . . well, his best friend.

Sooner or later, the time would come when he had to lie to Elliot and to his aunt and uncle. Would he be able to do it, even if it was for a good cause, perhaps the best cause of all?

Daniel was thinking about that when Roxanne said, "Here we are."

He looked up, his gloomy reverie broken by her comment, and saw that they had come to a stop in front of a tavern. The Salutation Tavern, in fact, where Elliot and he had shared more than one bucket of ale.

And also the tavern where he had seen the notorious Samuel Adams going into a back room the year before. Daniel blinked in surprise as that memory returned to him.

He said, "Wait a minute. I know this place. Everyone knows the rebels used to meet here—"

"Of course," agreed Roxanne. "And since everyone knows that, the committee would be much too smart to come back here, wouldn't they?"

"Oh . . ." Daniel thought he saw what she was getting at. "The safest place is sometimes the one where everybody has already looked, is that it?"

"Something like that," Roxanne said. "Come on."

Daniel opened the door and led the way into the narrow, high-ceilinged tavern with dark wood on the walls and heavy beams across the ceiling. Several oil lamps hung from the beams, but their yellow glow was not enough to dispel the shadows that lurked in the corners of the room. Quite a few people were standing at the bar, and others were seated at the tables.

Roxanne nodded toward one of the few empty tables and said, "We'll have to sit down and wait for a while, until Mr. Pheeters tells us it's all right to go on back."

"Mr. Pheeters?"

"The tavern keeper," Roxanne explained, indicating the burly, red-faced man behind the bar. He wore a soiled apron over his shirt and had short, iron-gray hair. From the look of his malletlike fists resting on the bar as he surveyed the room, he could tap a keg of ale without having to resort to a bung starter.

Roxanne went on, "Don't let that fearsome exterior fool you. He's really a dear and loyal man."

"I'll take your word for it," Daniel said.

As they sat down at the table, Daniel looked around. Most of the people here tonight were simple working men, although some, who were more well dressed, were probably merchants. The men outnumbered the women, and while many of the females were either serving wenches or trollops, there were enough respectable ladies in the tavern so that Roxanne did not look out of place. Daniel had enjoyed his previous visits to the Salutation, though it was now obvious he had not been aware of everything going on here.

Pheeters brought a bucket of ale and two mugs and set them on the table. As he leaned over, he growled softly, · "Give 'em about ten more minutes, miss, then you and yer friend can go on back. I'll give you a signal."

Roxanne nodded. "All right. Thank you, Mr. Pheeters."

Daniel paid the tavern keeper for the ale, and Pheeters shuffled back to the bar. After filling the mugs with the dark brown brew, Daniel slid one of them across the table to Roxanne. "To your health," he said, picking up his drink.

"To the cause of liberty," she replied, quietly enough that only Daniel could hear her over the hubbub that filled the tavern.

"I'll drink to that," he said with a grin. He tapped his mug against Roxanne's and then sipped the strong, bitter ale. "Wouldn't you rather have some sherry or a glass of sack? This ale might be a little potent for you."

"No, thank you." Roxanne took a healthy swallow of the ale. "This is fine."

"You're certainly a girl who's full of surprises."

"More than you'll ever know, Mr. Daniel Reed," she said with a teasing lilt to her voice. Then she became more serious as she went on, "It won't be long now. Another few minutes, and we can go back."

Daniel nodded. Despite the lighthearted tone he had taken, he was still edgy. He had admitted to being worried about British soldiers raiding this meeting, but he had another concern as well.

Once he attended the meeting and was introduced to the

Committee of Safety, there would be no turning back. He would be committed to working for their cause. It was a cause he supported, of course, but he had to admit, at least to himself, that one of the main reasons he was becoming more involved was Roxanne. If she had been older, plainer, perhaps even married, he might not have been so quick to agree when she asked him to spy for the patriots.

If that made him a hypocrite, so be it, he told himself. What was important were the results he might be able to obtain, more so than his motivation.

Besides, entire wars had been fought before over the beauty of a woman, he recalled from his studies of classical literature. One man could certainly become a spy for the same reason.

"Are you all right?" asked Roxanne, frowning across the table at him. "You look as if you feel ill."

Daniel shook his head. "Not at all. I'm fine. I was just thinking."

"If you're worried about Quincy, don't be. He'll be fine." They had left the lad at the apartment, despite his insistence that he be allowed to attend the meeting. Roxanne had been firm however; Daniel was the only one of the Reed brothers she was to bring. Quincy had not yet been taken into the inner circle of the committee, and it was deemed prudent to keep it that way for a while.

Daniel chuckled and said, "No, I'm not worried about Quincy. It won't hurt him to have to learn a little patience."

Roxanne was about to say something else, but at that moment, Pheeters gave her a high sign from the bar and she nodded to Daniel. "We can go back now."

His pulse beginning to race, Daniel stood up from the bench where he was seated and moved over beside Roxanne. They walked casually toward the door at the rear of the room. No one seemed to be paying any attention to them, and that was good.

He opened the door for Roxanne and let her precede him into a narrow, candlelit hallway with one door at the far end and another on the right-hand wall. Roxanne went to the nearest door and rapped softly. A voice came faintly from beyond it, bidding them to enter.

Daniel was not sure what to expect, but as he followed Roxanne into the room, he saw a normal-looking chamber dominated by a long table. In one corner was a small, unlit fireplace, and on the wall opposite the door was a window with heavy drapes drawn over it. Seated in chairs around the table were ten men, all of them well dressed and quite respectable looking. Daniel recognized Samuel Adams immediately, as well as the man's cousin, John Adams, and Dr. Benjamin Church, whose ability to inflame a crowd with his words was second only to the infamous Samuel Adams himself. The other men were unknown to Daniel.

He felt the scrutiny of all the men on him as he shut the door and turned to face them. Dr. Church, a tall, handsome man in his forties, was seated at the head of the table, and he rose as he said, "Welcome to our little gathering, Mr. Reed. You *are* Daniel Reed, I assume?"

"That's right." Daniel glanced over at Roxanne, but she had drawn back a pace, leaving him to face this stern-featured assemblage by himself.

"Allow me to introduce myself. I am Dr. Benjamin Church."

Daniel nodded, not wanting to tell the doctor that he was already aware of his identity. Dr. Church went on, "I'm pleased to introduce some of my compatriots and fellow committee members: Samuel Adams . . . Robert Paine . . . John Adams . . . John Hancock . . . Mr. Revere, the silversmith . . . Dr. Warren . . . James Otis . . . Silas DeBusk . . . and Jephtha Mason."

Each man in turn nodded to Daniel. He recognized all their names. These men were known throughout the colonies as the leaders of the revolutionary movement. In fact, a more notorious group could have hardly been gathered. If the British were to break up this meeting and arrest these men, the backbone of the insurrectionist cause would be broken, and that knowledge did not help Daniel's nervousness. Yet as he looked at the men sitting around the table, he saw that for the most part they were middle-aged and rather mild in appearance, hardly seeming like the firebrands and wild-eyed fanatics the British made them out to be.

"We're glad you've decided to join us tonight, Mr. Reed," said Samuel Adams in his thin, high voice.

"Not just for tonight, sir," Daniel said, knowing that they were expecting him to make some sort of response. "I am with your cause to the end."

"No offense, young man," Dr. Church commented, "but that's an easy thing to say and quite another thing to mean."

"I'll prove my meaning in my actions, Doctor."

"Quite an excellent answer," said the silversmith Paul Revere. Several of the other men nodded in agreement.

John Hancock spoke up. "We're told by Miss Darragh that some of your relatives are Tories."

"Yes, sir," Daniel replied, trying to keep his voice firm. "My uncle, Benjamin Markham, is a partner in the Markham and Cummings Shipping line."

"A well-known firm," said Dr. Church. "And well-known for their support of the British, I might add. You don't share your uncle's opinions, Mr. Reed?"

Daniel smiled slightly. "I've been exposed to them

frequently over the years, but they don't seem to have stuck."

Some of the committee members smiled, and a few laughed quietly. Samuel Adams was more solemn as he asked, "Are you prepared to use this relationship to gather information for us, my boy?"

"Yes, sir," said Daniel, nodding. "Miss Darragh explained what you want me to do, although not in detail, and I'm in complete agreement." He would have probably agreed to flap his arms and fly to the moon if Roxanne Darragh had asked him to do so, he thought.

Samuel Adams and Dr. Church looked at each other for a moment; then both men nodded. Church glanced around the table and got nods from each of the committee members. These were intelligent, decisive men, good judges of character, and it did not take them long to make up their minds. Dr. Church looked intently at Daniel again and said, "Do you declare your commitment to the cause of liberty?"

"I do, sir."

"You pledge never to divulge any information about this organization or its activities, even under the threat of death?"

"I do."

Dr. Church strode around the table and thrust out his hand. "Then I welcome you to our sacred fellowship, Daniel Reed. May God be with you . . . and may He have mercy on your soul if you betray us."

Daniel took the physician's hand and shook it. Just like that, he thought, he had become a latter-day son of liberty.

The men stood up, and each of them shook hands with him. The final one to do so was Samuel Adams, and he said, "We have no specific assignment for you right now, Mr. Reed. For the time being, you are to cultivate your relationship with your uncle, Benjamin Markham. Does he have any idea of your leanings toward our cause?"

Daniel shrugged. "Perhaps. I haven't been very out-spoken when I was at his house, but he may suspect that I'm sympathetic to the patriots."

"Then you must destroy any suspicion to that effect in his mind," Adams told him. "Your uncle must be convinced you are every bit the staunch loyalist he is. Can you manage that?"

"I'm sure I can."

"Very well. We'll be back in touch with you, probably through Miss Darragh. She will be your primary means of communication with us."

"That's fine with me." Daniel glanced at Roxanne and smiled. Any excuse for him to spend more time with her was welcome.

"You two go back out front and enjoy your evening," Dr. Church said. "The rest of us will be leaving by another route."

Daniel nodded but did not ask any questions, not want-ing to appear too inquisitive about things that were really none of his business.

Roxanne opened the door, and before he followed her into the hall, he stole one more glance at the members of the committee. These men were perhaps the most important individuals in the colonies, and he felt honored to have been in their presence.

He needed to put that behind him now and concentrate instead on the task ahead. It probably would not prove too difficult to convince his uncle that he had become a Tory; Benjamin would be eager to believe that he had finally convinced Daniel to see the light of reason. Elliot might be another story, though, since he knew him so well.

Daniel would have to cross that bridge when he came to it, however. Tonight, he could finally relax and enjoy spending a little more time with Roxanne.

They went into the main room of the tavern and resumed their seats at the table, which Pheeters had kept unoccupied in their absence. For appearance' sake, they finished their ale. Then Daniel said, "It would be my honor to escort you home, Miss Darragh."

"That would be fine," Roxanne said, and Daniel thought she meant it. Happy that he would be able to postpone saying good night to her a little longer, he stood up and offered her his arm.

They left the tavern and strolled down the cobblestone street, and as they walked, Daniel glanced over at her, studying her face in the yellow glow of the oil lamps they passed. She was undeniably lovely—but he had no idea where she lived. She had called for him at the apartment this evening, and they had come into Boston in Roxanne's buggy, which he had left parked some four blocks away.

"You know," he said, "it would be much easier to take you home if I knew where you lived."

Roxanne gave a low, throaty laugh. "That's right. You don't know a great deal about me, do you?"

"Only that you're a patriot—and a lovely young woman."

"Thank you . . . on both counts." She paused, then went on, "My father's house is on Salem Street. I'll show you the way."

"All right." Daniel hesitated. "Did you think the meeting went as it should?"

"Definitely. I think they were very impressed with you, Daniel, as was I. You're going to be a very valuable addition to our cause."

"I hope so." He turned his head and looked at her again. "You mentioned your father. Tell me about the rest of your family."

She smiled. "Have you started your information gathering already?"

"I'm practicing," Daniel assured her.

"Of course you are. . . . At any rate, my father is a printer, and a very good one. He prints a great many books, magazines, and pamphlets, which means that I get to read a great deal. I suppose that's why I'm as intelligent as I am."

"And modest as well," Daniel said.

She ignored his dry comment and went on, "I'm the youngest of six children, the only one still unmarried and living at home with my father and mother. Because I am the last of so many children, my parents allow me great freedom. I have been able to do many things my older sisters were never allowed to do. For example, they would never have dreamed of going to a tavern in the middle of the city."

"As independent and lovely as you are, your present marital situation surely will not continue much longer."

"Ah, you do like to flirt, don't you?"

Daniel merely shrugged and smiled.

"That's all right." Roxanne's expression suddenly became serious. "As long as you remember that what we're doing is very important . . . and perhaps very dangerous."

"I'm not likely to forget it," Daniel assured her.

They reached the buggy. After Daniel had helped Roxanne step up to the seat, he untied the single horse and took his own place on the bench. Lifting the reins, he flapped them and set the horse in motion. The buggy rolled down the street, bouncing slightly on the rough surface.

Roxanne gave Daniel directions as he drove and also told him more about her family, laughing as she mentioned some of the things her young nieces and nephews had gotten into. For his part, he told about his life growing up in Virginia. There was something bizarre about this, Daniel thought, even though he was thoroughly enjoying the conversation. This was the way any young couple might talk when they had been out for the evening, not exactly what one would expect from a courier and a spy for a band of rebels.

He brought the buggy to a halt in front of a good-sized house on Salem Street. The printing business owned by Roxanne's father was a successful one, though the family could not be considered wealthy. As Daniel hopped down from the vehicle and turned to assist her, he wondered if she would invite him in, perhaps introduce him to her parents.

Before he had a chance to find out, a rough voice said from behind him, "Evenin', mate. What're you an' the wench doin' out this late?"

Roxanne gasped, and Daniel turned to see four men sauntering out of the shadows of a nearby alley. Enough light came from the windows of the Darragh house for Daniel to see that they were all tall and broad shouldered and dressed in cheap clothing. Street toughs, Daniel thought, who had probably been drinking and were now out to harass anyone they could find for a bit of sport. And if they found someone with a purse worth stealing, so much the better.

"We'd best get inside," Roxanne said in a low voice as she stepped down beside Daniel.

He nodded. The ruffians were still several yards away, and if he and Roxanne could hurry across the small lawn in front of the house, they could reach the front door before being stopped—

One of the men sped up as if reading Daniel's mind, and two quick steps put him in position to cut them off if they tried to get to the house. "Here now," he said with a leering grin. "Don't go gettin' unfriendly on us. We just want a bit of talk."

"I don't think we have anything to say to you," Daniel snapped. "Let us pass."

Another of the men was close enough now to reach out and prod Daniel's shoulder. "Don't tell us what to do, mate."

Another one closed in. "Where ya been with that pretty redheaded wench, mister? And is she for hire?" He burst out with a raucous laugh.

Daniel glanced around as Roxanne crowded against him, trying to stay out of reach of the groping hands that nearly had them surrounded now. This was a quiet residential section of Boston, and the street was deserted at the moment, except for themselves and the four toughs.

"Whyn't you run along and leave the girl with us?" suggested the fourth man. "She won't mind. Will you, dearie?"

"This is my house," Roxanne said, inclining her head toward the brick structure. "I'm going to call for help if you don't leave us alone."

"Go ahead and yell yer pretty little head off," growled one of the men. "We don't care."

But as Roxanne opened her mouth to scream, one of the other ruffians leapt forward and clapped a big, dirty hand over her lips. Another swung a knobby fist at Daniel's head.

With a white-hot rage swelling within him, Daniel ducked the punch and threw one of his own. It connected solidly with the man's jaw, rocking him back. Before Daniel could follow up on the blow, however, clubbed fists smashed against the back of his neck, knocking off his tricorn hat and sending him staggering forward. Another man grabbed him from behind, long arms pinning his own and looping around his chest. The grip tightened, making it hard for Daniel to breathe.

The man holding him whirled around, and Daniel caught a glimpse of Roxanne struggling in the grasp of one of the men. Then that sight was blocked as the remaining two roughnecks loomed up in front of him and began alternating crushing blows to his face and midsection. Pain washed over Daniel as the punches rocked his head back and forth. The world was spinning dizzily now, and he knew he was on the verge of blacking out. He could not allow that to happen, because if he did, Roxanne would be left defenseless in their hands.

Daniel wished he were carrying a pistol, but even if he had been, it would not have done him any good now, not the way his arms were pinned. All he had free were his feet.

So he summoned all the strength he had, lifted his right leg, and drove the heel of his boot into the groin of one of his attackers.

The man howled in pain as he doubled over and stumbled backward. Somehow he stayed on his feet. His companion cursed loudly and launched a roundhouse blow at Daniel's head. It landed so hard that the impact tore Daniel from the grip of the man who had been holding him and sent him spilling to the street.

Daniel was barely holding on to consciousness now, but he was aware of the foot thudding into his side and rolling him over. Three men crowded around him, he saw through pain-blurred eyes. The one he had kicked in the groin had recovered enough to join his fellows in an attempt to stomp Daniel to death. He had no doubt that was what was about to happen.

There was a thud, a sharp crack, a cry of agony, and

then an unfamiliar voice saying calmly, "I wouldn'a be doin' tha' if I were you."

Daniel saw the three men looming over him turn their heads sharply. "Get outta here, mister," one of them growled.

"Wait a minute," said another. "He broke Dave's arm!"

"Aye, tha' I did," said the newcomer. "And I'll do tha' and more for the lot o' ye, if ye dinna scatter. I'll not be scared of a bunch o' gutter scum like you three."

"Get the bastard!" howled one of the men as they turned away from Daniel and leapt toward this fresh challenge.

Daniel clawed his way back to full awareness and pushed himself up on one elbow to see what was happening, gasping in pain as he did so.

He would never forget what he saw next.

It was like three curs challenging a mastiff. The toughs all attacked at once, but the man who stood tall and brawny in the street next to the buggy just laughed harshly. A fist that seemed to be all knuckles lashed out and sent one of the attackers flying head over heels, the shape of his jaw strangely distorted. Shrugging off punches as if he did not even feel them, the huge, buckskin-clad stranger, with hair the color of rusty nails, swung his other arm and backhanded a second man, swatting him away like an annoying insect.

The final man, seeing the odds on his side vanish in an instant, ducked back and reached toward his belt. "Come on!" he dared the stranger as he tugged a dagger from its sheath. "Come taste some cold steel, damn you!"

The stranger just grinned as he looked at the dagger. "Aye, and a taste is all tha' puny blade'd be." He bent slightly, and his hand dipped to the hilt of a knife sheathed in the top of his fringed, high-topped moccasins. As he straightened, lamplight glittered on the long, heavy blade. His grin widened as he went on, "While this is a full-course meal, me friend."

The dagger clattered to the cobblestones as the man dropped it, turned, and ran as if the devil himself chased him. His three companions, all moaning in pain, pulled themselves to their feet and staggered after him.

The man in buckskins stood there and started to laugh as the would-be toughs disappeared into the darkness. Then he sheathed the big-bladed knife, turned toward Daniel, and asked, "How be tha' lad o' yours, Roxanne? Ye be Roxanne, right lass?"

Daniel suddenly became aware that she had dropped to her knees beside him and was lifting his head to cradle it in her lap. "I think he'll be all right," she told the stranger, whose thatch of rumpled hair was every bit as red as her own. "I . . . I'm not sure who you are, but thank you—"

"Dinna ye recognize me, lass?" The question boomed out. " 'Tis ye cousin Murdoch, come back from the frontier!"

"Murdoch!" Roxanne cried. "Is it really you?"

"Who else? I know ye have'na seen me in quite a few years, but I dinna reckon I've changed much." The big man strode over to Daniel and Roxanne and bent over, resting his hamlike hands on his knees as he looked down at them. "Aye, the lad'll be fine once he gets his breath back. Be a mite bruised for a few days, though."

Every muscle in Daniel's body seemed to be aching, but he wanted to get back on his feet. He held out a hand to Murdoch and asked hoarsely, "Help me up, will you?"

Murdoch's fingers engulfed Daniel's, and with an effortless heave, the massive frontiersman pulled the younger man to his feet. Daniel swayed dizzily for a moment, but Roxanne slipped an arm around him to steady him.

"Thank you for helping us," Daniel said.

"Thanks for leavin' me a little t'do," Murdoch replied. "As t'was, ye'd almost softened up those heathens too much. You'd think four of 'em could put up a better fight."

Daniel grinned crookedly, and that hurt, too, as the expression pulled his battered lips. "Maybe next time it'll be more of a challenge."

"I hope there's not a next time," Roxanne put in. "Those men were dreadful."

The light from the houses and the streetlamps allowed Daniel to get a better look at Murdoch. The big man's blunt, rough-hewn features could not have been called handsome by any stretch of the imagination, but they did possess a certain power. His eyes were keen and penetrating and set in the permanent half squint of a man who had spent most of his life outdoors. He could have been anywhere from thirty to fifty, although Daniel suspected he was on the lower end of that span.

Daniel put out his hand again. "I'm Daniel Reed."

"Murdoch Buchanan," said the buckskin-clad frontiersman. Once again, his hand swallowed up Daniel's.

Roxanne said, "Murdoch's been exploring the wilderness for the past few years."

"Name a place west of the Appalachians, and I'll wager ye I been there." Murdoch grinned. "Me feet get restless if they stay in one place too long."

"What are you doing back here?" Roxanne asked.

"Just came for a visit. Hadn't seen any o' the family in such a long time, figgered I was overdue."

Daniel said, "Well, I'm certainly glad to meet you, Mr. Buchanan."

"Call me Murdoch, and you're Dan'l."

"All right. I—" Daniel's knees suddenly threatened to buckle underneath him. As he sagged Roxanne caught one arm, and Murdoch fastened his iron grip on the other. "I think I'd better go inside and sit down," Daniel finished weakly.

"Yes, come along," Roxanne said anxiously. "You've got some cuts and scratches. I'll clean those up."

Murdoch grinned. "An' I've got some good corn likker that'll brace ye right up, son."

With Murdoch on one side and Roxanne on the other, Daniel let himself be led into the house. He had been right about this being an eventful night, he thought ruefully. Eventful . . . and painful.

The tavern was a small, squalid place, full of the dregs of Boston's population. The surrounding neighborhood was a good place to get your throat cut for a few pennies. The well-dressed man sitting at a scarred table in the rear would never come here in the course of his normal activities.

Which made it a perfect rendezvous point for the men he had hired earlier in the day.

He was waiting for them now, his long cloak wrapped around him and his tricorn hat pulled low to partially shield his features. A glass of wine sat in front of him, but he had not touched it. His tastes ran far above the swill served in this tavern. As soon as his agents appeared and gave him their report, he could get out of here and go home.

Impatiently, the man watched the doorway, and finally he was rewarded. Two rough-looking men entered the tavern, spotted him at the back of the room, and came toward him. The waiting man frowned. There should have been four of them, not two. And one of these two had a huge bruise on his jaw, which was painfully swollen.

The two men sat down on the bench opposite him, both looking distinctly unhappy. The uninjured one said,

"You still owe us money. We'll collect for Dave and Rory, too."

"What happened? Did you find the Reed boy?"

"Didn't have no trouble findin' him. But you didn't say anything about that damned giant."

"Giant?" echoed the man who had been waiting. "What the devil are you talking about?"

"There was a big son of a bitch who was dressed in buckskins like some sort of redskin. He took a hand in the fight. Snapped Dave's arm like it was a piece of kindling and busted Rory's jaw into a dozen pieces." The other man pointed at his own jaw and made pained grunting noises, and the spokesman went on, "Oh, yeah, he did that to Mick, too. You're lucky we don't ask you for extra pay, mister."

"But what about Daniel Reed?" the well-dressed man asked coldly.

The uninjured tough shrugged. "We banged 'im around some, till that other bloke showed up."

"Did you hurt him badly enough that he'll be incapacitated for a time?"

"You mean will he be laid up? For a day or two, maybe, but that's all. If we'd had another five minutes, we'd've busted him up so good he wouldn't be no use to anybody for a couple of months, especially not that pretty redheaded lass with him."

"This is not good, not good at all. . . ."

The ruffian leaned forward, his ugly face tensing. "Listen, mister, it ain't our fault the job didn't work out. We'll be takin' our pay now, just like we agreed." The menace in his voice was unmistakable.

The well-dressed man grimaced. He seemed unfazed by the implicit threat, but he was plainly annoyed as he took a purse from inside his coat and counted out several coins.

"There," he said, shoving the money across the table. "Take with it the knowledge that you haven't earned it."

"That's where you're wrong, guv'nor. We earned ever' bleedin' penny of it, havin' to face that big bastard."

The man stood up, looking down disdainfully at his former employees. "I won't be needing your services again," he snapped, then turned away from the table and stalked out of the tavern.

He kept an eye out behind him as he walked quickly away from the grog shop toward the carriage he had parked several blocks away. It was possible the men he had just paid off would follow him and try to rob him of the rest of his money. Some other cutpurse might attempt to waylay him as well. If they did, they would be in for a surprise. He had a brace of pistols charged and ready underneath his coat, and he knew quite well how to use them.

No one bothered him, though, and he was left to contemplate the bitter taste of defeat. Tonight's beating was supposed to have left Daniel Reed in such poor shape that he would not be able to assist the insurrectionists for the foreseeable future. Instead, Daniel would be able to carry out any assignment he was given.

The man sighed and shook his head as he made his way down the darkened street. In the future, he was going to have to be exceedingly careful—if he was going to keep his fellow members of the Committee of Safety from finding out there was a traitor in their midst.

Chapter Ten

Daniel Reed had come to know Roxanne fairly well during his recuperation from the beating he had suffered. Her mother and father, Edward and Margaret Darragh, had been appalled when big Murdoch deposited the battered and bloody Daniel on the sofa in their parlor. To their credit, their reaction had been to his injuries, not to the blood that had stained the furniture and rug. Margaret Darragh and her daughter had worked to clean Daniel's wounds and make him comfortable, while Edward and Murdoch questioned him about the fight. As far as Daniel knew, he and Roxanne had simply had the bad luck to run into four toughs looking for trouble, and he said as much.

" 'Tis lucky Murdoch heard something and went out to see what was going on," Edward Darragh had said. "Otherwise those bruisers might have really injured you, my boy."

Daniel nodded, wincing a little as Roxanne dabbed at a small cut on his forehead with a wet cloth. "Yes, sir, you're right." He glanced at the big buckskin-clad frontiersman, who definitely looked out of place in this elegant parlor. "I think you saved my life, Murdoch."

With a wave of his big hand, Murdoch said, "Ye already thanked me, lad. No need t'make a habit of it. 'Twas an enjoyable fight—while it lasted."

Edward had at first insisted that Daniel spend the night there, but after Daniel had explained that Quincy was alone at the apartment, Murdoch had offered to drive Daniel home in the carriage. When he helped Daniel inside the apartment, Quincy had looked up at him in awe. The youngster had never seen anyone quite like Murdoch Buchanan.

Quincy saw quite a bit of Murdoch over the next couple of weeks, and of Roxanne as well. The two of them visited the apartment frequently to check on Daniel's recovery. Roxanne also brought him the news of the committee's decision to have her masquerade as his lady friend, although she was careful to do that on an occasion when Murdoch was not accompanying her. None of her family knew of her activities as an agent of the patriots, she explained, and she wanted very much to keep it that way.

"I believe both my mother and father are on the side of the colonists," she had told Daniel, "but I don't want to take the chance that my activities will endanger them, even though they might support my actions if they were aware of them."

Daniel had nodded in agreement. "A wise move," he told her. "I'd feel the same if my parents were here in Boston. I worry enough about Quincy knowing of my involvement—but of course I never would have gotten mixed up in this if not for him."

"Oh, I'm not sure about that. I think I know you well enough by now, Daniel Reed, to say that your sense of justice would have brought you over to our side sooner or later."

"Perhaps you're right," Daniel had said with a smile. And indeed, his indecision now seemed to be a thing of the distant past. He was firmly committed to the cause of the patriots, willing to do anything they asked of him.

Three weeks had passed since the beating Daniel had received at the hands of the four ruffians. His cuts and bruises had healed, and there was a spring in his step again as he walked down the streets of Boston with his cousin Elliot Markham.

"Then you and Quincy *will* be coming to dinner tomorrow night?" Elliot asked, continuing the discussion he and Daniel had been having.

"Of course. We wouldn't miss it."

"Bah," snorted Elliot. "You've missed plenty of dinners lately. I was beginning to wonder if you'd decided to disown us as relatives."

Daniel chuckled. "Don't be so sensitive, cousin. I've just been busy, that's all, what with the end of the school term. Lots of examinations to take, you know."

Both young men had put away their coats with the arrival of warmer weather. They wore lightweight shirts and had their tricorns canted to the backs of their heads. Their casual attire was in marked contrast to the sober garments of most of the men they passed on the street. This section of town was devoted primarily to business offices. The headquarters of Markham & Cummings Shipping was in the next block, in fact, and that was the destination of Daniel and Elliot.

As the two of them approached the building where Benjamin Markham and Theophilus Cummings had their offices, a young woman stepped down from a carriage that had stopped at the curb. She paid the driver and then turned away, and as her gaze swept over the cousins, she exclaimed in surprise, "Daniel!"

Stopping in his tracks, Daniel looked equally surprised to see her. He put a pleased smile on his face, though, as he said, "Hello, Roxanne. How nice to see you. What are you doing down here?"

"Oh, just a little business for my father." Roxanne switched her gaze to Daniel's companion without her smile losing any of its power. "And who's this with you?"

"My cousin." Daniel made the introductions formal. "Miss Roxanne Darragh, allow me to present Elliot Markham. Elliot, Miss Roxanne Darragh."

Unhesitatingly, Elliot stepped forward and took Roxanne's hand, bringing it to his lips. "I'm charmed to meet you, Miss Darragh," he said.

She looked lovely in a dark green dress and a felt hat dyed the same shade. Her hair hung in loose ringlets to her shoulders. She said, "And I'm very pleased to meet you, Mr. Markham. How is it Daniel never told me he had such an attractive cousin?"

Elliot shot Daniel a meaningful glance. "Oh, Daniel is very good at keeping secrets. For example, he never told me that he knew you."

"Well, we haven't known each other for long," Roxanne said with a laugh.

"Perhaps not, but I can certainly see why he's been keeping you to himself. And why you haven't been spending much time at my house, cousin. You *have* been busy, haven't you?"

"I suppose so," Daniel admitted. "But I've already agreed to come to dinner at your house tomorrow night, Elliot."

Roxanne made a face and repeated, "Tomorrow night? I thought we had an engagement tomorrow night, Daniel. Surely you haven't forgotten." Her voice was a little cooler now.

"Ah . . ." Daniel suddenly looked embarrassed and uncomfortable. He went on, "As a matter of fact—"

"As a matter of fact, I was just about to invite you to join my family and me for dinner tomorrow night, Miss Darragh," Elliot said smoothly. He gave Daniel a mock stern look. "You were planning on bringing Miss Darragh, weren't you, Daniel?"

He nodded quickly. "Of course. I'm sorry I forgot to say anything to you about it, Roxanne, but I've been so busy lately. . . ."

"All right," she said. "I suppose I'll accept that explanation—since I'm feeling so generous today." She stepped forward and brushed her lips across Daniel's cheek. "I'll see you tomorrow."

"Of course. Good-bye, Roxanne."

Elliot swept off his tricorn. "Good day, Miss Darragh. Again, it was a pleasure to meet you."

"Good day," she said to both of them with a smile. She went on down the street and vanished into one of the buildings that housed the offices of several firms.

Elliot let out a low whistle of appreciation. "You surprise me, cousin," he said. "I see you haven't been wasting all your time lately in the stuffy halls of Harvard."

"Well, as I said, the term is over for the summer." Daniel grinned. "A fellow has to have something to occupy his time."

They fell in step again along the sidewalk, and Elliot said, "Seriously, who is she, Daniel? Something about her name seems familiar to me, but I can't quite place it."

"You've probably seen the name Darragh on books and magazines. Roxanne's father is a printer, and a very successful one."

"Of course! Edward Darragh—I recall him now. I must say he has a very lovely daughter."

"That was nice of you, rescuing me from an awkward situation like that. I really had forgotten I had an engagement with Roxanne tomorrow night when I said Quincy and I would come to your house for dinner."

Elliot slapped Daniel on the back. "What are cousins for?" he asked. "I was glad to help out. Besides, I had a bit of an ulterior motive. This way, I'll get to see the lovely Miss Darragh again, instead of you keeping her all to yourself."

"Don't get any ideas," warned Daniel. "You've got Sarah, remember?"

Elliot shrugged. "I enjoy the company of lovely young women, whether I'm romantically involved with them or not."

Their arrival at the offices of Markham & Cummings put an end to the discussion. They went inside and were immediately shown into the private office of Benjamin Markham by one of the clerks.

"Good news, Father," Elliot said as he shut the door. "Daniel and Quincy will be having dinner with us tomorrow night."

Benjamin barely glanced up from the documents he had spread before him on his desk. "Good," he grunted. "Your aunt was beginning to worry about you, Daniel. She's convinced that you and Quincy probably aren't eating well since you stopped taking any of your meals at our house."

"Well, sir, Quincy and I have both been quite busy," Daniel said. "But I think things are beginning to change now. We should be able to see more of you and Aunt Polly, and I must say we're glad for the opportunity."

"That's not all the news we have, Father," Elliot said.

Benjamin picked up a quill pen and dipped it in an inkwell. "Oh?" he said as he made a notation on one of the documents.

"Daniel will also be bringing a young lady with him. A Miss Roxanne Darragh."

"Indeed?" Benjamin laid down the pen and showed real interest for the first time. "Is this young lady related to Edward Darragh, the printer?"

"He's her father," Daniel replied.

"Good man, Darragh. Does an excellent job. I wish he'd be more forthcoming about where he stands politically, but I suppose it's expedient for him to maintain a neutral posture, since both sides represent potential customers for him. At any rate, his daughter is quite welcome in my house, Daniel."

"Thank you, sir."

Benjamin switched his gaze to Elliot. "Now, I suppose you're here for a reason." His tone was curt.

"Of course," Elliot answered casually. "I should think five pounds would do nicely." His attitude was nonchalant, but Daniel saw something else lurking in his eyes. A mixture of anger and embarrassment, perhaps.

Benjamin opened a drawer in the desk, took out a coin purse, and slid several coins across to Elliot. "There," he said coldly. "Try to make it last a little longer this time."

Elliot nodded and without saying anything to his father scooped up the coins. "Come on, Daniel," he said jauntily. "Let's go."

Daniel followed Elliot out of the office, saying over his shoulder as he left, "Good-bye, Uncle Benjamin. We'll see you tomorrow night." His uncle had gone back to his work, however, and did not look up or make any response.

When they reached the street again, Elliot sighed and said, "Well, at least that's over. And it wasn't too bad this time. The old boy can be rather unpleasant on occasion."

Daniel could well imagine. Benjamin was well-known as a thunderer and a blusterer, and he seldom bothered to conceal his disappointment in his only offspring.

"You know, your father might not be quite so . . . brusque," Daniel ventured, "if you spent more time in the office."

Elliot laughed lightly, but Daniel heard the undertone of bitterness. "What? Waste a perfectly beautiful day like this by sitting in some dusty office? I think not, cousin! There'll be time enough for that when my father retires and I have to take over the business. For now, I'm going to enjoy myself, and you're going to enjoy yourself along with me. Now come along; I've heard about a new tavern over by the Charles where the serving wenches are supposed to be absolutely lovely!"

Daniel had a slight headache by the time he reached the apartment in Cambridge late that afternoon. He had downed only one drink for every three of Elliot's, but even at that rate he had consumed enough ale to make him a bit light-headed. In addition to the natural affection he felt for Elliot as a cousin, Daniel genuinely liked him, and today he felt rather sorry for him. Elliot worked so hard at being an idler. If he were to devote that much energy to a worthwhile cause, such as learning his father's business, he would be ready now to take over the operation of Markham & Cummings.

Quincy was waiting for him as he entered the apartment. The lad looked up from the book he was reading and asked, "How did it go? Was Roxanne on time?"

"Right on time," replied Daniel as he hung his hat on a hook just inside the door. "And she played her part well, which comes as no surprise."

"So she's going to dinner with us tomorrow night?"

Daniel nodded. "Just as we planned."

He had been surprised when Roxanne first told him about the ruse that had been concocted by someone within the Committee of Safety. It had been decided that Daniel could better insinuate himself in the social circles of the Tories if he had a pretty young woman on his arm, and no one was better suited for the part than Roxanne. Clearly, she had been a little uncomfortable with the arrangement, but she was not going to go against the wishes of her leaders in the patriot cause. If they wanted her to feign a romantic involvement with Daniel, she would do so.

She had made it clear, however, that a role was all it would be.

For his part, Daniel was satisfied with that. He could not deny to himself that he was very attracted to Roxanne Darragh, but he did not want to take advantage of the situation, either. If she was to have any genuine interest in him, he preferred that it come about naturally.

The dinner that was planned for the following evening would be the first step in linking himself and Roxanne as a couple in the minds of the loyalists, beginning of course with Benjamin Markham. Daniel had to wonder who in the inner circle of the committee had come up with the scheme.

Whoever it was, Daniel thought, he owed the man a debt of gratitude. Now he would be able to spend more time with Roxanne than ever before.

Daniel, Roxanne, and Quincy were the only dinner guests at the Markham residence this evening. Daniel and Roxanne were seated next to each other on Benjamin Markham's right, while Elliot and Quincy were opposite them on Benjamin's left. At the other end of the table was Polly Markham, and she took advantage of her proximity to Roxanne to have a long conversation with the redheaded young woman. Roxanne was getting along splendidly with the Markham family, and Daniel was grateful for that. So far, the plan was working perfectly.

Benjamin played into his hands by bringing up the continuing friction between the colonies and England, just as Daniel had known he would. "You would think the Coercive Acts would have shown those hotheaded fools they can't get away with defying the Crown," Benjamin said over dessert. "But instead they seem to be more defiant than ever. I hear that there's talk of having some sort of meeting in Philadelphia this summer, for the purpose of planning an open rebellion against England!"

"Perhaps it won't come to that," Daniel said, "but if it does, I have no doubt the troops will put a stop to it without much trouble."

Benjamin looked sharply at him. "You think so, do you?"

"I don't think a mob can stand up to His Majesty's finest soldiers, do you, Uncle Benjamin?"

"You sound as if you think that rabble should be crushed, Daniel." Benjamin seemed surprised.

Daniel shrugged. "I don't like to see anyone get hurt, but the rule of law must prevail. My time at Harvard has taught me that much, if nothing else."

"You know, lad, I don't believe I've ever heard you come out in such strong support of the Crown before."

"Perhaps I never saw clearly until recently what a lawless bunch these so-called patriots are, sir." Daniel smiled. "When dealing with outlaws, sometimes force is required." Out of the corner of his eye, he saw Elliot looking at him rather strangely. His cousin had never heard him express ideas like these, and Elliot was as puzzled as Benjamin seemed pleased by Daniel's statements.

"It's good to see that you're taking such an attitude, Daniel," his uncle said. "It's high time more people here in the colonies began thinking clearly." Benjamin looked at Roxanne. "What about you, Miss Darragh? What's your opinion of these matters?"

"Oh, I agree with Daniel," Roxanne said quickly.

"Well, that's fine. It's good when a young couple sees the world in the same light." Benjamin picked up his glass of wine. "To clear thinking," he toasted.

Daniel echoed the toast, concealing the grin that played across his face by taking a sip of his wine. Uncle Benjamin had reacted just as they had anticipated, and he seemed to be completely fooled by the act Daniel and Roxanne were putting on.

Benjamin switched his attention to the other side of the table and asked Quincy, "What about you, young man? Are you still a revolutionary, or are you coming around to your brother's way of thinking?"

Quincy shrugged. "Just because Daniel and I are brothers doesn't mean we have to agree on everything," he said noncommittally.

Benjamin glared at him for a second, then went back to his pudding. It had been decided before they came here tonight that Quincy would take a different tone from Daniel.

Given the past arguments Quincy had had with Benjamin, it had seemed unlikely that he would change his tone too quickly. Daniel, on the other hand, had always been fairly neutral in his comments when visiting his aunt and uncle, so his new pro-Tory stance would not come as a real surprise. Obviously, the plan had been successful so far.

"I think that's quite enough discussion of politics," Polly said firmly. "I'd much rather hear how Daniel and Roxanne met."

Elliot smiled and added, "That's a question to which I've never gotten a satisfactory answer, Mother." He looked across the table at the two of them. "How about it?"

"It's quite simple," Roxanne said. "We met at Harvard."

"Harvard?" Polly echoed in surprise. There were no female students at Harvard. Young women seldom had any education beyond perhaps a finishing school, if their parents were wealthy and could afford such. Polly would have been more shocked if she had known that Roxanne was more intelligent and better read than most of the men Daniel and Elliot knew.

"Yes," said Roxanne, "I was with my father when he delivered some material he had printed for the college. Daniel came along and was kind enough to help my father unload his wagon."

"I was just being polite," Daniel put in. "It was really nothing."

"On the contrary," Roxanne said. "I prefer to think of it as fate."

They had worked out this story ahead of time, too, and it seemed to be accepted without question by their dinner companions. Only Elliot appeared the least bit suspicious, but he did not ask any more questions. The conversation continued pleasantly for a time, then the ladies excused themselves, leaving Benjamin, Elliot, Daniel, and Quincy at the dinner table.

Benjamin slid back his chair, stood up, took a cigar from his pocket, and bent over one of the candles on the table to light it. "Come with me, Daniel," he said curtly.

"Sir?" Daniel asked.

"There's something I wish to discuss with you—in private." Benjamin turned toward the door. "Come along. We'll go into my study."

Daniel glanced at Elliot and saw the hurt expression on his cousin's face. Whatever it was Benjamin wanted to talk about, it was rather rude of him to demand the presence of his nephew and ignore his own son. But there was nothing Daniel could do about it, so he merely shrugged and followed Benjamin, leaving Elliot and Quincy in the dining room.

Considering his assignment from the Committee of Safety, it was wise to cultivate the favor of Benjamin Markham. Daniel's uncle could open more doors for him than anyone else in Boston. Still, Daniel felt uncomfortable as he closed the study door and faced Benjamin across the shipping magnate's big desk.

"The reason I brought you in here, my boy," Benjamin began without preamble, "was to ask you about Elliot."

Daniel waited silently while Benjamin took a couple of puffs on his cigar.

"You're probably closer to him than anyone else," Benjamin went on. "He doesn't confide in his mother or me anymore. Does he talk to you, Daniel?"

"Well, yes, sir," Daniel replied slowly. "We talk things over sometimes."

"How does he really feel about this trouble between

England and the colonies? Is he on the side of those damned insurrectionists or not?"

Daniel took a deep breath. "I don't know, sir," he answered truthfully. "The only times I've ever heard him comment on the situation, his statements have backed the British."

"Yes, but does he say that just because he knows how I feel and because I control the purse strings? Dammit, I just can't figure the boy out anymore!"

Daniel's discomfort was growing. He felt he had no right to be having this conversation, that he was somehow being disloyal to his cousin and best friend.

"I don't think you really have to worry about Elliot, Uncle Benjamin. He'll settle down one of these days—"

"Like you have? I'll admit, Daniel, for a time I thought you were being a bad influence on Elliot. Now I fear it may have been the other way around. At least you've been able to make up your own mind and come to the right conclusion about these troubles." Benjamin grimaced, and his fingers threatened to snap the cigar in his hand as they tightened on it. "The boy's got to make up his mind which side he's on," he declared pompously. "And he'd better decide damned fast. Things are coming to a head."

"Yes, sir," Daniel agreed. He did not know what else to say.

"Well, thank you for listening to me," Benjamin said with a heavy sigh. "It's a relief knowing I don't have to fret about you, my boy, and I chalk up Quincy's quarrelsome statements to his youth . . . but Elliot is a worry to me." He looked up from the desk, his blunt features a bit more animated as he went on, "Theophilus Cummings is having a party next week. Many of the best people in Boston will be there. I think you should come, too, and by all means bring that charming young lady of yours."

Daniel knew exactly what his uncle meant by "the best people in Boston." Benjamin was talking about the cream of Tory society—and those were exactly the kind of people with whom Daniel was supposed to begin making contacts. Benjamin was still playing right into his hands.

"Thank you, sir," he said with a smile. "I can promise you, Roxanne and I will be pleased to be there."

Chapter Eleven

T hat was the beginning of one of the longest summers of Daniel Reed's life. It was dominated by a seemingly endless series of parties, balls, and dinners given by Tory friends, acquaintances, and business associates of the Markham family. Daniel and Roxanne attended most of them, the only break coming when Geoffrey and Pamela Reed arrived from Virginia to visit their sons. Daniel became quite expert at mouthing the things the loyalists wanted to hear. In turn, he was accepted by them, and it was not uncommon for him to be included in groups that were discussing what the British plans were for dealing with the unrest in Massachusetts and elsewhere in the colonies.

Many times, the guest list at these parties also included high-ranking British officers. General Gage himself, bluff military man that he was, seldom attended such affairs, but several members of his staff did. After a few glasses of wine, some of them became rather loose-tongued, especially when they were surrounded by a gaggle of female admirers—one of whom was usually Roxanne Darragh. Either Daniel or Roxanne, or sometimes both, usually managed to pry some useful information out of their fellow partygoers.

They heard talk of troop movements, of orders direct from England, of contingency plans in case of war with the colonies. The rumors flew turbulently during August and September, when fifty-six delegates representing twelve of the thirteen colonies met in Philadelphia in what was called the First Continental Congress. To the surprise of many, the historic gathering did not produce a call for the colonies' independence from England, no doubt due to the presence of conservatives such as John Rutledge of South Carolina and Joseph Galloway of Pennsylvania, who counteracted the fiery radicals like Patrick Henry and Samuel and John Adams.

Instead, a set of resolutions known as the Suffolk Resolves, opposing the Intolerable Acts, was adopted. In response, once word of the Resolves reached Boston, General Gage canceled the Charter of Massachusetts and issued orders for military fortifications within the city to be built up.

Another dangerous step closer to war had been taken.

Daniel and Roxanne heard endless discussions of these events, but a common thread ran through all the talk. Although the Tories were outraged and incensed by the activities of the patriots, and although many gloomily predicted that a war was inevitable, none of them expected it to last long, and they were united in their belief that the forces of the Crown would easily emerge triumphant.

Daniel had to admit to himself that the situation made him a bit nervous. He had cast his lot with the patriots and would never desert them, but he had to wonder what chance they would have against the impressive military might wielded by King George.

One night, as Daniel and Roxanne drove back toward the Darragh house after attending one of the parties, he finally voiced his doubts. "When war comes," he said without looking over at her, "do you think we can win it?"

"Of course we can," she answered immediately. "We're in the right, aren't we?"

"I didn't ask whether our cause was just," said Daniel. "We both know that it is. But that won't serve as much protection from a musket ball fired from the barrel of a Brown Bess."

"If you're afraid, you don't have to help us any longer," Roxanne said stiffly, and he knew he had offended her, and that had not been his intention at all.

"I didn't say that." He was a little angry now himself. "I'm not talking about ideals, Roxanne. I'm talking about practicalities. *Can* we defeat the British?"

"I have to believe we can. Otherwise . . ."

"Otherwise what you and I are doing is futile, the risks we're running for nothing. Is that what you were going to say?"

For a long moment, Roxanne was silent. Then she looked at him with imploring eyes and whispered, "Damn you, yes."

He took a deep breath. He had not wanted to start an argument with Roxanne or to cause her pain. But they had grown closer in the time they had been working together, and he thought of her as a good friend. He had wanted to share his feelings with her.

"I'm sorry," he said quietly, his voice barely audible over the *clip-clop* coming from the hooves of the horse pulling the carriage.

They might have discussed the matter more, but they were nearing the Darragh house, and Daniel thought it wise to let the subject drop. Instead he was silent until he had pulled the carriage to a stop. The vehicle belonged to Roxanne's father, and after she had gone inside, he would return it to the carriage house and get his horse, which he had left there earlier.

He dropped down to the street and hurried around the carriage to assist Roxanne. When she was standing beside him, he said quietly, "You'll take the message to the committee concerning that shipload of troops?"

"Of course," she said with a nod. At the party earlier in the evening, they had overheard a British major boasting of how yet another English ship loaded with soldiers would soon arrive in Boston Harbor. Before long there would be more redcoats in Boston than civilians, Daniel had thought at the time.

He shifted his feet rather awkwardly as he looked at Roxanne. There was always an uncomfortable moment when they parted. They were supposed to be sweethearts, after all, and it would be the most normal thing in the world to end the evening with a kiss, yet Daniel had never seen a sign from Roxanne that she would welcome such a gesture. Usually they parted with a graceless "Good night."

"I did'na ever see the like." The deep, rumbling voice came from a clump of shadows nearby and made both Daniel and Roxanne jump slightly. "For a couple who's supposed t'be acourtin', ye seem 'bout as friendly as a pair o' surly ol' possums." A huge figure bulked up out of the darkness.

"Oh! You frightened us, Murdoch," Roxanne said. "We didn't know there was anybody else out here."

"Figgered as much," said the big Scot. His visit to

Boston, originally intended for a few weeks, had stretched out to several months now. He went on, "What I kinna figger out is how come this lad isn't bussin' ye soundly right now, lass."

"If I want to kiss her, I will," Daniel protested.

Murdoch Buchanan waved a hand. "Then go right ahead."

Daniel looked at Roxanne. "All right," he said abruptly. "I will."

Then, before she could stop him, he took her in his arms and brought his mouth down on hers. For a moment, she stood stiffly in his embrace, not fighting him but not cooperating, either. Then, gradually, her stance softened, and he felt the warmth of her body as she pressed against him. Her lips were just as warm and sweet as he had imagined they would be. His arms tightened around her, and he felt her responding to him—

" 'Course, maybe ye both be too worried 'bout this committee business t'think too much 'bout lovin'. . . ."

Instantly Daniel and Roxanne tensed again, and they stepped apart, the kiss forgotten. *Almost forgotten,* Daniel amended silently, because a faint taste of Roxanne lingered on his lips and in his mind.

"What are you talking about?" Roxanne demanded. "I'm sure I have no idea—"

"No use denyin' it, lass. The two of ye be up to somethin', an' ol' Murdoch wants to know wha'."

Roxanne started to protest again, but Daniel stopped her by putting a hand on her arm. "It's no use," he told her. "We both know what keen ears Murdoch has. He's heard too much."

"Aye, and just because I be an unlettered ol' woodsman dinna mean I've no idea wha's goin' on in the world,"

Murdoch said. "This committee . . . It'd be the Committee of Safety, the independence-minded gents who've been outlawed?"

Daniel had to grin. "Just how much did you hear?"

"Eno' to know that the two of ye be playin' a dangerous game, me friend. I think ye be spyin' on the bloody British for the patriots."

Daniel exchanged a glance with Roxanne. He had gotten well enough acquainted with Murdoch to know that it would be a mistake to underestimate the man. Uneducated he might be, but Murdoch possessed plenty of both cunning and common sense—and he kept up with what was going on in the world.

"We'd better go back to the carriage house," Daniel said. "This isn't the kind of thing we need to discuss in the street." Murdoch and Roxanne both nodded in agreement.

"I've been keepin' an eye on ye," Murdoch went on when the three of them were safely inside the stone walls of the small building behind the Darragh house. "What ye do is ye own business. But I dinna want t'see this pretty little cousin o' mine come to any harm, Dan'l."

"Don't blame Daniel," Roxanne said quickly. "The only reason he's involved with this is because of me."

"Because he be in love with ye, is tha' what ye mean?"

Roxanne flushed. Daniel was sure of that, even though he could not see her very well in the shadows. "That's not what I mean at all. I mean I'm the one who recruited him for our cause."

"You, lass?"

"That's right," Roxanne said with a toss of her head. "I was a patriot long before Daniel was."

"An' t'think the last time I saw ye a'fore this visit, ye

were playin' with a rag doll." Murdoch sighed. "Things have a way of changin', dinna they?"

"What's important is that we both believe in the work we're doing, Murdoch," Daniel said. "I hope that whether you agree with us or not, you won't betray us."

The Scot drew himself up to his full height, towering over his two younger companions. "Murdoch Buchanan never did wrong by a friend or relative, Dan'l. So I be ginna pretend I did'na hear ye say tha'. An' it just so happens I think the patriots be doin' the right thing. Folks got a need t'be free. Tha's somethin' ye'll learn, happen ye ever pay a visit to the frontier." He lowered his voice and went on, "In fact, if ye'll have me, I'd be honored if ye'd let me lend a hand wi' what ye be doin'."

Again Daniel and Roxanne shared a startled look. "You mean you want to help us spy on the British?" asked Daniel.

"Aye." Murdoch nodded emphatically.

"I'm sorry, Murdoch, but I . . . don't think that's possible," Roxanne said, her voice gentle.

"Dinna ye trust me?"

"Of course we do," Daniel said quickly. "It's just that . . . well, we have to be able to blend in with the Tories. I'm afraid, ah, that someone like you would just draw attention to us."

For a long moment, Murdoch did not say anything, and Daniel was afraid he had hurt the feelings of the big man. Then Murdoch chuckled abruptly. "I suppose ye be right. A gent like me, in buckskins an' coonskin cap, would stand out like a polecat in a hen house at these parties ye been goin' to. I dinna reckon I'd be much help after all."

"It's not that we don't appreciate the offer . . ." began Daniel.

"The patriots need all the support they can get," Roxanne added. "And if there's ever anything you can do, be sure we'll let you know, Murdoch."

The big redhead nodded. "Suppose I must be satisfied wi' tha'." He grinned. "Then this romance a'tween the two of ye, tha's all for show, t'fool the Tories?"

"Of course," Roxanne said immediately, before Daniel could frame an answer. He blinked, a little surprised at the quickness of her reply to Murdoch's question. Obviously, she had no doubt in her mind as to their true relationship.

And now, Daniel supposed, he had no doubt in his, either.

"Well, I won't apologize for interruptin' ye, then— although tha' kiss looked like the real and true thing t'me, lass." Murdoch shrugged his massive shoulders. "Still, I suppose ye got t'have some actin' talent if you're ginna be a spy."

"That's right," Daniel said. "You've got to be able to conceal your true feelings." Roxanne glanced at him when he said that, but he did not meet her gaze. Instead, he continued, "I need to be getting home. The hour is late."

"I'll unhitch the horse from the carriage for ye," Murdoch volunteered.

Daniel turned to Roxanne and said, "Don't forget to pass along that message."

"I've been at this longer than you have," she reminded him, her tone rather cool and formal.

Daniel nodded and began putting the saddle on his horse. He performed the task in silence, then swung up onto the animal. " 'Night, Murdoch," he said to the frontiersman, then added, "Good night, Roxanne."

"Good night, Daniel." She still sounded reserved.

Daniel gave a mental shrug. There was no need for her

to continue the masquerade that they were lovers, not here in the sanctuary of the Darragh carriage house where they were unseen by anyone except Murdoch. So if that was the way she wanted to play things, it was fine with him.

He flipped a hand in a wave to Murdoch, turned the horse around, leaned over to open the door leading out of the building, and rode away into the warm, muggy night.

Not surprisingly, Daniel did not sleep well that night. There was the heat, for one thing, an unseasonable heat that should have passed in August, not lingered on into late September. Although the windows in the apartment were open, not a breath of air was stirring. He tossed restlessly in his bed, hoping that he was not keeping Quincy awake in the other bed across the room. The sound of his brother's deep, regular breathing told Daniel that Quincy was undisturbed.

The real thing that was bothering him, he thought, was Roxanne's attitude. He could not make sense of it. When she had been in his arms, kissing him, he sensed a strong passion within her, a passion he had thought was aroused by his touch. Later, though, she had seemed adamant that the so-called romance between them was so much pretense.

Which had been the truth? The kiss—or the cold words?

Daniel had no way of knowing, and the uncertainty was keeping him awake. He tried to put Roxanne out of his thoughts, but that was next to impossible.

Finally, not long before dawn, he dozed off, his exhausted body finally overcoming the turmoil in his mind.

He was awakened by a pounding on the door of the apartment. Rolling over in his tangled sheets, Daniel let out a groan and forced his eyes open. He heard Quincy's footsteps crossing the floor of the other room, and then the door opened. Elliot Markham's voice asked curtly, "Where's Daniel?"

"He's still asleep," Quincy replied.

"No, I'm not," Daniel called out as he sat up and swung his feet off the bed onto the floor. His eyes felt as though they had sand coating their sockets. He tried to rub away the gritty, unpleasant feeling with his knuckles as he yawned and stood up. Clad only in the pants of his long underwear, he stumbled into the other room and saw Elliot, his tricorn hat clutched tightly in his hands, standing just inside the door alongside Quincy.

"Sorry I woke you," Elliot said, but he did not sound very regretful. He went on in an agitated voice, "There's something important I have to talk to you about, Daniel. You, too, Quincy."

Daniel lifted his head and blinked his eyes. Elliot sounded quite serious, which was very unusual for him. There was no trace of the bantering tone he often used. Daniel nodded and said, "Sit down, both of you. Whatever's bothering you, Elliot, let's hash it out now, and perhaps I can get some more sleep." A glance out the window told him that the sun was up, but he could tell the hour was early.

"Rather weary this morning, are you?"

The sharpness of the question made Daniel look at Elliot again. "Yes, I am," he said. "I didn't sleep well last night."

"Out late with Roxanne Darragh again?" Elliot had not sat down, but Daniel and Quincy had, and they both frowned sleepily at him. This was not like the easygoing Elliot they knew at all.

"As a matter of fact, yes," Daniel said. "We went to a party at Jeremy Lloyd's house. I assumed you would be there, too. I was a little surprised when we didn't see you."

"Oh, I was there—for a few minutes. But I'm not surprised you didn't notice me. You were too busy listening to every word that British major had to say."

"I was just trying to be polite," Daniel said. He felt uneasiness growing inside him at the way this conversation was going.

"Just as you were trying to be polite at all the other parties and dinners every time some British officer began to boast about how the Crown's forces will crush any rebellion that comes?"

Quincy looked anxiously at Daniel and started to say something, but Daniel stopped him with a curt gesture. His weariness had vanished. He stood up and walked over to face Elliot. "Just what is it you're trying to say?"

"I'm saying that you've been acting very suspiciously the past few months, Daniel. My father hasn't questioned your behavior because most of the time you're agreeing with him. But I know you—or at least I thought I did—and this isn't like you. You're not the type to become a devoted Tory overnight."

Daniel shrugged and insisted, "I finally thought things through and came to some conclusions, that's all."

Elliot shook his head. "No. You're lying, Daniel." His voice rose in anger. "You've been lying all summer, and I'm tired of it! We used to be friends as well as cousins, you and I, but that doesn't seem to be the case any longer."

"I'm sorry, Elliot, but I think you're imagining things—

" Daniel began, hoping he could settle Elliot down before the situation became worse.

But it was too late for that. Elliot shook his head and said, "You used to trust me, but you don't anymore, neither one of you. I'm not imagining *that*. Just as I'm not imagining the way you've been insinuating yourself into a position where you can pick up plenty of information about what the British might be planning."

For the first time since Elliot's arrival, alarm bells went off in Daniel's mind. Elliot's observations were coming dangerously close to the truth. In a flat voice that betrayed no emotion, Daniel asked, "What do you mean by that?"

"I mean I've finally figured it out, cousin." Elliot laughed humorlessly. "You're a spy for the patriots."

Thunderstruck, Daniel stood there silently. Clearly, he had underestimated Elliot's intelligence, or perhaps he himself had not been as clever as he thought. He had to make some response to the accusation, he realized, so he said slowly, "And if I am? What would that mean to you?"

Elliot's determination appeared to falter slightly. "I . . . I don't know," he said. He took a step back and sat down clumsily in a straight chair. "I expected you to deny it. I hoped I was wrong . . . that I had made some mistake . . ."

"I didn't say you weren't wrong," Daniel pointed out, keeping a tight rein on his own emotions. He had to stay calm right now. "I asked what you would do if you were right."

"My father is one of the most fervent loyalists in the colonies. By all rights, I would have to turn in anyone who was spying for the rebels."

"Even your cousins?" Quincy asked.

Elliot grimaced. "I don't know."

He still had to proceed carefully, but the time had come to take a chance, Daniel thought. He said, "Your father is always pressing you to take a stand, Elliot. Now *I'm* asking you: Which side are you on?"

For a few interminable seconds Elliot said nothing, his gaze riveted to the floor. When he finally looked up, his features were twisted with confusion. "I think the British are wrong," he said. "I . . . I can't believe that the right thing to do is for the colonies to break away, but something should be done—"

"The British are forcing that break," Daniel interrupted. "The Intolerable Acts have seen to that." He walked over to his cousin and put a hand on Elliot's shoulder. "Listen to me. Quincy and I *are* working for the patriots. You were right about everything you thought. But if you tell your father about us, Quincy will no doubt be arrested and put in jail, and I will probably be hanged as a traitor. Is that what you want, Elliot?"

The younger man's head jerked up. "God, no! I just wanted the truth—or at least I thought I did. Now, I don't know. . . ." Elliot caught Daniel's hand. "Tell me what to do, Daniel."

"Work with us," Daniel said softly, scarcely believing that he had dared to speak the words.

Quincy exclaimed in surprise, and Elliot looked shocked as well. He shook his head. "I don't understand."

"You know that you can't turn us in," Daniel said, "just as you know deep inside yourself that our cause is just. You've been drifting ever since you finished school, Elliot. Help us, and let the cause of liberty be your rudder."

My God, thought Daniel, *I'm making a speech just like Samuel Adams or one of the other firebrands.* The words felt clumsy and forced, but they came out anyway, and from the look on Elliot's face, they had an effect.

"I could do it," Elliot said, as much to himself as to Daniel and Quincy. "Everyone knows where my father stands, and they all assume I go along with everything he says. He has a great many contacts in the military because of his business. All those officers would trust me—if they gave the matter any thought at all."

Daniel put his hand on Elliot's shoulder again and tightened his grip. "You could be an enormous help to us."

A grin suddenly spread across Elliot's face, and he looked more like himself again. "It would be quite an adventure, wouldn't it? A bit of a lark before I have to settle down to a life of paperwork?"

"You could look at it that way," Daniel admitted somewhat dubiously. Considering his initial motivation—the beautiful Roxanne Darragh—any incentive was better than none, he supposed.

"I'll do it!" Elliot exclaimed, springing to his feet. "I can introduce you to some people and get you into higher circles than you've managed so far. Not that you haven't been doing a good job. You and Roxanne are a fixture now at most of the parties—" He broke off and stared at Daniel. "Roxanne . . . ? She can't possibly be—"

"Leave Roxanne out of this," Daniel advised firmly. "Your contacts will be with Quincy and me."

"Of course. No more awkward questions, eh?" Elliot slapped Daniel on the shoulder. "My own cousin, a master of spies! Who'd have thought it?"

Certainly not myself a few months earlier, Daniel mused. His whole life had changed since the day last December when Quincy had been part of the Boston Tea

Party. They had started down this path on that day, and now there was no leaving it. Too much had happened.

For one thing, in the space of less than twelve hours, both Murdoch Buchanan and Elliot Markham had stumbled onto his secret. The frontiersman had been too observant, and Elliot simply knew his cousin too well to be fooled completely. Daniel, a nagging doubt very present in his mind, hoped that none of the British officers had such keen eyes and minds.

Quincy stood up and walked over to them, and Elliot put a hand on the shoulder of both of his cousins. "From now on we work together," he declared. "Partners."

Quincy grinned. "I like the sound of that."

So did Daniel.

Chapter Twelve

Roxanne Darragh took a sip from the glass of wine in her hand and was glad, not for the first time, that she seemed to have a good tolerance for the stuff. Otherwise, she would have been light-headed and giddy, like most of the women at this party, and of no use at all to her fellow patriots and the cause they served.

Daniel leaned closer to her. "Are you all right?" he asked in a whisper.

"I'm fine," she told him, the smile never wavering from her face. "Just go on about your business."

"Of course." Daniel was smiling, too, but Roxanne could tell he was not happy.

Things had not been the same between them since that night several months earlier when their ruse had been discovered by Murdoch Buchanan. Forced by her cousin's probing questions to declare her feelings for Daniel, she had said the only thing she could—that they were working together and nothing more. Obviously, from the way Daniel had treated her ever since, he had believed her wholeheartedly. In public, whenever it was necessary for them to fool someone, Daniel was as loving and attentive as ever, and Roxanne managed to put up the same sort of façade. But it cost her an effort, a greater effort than Daniel Reed would ever know, damn him. . . .

"I'll go talk to Major Briggs," Daniel said. He started across the room toward a small group of men clustered around a red-coated British officer.

They were in the elegant ballroom of Cyrus Wallingford's Beacon Hill mansion, several blocks away from the Markham house. The walls of the ballroom were covered in gold damask cloth, which glowed in the light of huge candle-filled chandeliers that hung from the ceiling. The gleaming parquet floors were laid in a diamond pattern copied from a grand house in England.

Benjamin and Polly Markham were in attendance, as was all the cream of Tory society. Elliot Markham was only a few feet away, in fact, talking and laughing with Sarah Cummings. Roxanne had met Elliot's gaze a time or two tonight, and each time she had seen the knowledge in his eyes. Elliot was well aware that she was working with Daniel, although Daniel had never come right out and admitted as much to his cousin.

Roxanne knew, of course, that Elliot had figured out why Daniel was playing the role of a loyalist sympathizer. Daniel had told her all about the visit Elliot had paid to the apartment several months earlier. Elliot had agreed to help Daniel in his mission, and since then, Roxanne had to admit that things had been proceeding quite smoothly. Daniel had been introduced to many more British officers, and he was known throughout Boston as one of the brightest young lights of the Tory cause. He was back at Harvard, continuing his study of the law, and there was no doubt that when he was finished, he would be offered a position in one of the city's leading firms—unless, of course, war had turned everything upside down by then.

That war was inevitable was still accepted by most people, but in this winter of 1774, no one seemed to know exactly how or when it would start. The conflict between the colonies and the British had settled into an interminable pattern of speechmaking and name-calling. All through the colonies a feverish amount of pamphleteering was taking place on both sides of the issue, and Roxanne's father was kept busier than ever printing the fiery documents. There had been no violence, although General Gage frequently sent troops out into the countryside to search for stockpiles of guns, powder, and shot hidden by the colonists. Sometimes the redcoats found and confiscated such caches; sometimes they did not. On one such occasion, a group of well-armed farmers in the community of Salem had turned back a search party of British troops, but no fighting had broken out.

Although it would have seemed impossible a year earlier, the tension in the air had grown tenfold since then. A few people still held out hope of a peaceful end to the troubles, but most citizens of Massachusetts knew that was impossible. The only real question now was when the crisis would come.

And who would die when it did . . .

"My, you certainly look more appealing than ever tonight, Miss Darragh."

Startled by the voice close beside her and the warm breath on her neck, Roxanne gasped and stiffened. Her head snapped around, and she saw the smoothly handsome features of Avery Wallingford looking at her. Avery was smiling slightly, the same faintly arrogant expression he wore most of the time.

Roxanne had been introduced to Avery when she and Daniel first began making the rounds of the parties the previous summer. As the son of one of the town's leading bankers, Avery was invited to every gathering. He attended with a different girl on his arm each time, and Daniel had warned Roxanne that Avery fancied himself quite a ladies' man—but that had been obvious to her as soon as they had been introduced.

This evening Avery took her hand and lifted it to his lips, pressing them to her fingers longer than was necessary to be polite. And during their brief conversation, his gaze frequently strayed to the gentle swell of her breasts above the soft yellow silk of her gown. He even had the effrontery to touch the lace that decorated the bodice of her dress and pretend to care whether or not it was imported. He had always made Roxanne feel uncomfortable, and tonight was no different.

"How nice to see you, Avery," she forced herself to say in a civil tone. "I was just wondering when the dancing would start."

"Ah, you like to dance, do you?"

"Of course. Don't you?"

She saw his eyes light up and realized too late that she had played right into his hands. "I certainly do," he said. "And I'd love to dance with you right now." He signaled to the musicians on the far side of the room, who had been instructed to wait for just such a sign, and then stepped forward to take her hands. The musicians began a waltz, and the partygoers instantly paired off and moved onto the parquet dance floor.

"I really should dance with Daniel—" Roxanne began quickly.

Avery's grip on her hands did not loosen. "I'm sure Daniel will understand." With surprising strength for one so slender, he pulled her close to him, sweeping her into his arms and onto the dance floor.

Roxanne caught a glimpse of Daniel hurrying toward her, but he stopped when he saw that she was already in Avery's arms. In the brief moment in which their eyes met, his expression was unreadable, and then Avery twirled her away.

The dance seemed to go on forever. Roxanne had to admit that Avery moved smoothly, but she had no interest in dancing with him no matter how good at it he was. She was at this ball to do her duty, not to enjoy herself. As soon as it was possible to do so politely, she would disentangle herself from Avery.

However, he did not give her that chance. Their path around the dance floor took them past an open door, and before Roxanne knew what was happening, Avery had steered her through it and closed it behind them with a deft move of his heel. They were in a small sitting room to one side of the ballroom. The chamber was softly lit by a crystal chandelier, a miniature version of the elaborate ones in the ballroom, and the fire in the fireplace added romantic shadows to the room. The music of the waltz was clearly audible through the door, and Avery kept dancing.

Roxanne had had enough. She put her hands on his chest and pushed, breaking away from him and taking a stumbling step backward. Avery lost his balance for a second but recovered it quickly. A look of annoyance flickered across his face but was gone in an instant, replaced by his usual smirk.

"Really, if you were tired of dancing, you could have said so, my dear," he murmured.

"Why did you bring me in here?" Roxanne demanded.

"I should think it would be obvious. I wanted you to myself for a little while. Daniel Reed is a fine chap, of course, but a bit tiresome at times. I want to know you better, Roxanne."

She took a step toward the door. "I think we should go back to the ballroom."

Effortlessly, Avery blocked her way. She could tell from his manner that he had done this sort of thing before, probably many times.

"A few moments of conversation, that's all I want," said Avery. "Surely you won't deny me that. After all, I am one of your hosts."

Roxanne took a deep breath. It was important to stay on the good side of the most influential Tories, and Avery Wallingford and his family definitely fell into that category. She could let him play his little game, at least for a while.

"All right," she said, forcing a smile onto her face. "What do you want to talk about?"

Avery moved closer to her, and again she had the uncomfortable sensation of his gaze sliding over her body. "I want to know just what it is you see in an ill-bred country lout like Daniel Reed."

Roxanne caught her breath. "You shouldn't talk that way about Daniel," she scolded. "I thought you said you liked him."

"Oh, I do, but that doesn't make me blind to his shortcomings. I just can't understand how he managed a liaison with such a lovely creature as yourself." Avery lifted a hand and let his fingertips stray over the skin of her shoulder, left bare by the neckline of her gown. "He must be an excellent lover to hold your interest."

"You . . . you speak too plainly, Mr. Wallingford. Please remember, I am a lady."

"A lady, yes," breathed Avery, much too close to her now. "But also a woman, with a woman's needs and desires." He leaned even closer to her, his mouth approaching hers as his hand moved down to caress the soft swell of her breast.

The click of the doorknob turning made Avery spring back as if he were on strings controlled by a particularly rough puppeteer. Almost instantly, he had put several feet between himself and the breathless Roxanne. As the door swung open, he said, "And so I told Reggie, you can't possibly intend to wear that outfit, old man, it makes you look like a veritable Hibernian! Haw!" Avery threw back his head and laughed.

"So there you are," Daniel said from the doorway. "I wondered where the two of you had gone off to."

Roxanne's heart was beating wildly. She had been on the verge of kneeing Avery in the groin when Daniel interrupted them. His arrival had freed her from the necessity of that, but it would take several minutes for the anger and revulsion within her to dissipate.

"Roxanne brought me in here to sing your praises, dear boy," Avery said, his voice quick and nervous. "Daniel, Daniel, Daniel—that's all I've heard the past few minutes."

"Well, it's good to know she thinks so highly of me," Daniel said lightly, taking a sip of wine. He looked at her with a mocking smile on his face.

"I believe I need some wine," she said as she started toward the door.

"I'd be glad to get it—"

"I'll get it myself, Daniel. Thank you anyway." With that, she brushed past him. Behind her, she heard Daniel chuckle and make some comment under his breath to Avery.

Damn him! He could have at least been upset, she thought. *He should have been able to see that he had almost caught Avery in the act of pawing me. He should have knocked that arrogant bastard on his skinny little Tory ass—!*

Roxanne caught herself and forced those thoughts out of her mind. Daniel had no real reason to be jealous. As far as he knew, they were just playing a game. A dangerous one, to be sure, but still a game of masks and false faces where nothing was what it seemed.

But if that was true, she asked herself, why was she so upset right now?

It was all Daniel could do not to ball his fists and smash them into Avery's face until his aristocratic features were nothing but a bloody pulp.

That would never do, though, not for the role he was playing now. He could do nothing that might alienate Avery, and that meant he had to act as morally bankrupt—or nearly so—as Avery himself.

"Quite the little spitfire, isn't she?" he asked with a grin as Roxanne left the room. He could tell by the stiff set of her back that she was angry, and with good reason. The guilty look on Avery's face when Daniel came into the room was enough to tell him that Avery had been up to something. Given the young Tory's reputation, there was only one thing it was likely to be.

Avery relaxed a little, seeing that Daniel did not seem upset. He grinned back at him and said, "She's a very lovely girl, and you're a lucky man, my friend. If she were mine, I'd never leave her alone with a bounder such as myself."

"Oh, I don't worry about Roxanne. There are no strings on either of us. We each do as we please."

"Is that so?" purred Avery, his thoughts completely transparent to Daniel. He was considering making another play for Roxanne, and Daniel could do nothing to stop him. Seething inside, Daniel tried to keep the fires of rage carefully banked.

It was true that there were no strings on them, he thought. Roxanne herself had seen to that. She had made it clear that she valued his friendship and the potential contributions he could make to the patriot cause, but that was as far as it went. Their masquerade was simply a matter of duty.

He had been trying to convince himself for months now that he felt the same way. He had taken great pains to conceal his true feelings from Roxanne, hoping that the pretense would eventually become the reality.

But as soon as he had seen Avery Wallingford spirit her into this sitting room, he knew that all his pretending had been futile. He was as strongly attracted to her as he had ever been, and it had taken a tremendous effort of will to make himself walk calmly and slowly across the ballroom to open the door and confront them.

Now he said to Avery, "I'm afraid that for all her loveliness, Roxanne is a bit lacking in intellectual capacity." That was the farthest thing from the truth, of course; he had already realized that if anything Roxanne was smarter than he was. But Avery was not the type to admit that a woman could be that intelligent. Daniel went on, "I sometimes grow tired of having to explain to her what's going on with those upstart rebels."

"Well, those insurrectionists are rather tiresome anyway, aren't they?" Avery asked with a laugh.

"Of course. But take the munitions situation," Daniel said, warming to his subject. "Fighting ability is one thing, but it is the army with the most guns that usually wins."

"The Crown's troops won't have to worry about that. General Gage's men have seized huge quantities of weapons and ammunition. If the rebels are foolish enough to start a shooting war, they'll quickly find themselves outgunned."

"I wonder what they've done with all the rifles they've confiscated," Daniel mused, sounding only mildly curious. He finished the wine in his glass.

"Well . . ." Avery looked around needlessly, since they were alone in the sitting room, then dropped his voice to a conspiratorial tone. "I don't know what they've done with the colonists' rifles—destroyed them, I imagine, because the crudity of the weapons really makes them useless to experienced fighting men—but I do know where the British have stockpiled their own munitions."

Daniel tried to keep the sudden intense interest he felt from showing on his face. He had started this conversation with Avery in the hope of finding out some valuable information, and now it looked as if he had stumbled onto something very important indeed.

"Really?" he said, matching his own tone to Avery's and leaning closer. He could not afford to be too aggressive now. He had to let Avery think that spilling this information was his own idea.

"That's right. Perhaps I shouldn't say anything about this, but I heard one of the officers on General Gage's staff talking about a warehouse they've taken over down near

Amory's Wharf. From the way he was talking, it's packed full of rifles and powder and shot."

"How interesting!" Daniel shook his head. "I almost pity those poor rebellious oafs. Once the fighting starts, they'll never know what hit them."

"How right you are," Avery agreed. He gestured at the empty glass in Daniel's hand. "I say, you need some more wine."

Daniel looked at the glass as if surprised to see it was empty. "You're right," he said. "What say we go get some?"

"Excellent idea."

Side by side, giving every impression of being new-found friends, Daniel and Avery left the sitting room and headed across the ballroom. Daniel saw Roxanne standing by the wall, still looking rather put out, and when she spotted Daniel, she quickly went to one of Avery's friends, a weak-chinned young man whose father owned property all over Boston, and spoke to him. The young man looked surprised, but he nodded eagerly and took Roxanne in his arms, spinning her out to join the dancing.

"I'd say your little minx has her nose out of joint," Avery gibed from beside Daniel.

"She'll get over it," he replied with an unconcerned shrug. "But perhaps I'd better hurry her along a bit." He handed his empty glass to Avery. "Sorry I won't be able to join you in a drink after all."

"Go to it, old man. Have to keep our priorities straight and all, you know." With an oily grin, Avery proceeded on toward the far side of the room while Daniel veered toward the spot where Roxanne and her new companion were dancing.

Acting quickly and taking them by surprise, Daniel moved up beside them and tapped the young man on the shoulder. "Thanks, friend," he said, "but I'll take over now."

The young man jerked to a halt and started to stumble out an apology. Daniel waved off his anxious words and then took Roxanne in his arms. As they began dancing, he looked into her eyes and began, "I know you're angry—"

"Whatever makes you think that?" Roxanne snapped. Her eyes were wide and flashing with emotion.

"Look, what did you expect me to do?" Daniel asked in a whisper, keeping a smile on his face. "Fighting with Avery Wallingford wouldn't have done any of us any good. But by playing along with him, I've just found out where the British are stockpiling their munitions."

Roxanne's steps faltered, but only for an instant, and then she continued dancing without missing another beat. "Are you sure?" she asked.

Daniel nodded solemnly.

"We have to act on this knowledge right away," Roxanne said. "Do you think if I claimed to feel unwell, we could leave now without arousing suspicion?"

"I don't see why not."

"All right. Let's stop dancing. Walk with me over to the punch bowl."

The two of them began making their way toward the far side of the room. As they went, Roxanne massaged her temples, grimaced, and gave every impression of someone suffering from a severe headache.

Elliot suddenly appeared in front of them, with Sarah Cummings beside him. "Is everything all right?" he asked anxiously.

"Ah, Roxanne doesn't feel well," Daniel replied quickly.

She put a pained smile on her face. "I hate to spoil things, but could you be a dear and take me home, Daniel? I don't think I'm going to be able to dance anymore."

"Of course," Daniel answered without hesitation.

Sarah put a hand on Roxanne's arm and said, "I'm so sorry you're feeling ill. Is there anything Elliot and I can do . . . ?"

Roxanne shook her head. "I'll be fine. I just want to go home and lie down."

"I'll take good care of her," Daniel said, slipping an arm around her waist.

After saying their good-nights to their host and hostess, Avery's parents, and apologizing for leaving the ball early, Daniel found Roxanne's heavy black velvet cape and his own greatcoat in the cloak room. They went out into the cool, blustery night.

A liveried servant brought up their carriage, and Daniel took the reins to drive away from the Wallingford mansion. "Where now?" he asked Roxanne when they were well away from the house. "The Salutation Tavern?"

Using a small hand mirror she had taken from her bag, she was unobrusively checking to make sure no one was following them. "I don't know if any of the committee members will be at the tavern," she said without taking her eyes from the mirror's reflective surface. "But that's usually the quickest way to contact them." She nodded in satisfaction. "There doesn't seem to be anyone trailing us. Yes, head for the Salutation."

Daniel pushed the horse to greater speed, sending the carriage rattling over the cobblestoned Boston streets.

This was perhaps the single most vital piece of information either of them had turned up, Roxanne thought. A warehouse full of British munitions was a most tempting target. If the patriot forces could capture those guns, the weapons would more than replace those confiscated by the redcoats. Failing that, the destruction of the rifles would at least make sure that none of them would ever be used against the colonists. She was sure that once the committee heard what she and Daniel had to say, they would act quickly.

"You had better tell me what you know," she said to Daniel. "Just in case anything happens."

"Of course. That's a good idea. The warehouse is at Amory's Wharf. That's down on Boston Neck."

"I know where it is. Do you know which warehouse?"

Daniel shook his head. "Avery didn't say. But I'm sure anyone keeping a watch on the area would be able to determine which one it was. The British probably have a guard on it, although a small one so as not to draw too much attention."

"That makes sense," replied Roxanne, nodding.

How easy it was to talk to him about things like this! At first she had not been convinced of his loyalty, thinking that perhaps he became involved because of his brother—or even because of her. Perhaps there had been some truth to that at the outset, but now it was different. Daniel was different. He would probably be willing to give up his life in the pursuit of liberty, like so many of them. They certainly had that in common.

But was that enough on which to base anything but a friendship and a working relationship? Roxanne was not sure she wanted anything deeper with Daniel, regardless of how she might feel about him. Becoming romantically involved with him could direct her energy away from her real goal, which was to help win freedom for the colonies.

And if she were to give her heart to Daniel, she would face the terrible possibility of seeing that love destroyed by the muskets of the redcoats when the inevitable war finally came.

No, she thought as the carriage rocked and swayed toward the Salutation Tavern, with all the burdens she was already carrying, she did not need the extra weight of love.

A little later, as the carriage came to a stop at the curb near the Salutation, Daniel said, "Here we are!" and hopped down to give her a hand. They went inside, glad to be out of the blustery winter air.

Pheeters, the tavern keeper, was behind the bar as usual and saw them come in. Daniel noticed the quick glance that passed between Roxanne and the man, and he knew the tavern keeper had understood her message. They went to a table and sat down, and less than a minute later, the burly Pheeters brought them a bottle of wine and two glasses.

"Drink one glass of wine and then go to the back," he told them in a low rumble. Roxanne gave a minuscule nod in acknowledgment of the order.

They took their time with that glass of wine, lingering over it even though the delay chafed at them. Finally, Roxanne took the final sip from her glass and said, "I think that's quite long enough."

Daniel drained his own glass and nodded. "I agree."

He stood up first and held her chair for her, then took her arm as they started toward the rear door. No one seemed to be paying any attention to them. Roxanne wondered if the men they were going to see had been in the back room all along, or if Pheeters had summoned them some way.

They moved into the narrow corridor, then knocked on

the door on the right. A man's muffled voice told them to come in.

Three men were sitting around the table in the room. Roxanne recognized them immediately, even though they had their coats off and were not wearing their usual powdered wigs. Papers were spread over the table, and from the weary looks on the faces of the men, they had been working for quite some time.

Samuel Adams took off his spectacles and looked up at Daniel and Roxanne. "Young Mr. Reed," he said in his thin voice. "We haven't seen you for quite some time, although we've had good reports on your work. What have you and the fair Roxanne for us tonight?" His companions, the physicians Joseph Warren and Benjamin Church, looked on with equal interest.

Roxanne began, "I thought this information was important enough to come directly here, rather than going through our usual channels. Daniel and I have discovered where the British are caching their weapons here in Boston."

Adams, Warren, and Church all sat up straighter in their chairs. "Indeed?" muttered Dr. Church.

"Are you sure about this?" asked Joseph Warren.

"Yes, sir," Daniel replied. "We have it on good authority that the British are using a warehouse at Amory's Wharf for their surplus munitions."

"Which warehouse?" Samuel Adams asked sharply.

Daniel shook his head. "We don't know, sir, only the general location."

Adams waved a hand and said, "That's not really important. What you've told us is sufficient. We'll set up a watch on the area immediately, and we should know within a week or less which warehouse is the one."

"That's what Miss Darragh and I thought, sir."

"Good thinking, my boy. And good work, both of you." Adams smiled at Roxanne. "I certainly didn't mean to slight you, my dear."

"No, sir," Roxanne said. "I urge you, Mr. Adams, to launch a raid on this warehouse as soon as possible. Those guns should be either captured or destroyed."

Adams's smile was tolerant. "Of course. Excellent thinking, Miss Darragh."

"And I'm going along when you raid the place," Daniel said.

Four pairs of eyes swung toward him in surprise. Roxanne was the first to respond to his declaration. "You can't do that!" she said.

"I'm afraid Miss Darragh is right," Dr. Warren added.

"But why not?" Daniel asked, his voice echoing the displeasure that was visible on his face. "I can handle a gun, and it's time I did more than simply skulk around."

"Your skulking around, as you call it, is vital to us, young man," Samuel Adams scolded. "Besides, Mr. Reed, what experience do you have in combat?"

"Well . . . none," Daniel admitted grudgingly, "unless you want to count a few scrapes I've gotten into since coming to Boston."

"A brawl or two is hardly the same thing as going up against highly trained guards," Dr. Church said with a frown. "Mr. Adams and Dr. Warren are right. You've done your part, Mr. Reed, and from here on out, let us handle the matter."

"You'll be much more valuable to us in the long run," Dr. Warren added.

Daniel sighed, and Roxanne could tell how deeply disappointed he was. She hoped he would not go against the wishes of the committee members, however.

"All right," he said. "You have to do as you see fit. I'll abide by your decision."

Roxanne relaxed slightly, pleased that the men had persuaded Daniel to abandon his idea of going on the raid against the British warehouse. Such a course would have been much too dangerous. He would have been risking his life—

Suddenly she felt ashamed. The patriots who ultimately made the foray against the British would be risking their lives, and they had people who loved and depended on them, too. She had no right to be happy that Daniel would be at least relatively safe if he continued in his current role.

But she was happy—or at least relieved—and there was not a thing she could do about it.

Samuel Adams stood up and extended his hand to each of them in turn. "Keep up the good work, you two," he said. "It's only a matter of time now until victory."

Yes, thought Roxanne, only a matter of time . . .

Chapter Thirteen

For the second time in a month, Daniel was back at the Wallingford mansion, and he was not any happier about it now than he had been the last time. For one thing, he was alone tonight. Although Roxanne had also been invited to this party, she had sent her regrets. *A previous engagement,* she had penned on the note she had returned to Avery Wallingford.

And a very important previous engagement, at that, Daniel thought. In truth, Roxanne was at the Salutation Tavern, in the back-room headquarters of the Committee of Safety, on hand to do anything she could to help coordinate the raid that would take place in a few hours on the British munitions storehouse.

During the weeks since Daniel had discovered the location of the stockpile, the committee had been very busy. He had heard most of the details from Roxanne, although Quincy had also managed to involve himself through his friend Roger Malvern. Roger's father was one of the men who would take part in tonight's activities.

It had proven no great challenge to determine the exact location of the warehouse being used by the British. A week's surveillance had told the patriots which warehouse along Amory's Wharf was being visited, usually late at night, by British troops. The redcoats had attempted to keep their visits secret, but with their usual overconfidence, it had not been difficult to keep track of their comings and goings. Samuel Adams had ordered another week of watching the place, though, just to be sure they had the right target.

Once that was certain, all that had been left was to plan the raid and wait for the proper time—tonight, when the moon was only a thin sliver and a layer of clouds blocked off over half the starlight. Under cover of deep darkness, a group of patriots would approach the wharf in small boats from Boston Harbor, go ashore just east of the warehouse, and sneak up on the small force of redcoats placed there as sentries. Most of the committee members hoped the guards could be overpowered quietly, without any loss of life, and then the weapons stored in the building could be spirited out and carried away in the boats. Failing that, however, the raiders had orders to put the storehouse to the torch, setting off the powder and destroying the crates of Brown Bess muskets.

Either way, the British would not be crippled by tonight's raid—but they would be hurt enough to feel it.

"Hello, there, old man. Sorry to hear that redheaded minx of yours couldn't be with you tonight."

The young Tory's voice put Daniel on edge, but he hid his reaction with the practiced ease of a veteran spy. "Good evening, Avery," he said. "Yes, it's a shame Roxanne couldn't be here. I'm sure she would have loved to see you again."

"Well, there'll be other parties," Avery said lightly. He cocked an eyebrow. "In the meantime, look around. There are plenty of girls here for kindred spirits like you and me."

Although the idea of being a kindred spirit to Avery Wallingford made Daniel's stomach clench, he kept the smile on his face and glanced around. It was true, there was an abundance of young women here tonight. In fact, all the guests were young. This was Avery's party, not his parents', and so he had invited only those of his approximate age.

Daniel saw Elliot and Sarah nearby and nodded to them. Avery was yammering on about something, but Daniel paid little attention to him. He was thinking instead about how the patriots would be gathering to begin their mission. He wished he were with them, wearing a dark sweater, pants, and a cap rather than the knee breeches, cutaway coat, frilly shirt, and silk cravat he currently sported. He was even wearing a powdered wig tonight, an affectation he usually disdained.

Suddenly realizing that Avery was staring at him and blinking stupidly, as if waiting for an answer, he said, "I'm sorry, Avery! Did you ask me a question?"

"I simply inquired as to whether or not you want me to introduce you to Mildred Carstairs. That's she right over there. I'm sure she'd be very impressed with you, Daniel."

Daniel looked in the direction Avery indicated and saw an attractive, though rather vapid-looking brunette who was standing across the room. He smiled and shook his head, saying, "I appreciate the offer, Avery, but I think not."

"Don't tell me you have some utterly foolish notion of remaining faithful to Roxanne?" Avery sounded appalled. "I thought you said the two of you have no strings on each other."

Daniel shrugged. "I guess I'm just not really in the mood for socializing."

"Then why are you here?"

"That's a good question." Daniel chuckled. Avery stiffened and looked vaguely offended, as if he knew he had been insulted without fully comprehending how, but Daniel could not very well explain the real reason for his amusement. He was here only so that no one could ever connect him with the raid on the munitions warehouse. Avery was his alibi—and the concept of that was what made Daniel laugh.

Because of all the men in Boston, there was no one he despised more than Avery Wallingford.

Roxanne had never told him the details of what had gone on between Avery and her at the party a month ago, but Daniel did not need a verbatim account to know that Avery had tried to force his attentions on her. He had probably tried to embrace her, might have even gone so far as to kiss her or attempt to fondle her. Daniel did not really want to know. If he had, he might have taken a horsewhip and gone after the Tory bastard.

Ah well, he told himself sternly, no use harboring thoughts like that. He had to keep up the friendly façade, no matter how much effort it cost him.

Avery offered to introduce him to several other young women, but each time Daniel refused. Finally, growing exasperated by Daniel's lack of cooperation, Avery wandered off to mingle with his other guests.

"I don't know how you stand it."

Daniel looked over to see Elliot beside him. Sarah

was on the other side of the room, one of a group of young women chattering among themselves. Elliot looked very elegant tonight in a deep blue suit, his blond hair concealed underneath a wig of his own.

"You're talking about Avery?" asked Daniel.

"Of course. I should think you'd want to wring his bloody little neck."

"It's an appealing prospect," Daniel said with a slight smile.

Daniel had told Elliot a little about what happened on the night of the previous ball. He had also mentioned the discovery he had made that night, and although Elliot knew the patriots would be launching a raid on the British warehouse, he was not aware of the exact timing. Still, Elliot's brain could work quite keenly when he put the effort into it, and he went on, "I imagine Roxanne's absence tonight means something."

"It means she had a previous engagement," Daniel said with a shrug.

Elliot nodded sagely. "I see. You probably wish you were with her."

"I do," Daniel said fervently. "Or at least nearby."

He took a deep breath. Friends of his would be going into danger tonight—partially because of him. He should be with them, he thought for perhaps the thousandth time.

"You look as though you could use a drink," Elliot said. He took hold of Daniel's arm. "Come on."

Daniel allowed his cousin to lead him toward the bar. Elliot was right. It was time for a good stiff drink, past time, in fact.

Tonight, he would celebrate like the good Tory he was supposed to be.

Sarah Cummings was not sure exactly how Avery Wallingford had gotten her into this sitting room with the door closed behind them. One minute, she had been talking to her friends, and the next she had been walking along with Avery, who had his hand on the skin of her arm, left bare by the short, puffed sleeve of her gown. "I just need to steal Sarah away for a moment," he had said with a charming smile at her companions, and he had moved so smoothly she had not resisted. Nor had she objected when he steered her into this room and closed the door.

She had been here before, and she knew what was going to happen next. Avery stood close to her, less than a foot away, and cupped her chin so that he could tilt her head back and gaze down into her blue eyes. That arrogant, mocking smile was still on his face as he said, "It's been a long time, Sarah. Too long, much too long."

"Avery, I shouldn't be in here—" she began.

"Why not?" he cut in. "Elliot was off talking to that hayseed cousin of his. If he's foolish enough to neglect you, then he has only himself to blame if someone else spirits you away."

"I suppose you're right. . . ."

"Of course I'm right."

She had agreed with him out of habit. For years now, Avery had fancied himself Elliot Markham's chief rival for her affection, and he was right, she supposed. He could be quite charming when he wanted to, and there was no denying that he was handsome, just as there was no denying that his father was very wealthy. All of those were definitely things to consider.

As was the way he could make her feel.

His mouth came down on hers, hard and cruel, his tongue insistently forcing its way past her lips. Sarah wanted to pull away, wanted to slap his face and demand to know what he thought gave him the right to treat her this way. But as an urgent warmth grew and spread in her belly, she knew all too well what gave him the right. She pressed herself against him, moaning low in her throat as his hand closed over her breast. His thumb strummed the erect nipple prodding against the thin fabric of her gown, and the touch made a shiver of longing race through her.

He took his lips away from hers and whispered, "You remember, don't you? You remember the carriage ride . . ."

She blushed hotly. Every detail of that carriage ride they had taken into the country near Cambridge the previous fall was etched into her memory, along with every detail of what they had done under the spreading limbs of a thicket of chestnuts well off the path. Her heart began to pound more quickly now as she recalled the way he had so expertly inflamed her passions and how he had taken her there.

Nothing like that had ever happened to her before, nothing. And she still shuddered as she thought about it, but it was a shudder of desire and need.

"You never spoke of that day to Elliot, did you?"

"I'm not a fool," she said hollowly. "He knows nothing. I . . . I would never hurt him that way."

"Come with me now into the garden," murmured Avery. "The night's not too cold, and Elliot will never miss you."

Sarah forced her head to move back and forth. "No, I can't," she said miserably, torn by her loyalty to Elliot and the feelings that Avery stirred in her. She did not love Avery; there was no question of that. He was a pompous, overbearing twit. But he was rich, and he was a wonderful lover. . . . "I just can't," she said, trying to sound more forceful this time.

"I think you can," he replied smugly, then kissed her again.

And as she caught her breath and felt her stomach thrust involuntarily against him, she knew he was right.

There was a knock on the door.

"Goddamn it!" Avery said, jerking away from her. "Not again."

The knock was repeated, a soft, diffident rapping, and Sarah did not pause to wonder what Avery meant by his comment. She took several quick steps to put more distance between herself and him, then said, "You . . . you'd better see who it is."

"I suppose you're right," Avery growled. "The bastard doesn't seem to be going away." He stalked across the room, jerked open the door, and demanded, "What is it?"

The short, bald-headed man who stood there wore butler's livery, and Sarah recognized him as one of the Walling-ford servants. He looked nervous, and he had to lick dry lips before he was able to say, "There . . . there's a gentleman to see you, sir."

"Blast it, Osborn, you know I'm not to be interrupted when I'm in this room——" began Avery.

He stopped short when he saw the man standing behind the butler. The newcomer was a tall, handsome man in the dashing uniform of a major in the British army. He stepped around the anxious butler and said in an urbane voice, "Sorry to disturb you, Mr. Wallingford. I would not have done so had this not been a matter of the utmost importance."

Avery's smooth veneer was not shattered, but it was shaken a bit. "Of course, Major," he said. "Please excuse my impatience. I'd be honored to speak with you, although I'm sure I have no idea how I might be of assistance to His Majesty's army."

The officer stepped into the room. "I'm Major Alistair Kane." He cast a meaningful glance at Sarah.

Avery reacted quickly. "Miss Sarah Cummings. Sarah, this is Major Kane."

"Very pleased to meet you, ma'am," Kane said stiffly.

"Major," she murmured, nodding.

Avery took her arm. "I'll speak to you again later, darling. Right now, I'm sure you'll excuse us." Without giving her a chance to protest, he ushered her out of the sitting room.

Sarah felt a surge of anger go through her. He had kicked her out as peremptorily as he had gotten her in there. She had a good mind to stay right here and give Avery Wallingford a piece of her mind when he emerged from his discussion with the British major.

Instinctively she turned toward the doorway as that thought went through her mind, and she saw that Avery had neglected to push the door completely shut. It was still open a couple of inches, and as she leaned toward it, she heard the voice of Major Kane saying, "—have here a warrant of arrest."

"Arrest?" echoed Avery, his startled voice coming clearly to Sarah's ears. "You want to arrest someone at my party?"

"Yes, sir."

"My God, who? And what are the charges?"

Major Kane said, "The charges are espionage, conspiracy, and treason against the Crown. And the man I'm after, Mr. Wallingford, is named Daniel Reed. I'd appreciate it if you could point him out to me."

Daniel and Elliot were chatting idly on the other side of the room when Sarah came up to them. Her fair-skinned features were even paler than usual, and her eyes were wide with surprise and perhaps a little fear.

Both young men saw immediately that something was amiss. Elliot stepped forward and put a hand under her elbow and said, "Good Lord, Sarah! What's wrong? You look as if you've had a shock."

"Not as much of a shock as your cousin is going to get in a few minutes," Sarah said. She switched her gaze to Daniel and went on, "There's a British officer here with a warrant for your arrest."

The words hit Daniel like a hard blow to the belly. His eyes narrowed, and his breath hissed between suddenly clenched teeth. The reaction lasted only a second before he controlled it. As he ordered himself to remain calm, he said to Sarah, "There must be some mistake."

She shook her head. "I overheard him talking to Avery just now." Pointing across the room, she added, "They're in that sitting room over there."

Daniel knew the sitting room of which she spoke, remembered it all too well, in fact. He cursed himself silently for not noticing the British officer's arrival, even though the room was crowded. Could he brazen his way out of this?

"This is insane," he said with a little laugh. "I've never done anything to be arrested."

"The major said the charges were espionage, conspiracy against the Crown, and treason."

The British knew! Somehow, they knew, Daniel thought wildly. His masquerade was shattered, destroyed.

Sarah looked at Elliot with accusation in her eyes and asked, "Did you know anything about this?"

Before Elliot could answer and possibly incriminate himself, Daniel said quickly, "Elliot didn't know anything because there's nothing to know, Sarah. It's a mistake, I tell you."

"Well then, you'll have to explain that to Major Kane, won't you? He asked Avery to point you out to him."

Despite Avery's pretense of friendliness, Daniel knew the young Tory cared about no one but himself. Avery would not hesitate to point out anyone this Major Kane wished to have identified.

"We'll handle this, Sarah," Elliot said. "You go back to your friends. I'm sure we can straighten everything out."

"I hope so." Sarah looked at Daniel. "I like you, Daniel, and I'd hate to see you get into trouble. I hope for Roxanne's sake this doesn't amount to anything."

"It doesn't," Daniel assured her, but even as he spoke, he was keeping an eye on the sitting room where Avery was conferring with Major Kane. The door was bound to open at any second, and then the major would emerge along with Avery.

As Sarah started toward the group of young women she had been talking with earlier, Elliot said quietly to Daniel, "Let's start moving toward the garden."

"My thinking exactly," Daniel agreed, his voice little more than a whisper.

Luck was with them. Just as Avery and Major Kane emerged from the sitting room, a group of several partygoers moved past them, blocking their view of Daniel and Elliot, who stood by the terrace doors. "Let's go!" Daniel hissed at Elliot. He walked quickly to the doors, opened them, and stepped outside.

There was no way of knowing if anyone had noticed them leaving the party. Elliot shut the doors behind them. Daniel paced out onto the terrace, his hands clenching into fists. "How could this have happened?" he asked in a low voice as Elliot followed him.

"I don't know, but the important thing now is to get you out of here," Elliot said. "Can you climb over those garden walls?"

Daniel nodded. That was the only way out. He certainly could not go back through the house.

The garden was fairly small, no more than fifty feet deep. Daniel and Elliot went down the terrace steps toward the brick wall that surrounded it, following a stone walk through flower beds that would be a riot of color when the flowers bloomed in the spring. Daniel's mind was racing. His chief worry now was what sort of story Elliot should tell when confronted by Major Kane. Evidently, the major had no idea that Elliot was aware of his cousin's espionage activities.

Daniel paused before he reached the wall and stopped Elliot with a hand on his arm. "Tell the major you have no idea why I ran away," he whispered. "You have to protect yourself."

In the darkness of the garden, Daniel could not see Elliot's face, but he heard the surprise in his voice as he said, "But I'm going with you."

"No, you're not," Daniel insisted. "There's no need for you to get in trouble, too—"

He broke off his argument, and both young men stiffened as they heard the steady tramp of heavy footsteps from the alley just behind the garden. There was no mistaking the telltale sound of soldiers marching.

Daniel's hand tightened on Elliot's arm. "They've covered the back," he breathed.

At that moment, the door from the house opened, spilling light into the garden.

"Hit me!" Daniel said.

"What?" asked Elliot, flabbergasted by the request.

Looking past Elliot, Daniel saw two figures come out of the mansion, one of them slender and no doubt belonging to Avery Wallingford; the other, tall and well built, would be Major Kane.

Daniel leaned closer to Elliot and said, "There's no way out for me now, but we can still save you. Struggle with me, pretend you've apprehended me in order to turn me over to the British!"

"I can't do that!" Elliot protested as Major Kane and Avery started toward them.

Daniel grabbed his shoulders. "You've got to!" he whispered desperately. "Go to the Salutation Tavern and find Roxanne when this is over! Tell her that I've been arrested and that the British may know about the raid on the warehouse later tonight!"

Still Elliot hesitated. "But . . . but it wouldn't look realistic for me to have captured you so easily."

"You're right," Daniel said.

Without warning, he slammed a punch into Elliot's jaw.

Elliot staggered backward from the impact of the blow and then toppled, his powdered wig falling askew over his eyes. With a shout of anger—whether real or feigned, Daniel could not tell—Elliot slapped the wig off and surged to his feet. He sprang at his cousin even as Daniel turned to flee. Elliot's flying tackle sent both the young men sprawling to the ground.

The breath was knocked out of Daniel when he landed. Over the blood roaring in his ears, he heard Major Kane shouting, "Sergeant! Sergeant!"

Daniel gulped air into his lungs and grappled with

Elliot. They rolled over and over, winding up in a flower bed.

Rushing footsteps pounded up the path. Men cursed. Daniel felt strong hands grasping him, pulling him away from Elliot, hauling him roughly to his feet. He hung there in the grip of two redcoat soldiers. Another trooper jammed the muzzle of a Brown Bess painfully into his back. A few feet away, Elliot was receiving the same treatment, Daniel saw in the light coming from the open doors. Most of the party guests had spilled out into the garden, too, drawn by the commotion, and they were standing by, watching in amazement.

"Stand still, both of you!" ordered Major Kane. He stood in front of them, hands clasped behind his back. Turning his head to look at Avery, who stood nervously beside him, the major demanded, "Which one of these men is Daniel Reed?"

"Th-that one," Avery said, pointing a slender finger at Daniel. "The other one is his cousin, Elliot Markham."

"Cousin, eh?" Major Kane said suspiciously, turning his attention back to the captives.

"Cousin no longer," Elliot said harshly. "I wouldn't claim a damned traitor as a relative of mine. Now tell these brutes to get their hands off me!"

As desperate as his own situation was, Daniel had to stifle a grin at the act Elliot was putting on. He had hit exactly the right offended, self-righteous tone and sounded just like a good Tory should have at this moment.

Major Kane concentrated on Elliot, saying, "Your father is Benjamin Markham, isn't he?"

"That's right, and he's not going to be happy when he hears how your soldiers manhandled me!"

Kane made a curt gesture, and the men holding Elliot

released him. Elliot squared his shoulders and straightened his coat, then brushed himself off. "That's better," he went on. He nodded toward Daniel, who was standing stiffly, with his head up, a defiant look on his face. "I had just stepped out into the garden for a breath of air with my—with this gentleman here when we heard your soldiers coming. Daniel panicked and blurted out that he was some sort of . . . of rebel spy and asked me to help him get away! You can imagine how shocked I was."

"Indeed," murmured Major Kane.

Don't overplay it, Elliot, Daniel warned silently.

The major continued, "Naturally, you tried to stop him when he attempted to flee?"

"Of course. I didn't understand any of this—still don't, really—but I wanted to get to the bottom of it." Elliot sighed heavily and shook his head. He looked at Daniel. "I'm sorry, old man. But you can see what a dreadful predicament you put me in."

"Tory bastard," growled Daniel. "You're right, Elliot. You're no cousin of mine, you damned—"

"That'll be enough of that," Major Kane said sharply.

Avery put his hands on his hips and glowered at Daniel. "I can't believe it. I simply can't believe it! Here I've been inviting you to all my parties, Daniel, and this is the way you turn out. I have to say I'm very disappointed in you."

Daniel wanted to laugh in Avery's face, but instead he just ignored the young Tory.

"Get him out of here," Major Kane ordered his men. Jerking him about roughly, the soldiers pulled Daniel away from the house.

It was certainly an ignoble departure, Daniel thought. But at least Elliot appeared to be safe, and he could carry the warning to the other patriots.

As for himself, Daniel saw only bleakness in the future—jail, a quick mockery of a trial, then the gallows. His parents would be devastated when they heard the news, and as for Quincy . . . Well, Quincy would take it badly, Daniel had no doubt of that. But perhaps his death would make everyone who had known him more determined than ever to liberate the colonies from the brutal grip of the British. If that was the result, his death would not have been in vain.

He had one regret, though, that loomed over all the others. He had never told Roxanne he loved her. . . .

"I'm still having a great deal of difficulty believing this," Elliot said as the British troops took Daniel away. "If I hadn't heard him admit his treason, I still wouldn't believe it!"

Avery clucked his tongue disapprovingly. "And here you've been taking him around all over Boston and introducing him to the best people."

"All the time he was just using me to further the cause of those damned insurrectionists."

"Well, he'll trouble no one else," Major Kane declared. "His Majesty's justice will see to that." He bowed to Avery and went on, "Sorry to disturb your party, Mr. Wallingford. We'll take our leave now." He strode out of the garden, and the detail, with its prisoner, followed him.

Elliot was still straightening his clothes and brushing dirt and dead grass off his breeches. Sarah came up to him and asked anxiously, "Are you all right, Elliot?"

"I'm fine—No, actually, I'm quite miserable. It's not every night one discovers that one's best friend is a traitor." He looked intently at Sarah, hoping she would not mention the conversation she had overheard between Avery and Major Kane.

"We might as well go back inside and get on with the party," Avery said. "No need to let this spoil the evening."

"I'm sorry, Avery," Elliot said quickly. "But I don't really feel up to that right now. In fact, I'd be very grateful to you if you'd see to it that Sarah gets home safely."

"Elliot!" exclaimed Sarah. "What are you talking about?"

"I have to inform the family of what's happened, and I'm not looking forward to it. My father is going to be livid when he finds out he sheltered a rebel spy under his roof. But the best thing to do, I suppose, is get it over with."

Avery put an arm around Sarah's shoulders. "I'd be more than happy to escort Sarah home, Elliot. Don't you worry about her at all."

Elliot saw that Sarah was displeased, but there was nothing he could do about it now. He would have to make this up to her later. At the present, the most important thing was to get to the Salutation Tavern and find Roxanne. He had no idea what she was doing there, but he guessed it had something to do with the raid the colonists were going to carry out on the British arms warehouse. Obviously, from what Daniel had said, the attack was scheduled for later tonight.

And Daniel was right, Elliot realized—if the British knew he was a spy, they probably knew what the patriots were planning, too.

Elliot stalked through the mansion, speaking to no one as he got his hat and overcoat and had one of the servants fetch his carriage. With his face grim, he took the reins and sent the vehicle rolling off into the night, carrying a message he wished he did not have to deliver.

Chapter Fourteen

Quincy Reed was utterly thrilled. This was surely the most exciting night of his life, just as he was surely the only youngster who was being allowed this close to the inner circle of the Committee of Safety on such a momentous evening.

He was sitting in the Salutation Tavern at a small table near the rear door. Mr. Pheeters had given him a glass of milk—Quincy would have preferred ale, but he knew better than to ask for it—and Roxanne had sat him down with firm orders not to budge unless there was an emergency, such as a raid by British soldiers. In that case, he was to enter the rear corridor, knock three times on the door to the back room, then run to the door leading to the alley behind the building. His horse was tied up there, and in the event of trouble, after giving the warning, he was supposed to head for Cambridge and home as fast as he could.

Even serving as a lookout for the committee was an

honor, Quincy thought, and he probably would not have been chosen for the duty if he had not arrived at Roxanne's house just as she was leaving to go to the tavern. He had told her in no uncertain terms that he was going with her, and there was no time for her to argue with him—just as Quincy had planned.

He took another sip of his milk and watched the goings-on in the tavern. The place was crowded, and Pheeters and his serving girls were being kept busy serving ale and wine and whiskey to the drinkers who crowded the bar and the tables. An old man with a fiddle was holding forth in a corner, dancing a sprightly jig as he sawed away with his bow. Several patrons stood around him clapping and singing a mildly bawdy song to the tune he played. The infectious melody had Quincy tapping his toe. He was grinning at the lyrics of the song when the door opened and a well-dressed young man came hurrying in from the street.

Quincy glanced at the newcomer and then away before recognition suddenly jerked his gaze back. The man was Elliot Markham, and he stood just inside the doorway looking around anxiously as if he was searching for someone.

A shiver of apprehension went through Quincy. He had no idea why Elliot was here or why his cousin looked so disturbed, but every instinct in Quincy's young body told him there was trouble. He stood up and lifted a hand, trying to catch Elliot's eye.

Elliot finally spotted him, looked shocked to find him here, and then started quickly across the room, skirting the group that was still growing around the spry old fiddler. As Elliot hurried up to Quincy, he gripped the younger man's arm. "Do you know where I can find Roxanne Darragh?" he demanded.

Quincy hesitated. Over the past months, Daniel and he

had kept few secrets from Elliot. He knew almost everything about their activities on behalf of the patriots, and Daniel trusted him completely. So did Quincy, for that matter. But this was no longer just a question of trusting Elliot. With Roxanne in that back room were Samuel Adams and the leaders of the Committee of Safety. Quincy was not sure how they would feel about being interrupted.

Elliot's fingers tightened on Quincy's arm when he did not answer. "Damn it, lad, this is important!" he said in a harsh whisper. "Daniel's been arrested!"

Quincy's jaw dropped in astonishment. The world seemed to spin crazily around him for a few seconds, and only after it had righted itself was he able to croak, "What?"

"You heard me. The British have him." Elliot leaned closer and dropped his voice even more. "They know he's been spying for the patriots. And they probably know about what's going to happen tonight!"

Quincy had not known Elliot was aware of the raid planned for tonight, but obviously he was. Equally obvious was the fact that Elliot's news was serious enough to warrant interrupting the meeting in the back room. Quincy was stunned and horrified by the news of Daniel's arrest, but he had to bring his emotions under control. There were things afoot that were larger than the arrest of one young man.

Even when that young man was his brother . . .

"Roxanne's back here," Quincy said after taking a deep, ragged breath. "I'll take you to her."

"Quickly," Elliot said.

Quincy opened the door and stepped into the rear corridor with Elliot following closely behind him. He went straight to the door and rapped on it, but only once, being careful not to give the signal that would indicate a raid by the

British. Nervousness made his mouth and lips dry as he waited for a response. It was not long in coming.

The door swung back a few inches, and Roxanne's green eyes peered out at him, widening slightly in surprise as she saw him. "Quincy!" she exclaimed. "What is it?"

Rather brusquely, Elliot pushed the door open, forcing Roxanne to step backward quickly. Elliot moved into the room, followed by Quincy.

The youngster's gaze darted around, and he almost gasped as he saw the men around the table. The Adams cousins, Hancock, Revere, Warren, Church, Otis, Dawes— the inner circle of the committee was here tonight.

"What's the meaning of this, young man?" Dr. Benjamin Church demanded thunderously. "And just who are you?"

"My name is Elliot Markham, sir. I'm Daniel Reed's cousin."

Roxanne caught Elliot's arm. "What is it?" she asked anxiously. "Has something happened to Daniel?"

Elliot nodded grimly. "I hate to tell you this, Roxanne, but—he's been arrested by the British."

"Arrested?" she cried, and the men in the room echoed her astonishment.

Samuel Adams came forward, his penetrating gaze fixed on Elliot. "What were the charges?" he asked.

"Espionage, conspiracy against the Crown, and treason," Elliot recited.

Quincy felt sick to his stomach. Despite the fact that he had been aware of the danger Daniel and he were in every time they carried out an assignment for the committee, he could hardly imagine Daniel in the hands of the British. No mercy could be expected from the redcoats, that was certain.

They would surely want to make an example of any rebel spy who was caught.

Everyone in the room looked shaken. "This is a disaster," said Paul Revere, and several of the men nodded in agreement with him. The silversmith went on, "If the British were aware of young Reed's activities, they probably know what our plans are for tonight, too."

Samuel Adams nodded gravely. "That's exactly what I was thinking. Our men are probably headed right into a trap." He looked around the room. "We have to warn them somehow—"

His gaze fell on Quincy Reed.

Thrusting out his hand, Samuel Adams said, "Someone give me a pistol!" William Dawes slid a flintlock pistol from his waistband and passed it across the table to Adams, who turned and came toward Quincy, clutching the gun tightly in his hand.

Quincy swallowed nervously. What did the patriot leader intend to do with that pistol? Had the old firebrand gone mad? Did Adams blame him for the fate that had befallen Daniel and thus the raid on the warehouse?

Adams reversed the pistol and extended the butt toward Quincy. "Take it, my boy," he said urgently. "You've got to get down to that warehouse and warn our men to call off the raid, and there's not much time left!"

Quincy could not have been more shocked by any request. He had never expected Adams to entrust such an important mission to him. Obviously, neither had Roxanne, because she said, "But Mr. Adams, Quincy's only a boy! He can't be asked to do such a thing, to take such a chance."

"I'm not asking," Samuel Adams said, his eyes narrowing and his thin voice rising. "The lad is the lightest and therefore the quickest rider."

"I can go," Elliot volunteered.

"Do you have a horse?" snapped Adams.

"A carriage, but that will do."

"No, it will not." Adams swung back to Quincy. "We're wasting time. I won't force you to go, lad. But decide now."

"I'll go," Quincy said, not even waiting to consider the issue. He took the pistol from Adams, tucked it into his belt, and started toward the door. "It will be my honor."

"Wait!" Roxanne said. "Quincy, you can't—"

He turned toward her, his face and voice hard as he said, "I have to, Roxanne. For Daniel . . ."

She caught her lower lip between her teeth, looked at him intently for a moment, then nodded. "I understand," she whispered. "I just wish I were going with you."

"Good luck, lad!"

"Godspeed!"

"The Lord be with you!"

The calls of encouragement and support came from the men in the room. Quincy smiled weakly, determined to go through with this but well-nigh overwhelmed by the whole thing. He had never expected the night to turn out like this.

As soon as Quincy was gone, Roxanne turned to Elliot and said, "Tell me everything that happened." The committee members nodded and watched Elliot, also anxious to hear the story.

Quickly, Elliot told them what had gone on at Avery Wallingford's party, at least what he knew of the details. Some of it was still rather fuzzy in his mind. The most important things were crystal clear, however: Daniel's masquerade had been uncovered, and he had been taken away from the party and no doubt thrown into a jail somewhere in Boston.

"They've probably taken him to the stockade on Brattle Street," John Hancock said. "That's where most of the political prisoners have been taken lately."

Paul Revere nodded in agreement. "I've been told more than once that I'll wind up in the Brattle Street jail," he said with a wry grin. "That's where young Reed will be found."

"What are we going to do, gentlemen?" Roxanne asked rather tentatively. She knew it was unusual for a woman, and such a young one at that, to have been allowed to attend this meeting. She was only here, she figured, because she and Daniel were the ones who had provided the crucial information about the British munitions storehouse. Being temporarily admitted to the inner circle was in the nature of a reward for their work.

Samuel Adams said, "I'm afraid there's not much we can do, my dear. The British have the jail well guarded, and we cannot risk a full assault on it simply to free one prisoner, no matter who he is. Why, if I myself were incarcerated there, I would not expect my fellow patriots to waste their lives in a vain effort to liberate me."

"But that's not fair." Roxanne knew she was being dreadfully bold to speak this way to these men, but ever since she had heard Elliot's news, her mind had been in a turmoil. "Daniel's in trouble because he tried to help!"

"He knew the risks, Miss Darragh," Dr. Warren said gently. "All of us do."

Roxanne turned away, her hands clenching into fists. Anger and fear, fear for Daniel, boiled up within her.

He might well die in that prison, she thought, and if he did, he would go to his grave without ever knowing the truth, without ever realizing that she did care for him, that she . . . loved him.

Her breath caught in her throat. Yes, she loved Daniel Reed. There was no point in denying it, not now.

A touch on her arm made her gasp and turn halfway around. Elliot stood there, his handsome features grown taut and bleak. "We have to do something," he said. "We can't just leave Daniel there to rot in prison or be strung up from a gallows."

"As Mr. Adams said, what can we do?" Roxanne asked dully.

"We can get him out of there! You and I alone if need be—but we'll get him out."

Elliot's determination was contagious. Roxanne felt her spirits rising. "All right," she said. "Let's work out a plan."

She glanced at the table and saw that the committee members were deep in discussion about moving their headquarters. With Daniel captured, they risked exposure here. They would have to find another place in Boston to hold their meetings and plan their activities, and that problem had them fully occupied now.

"Come on," Roxanne told Elliot. "We'll talk outside."

As they left the room, Roxanne looked at the committee members one last time, and it struck her that someone was missing, someone who had been there earlier. With everything that had been going on, one of the men could have slipped out without her noticing, she supposed. She was in no mood to worry about that, however. The question of Daniel's rescue was uppermost in her mind, and besides, she had no right to question the comings and goings of the inner circle.

Taking Elliot's hand, she led him from the room. Already, a desperate plan was forming in her mind, and she was anxious to know what he thought of it.

To Quincy, it seemed that his heart was pounding even more loudly than the hooves of his horse on the cobblestone streets. As he rode through the darkened avenues, he thought about how he might be able to warn off the men who were supposed to raid the warehouse.

He knew its exact location, having been one of those assigned to watch the warehouses along Amory's Wharf. The patriots would come ashore to the east of the building and then approach it across an empty lot. There were a couple of storage sheds they could use for cover, but that was all. Still, it was a more likely route of access than the one to the west, which was completely wide open. His best bet, he decided, would be to work his way down to the waterfront east of the warehouse and try to intercept the raiders as soon as they came ashore. That is, if he arrived on the scene in time.

If he was too late for that, he had no idea what he would do.

His year and a half in the Boston area served him in good stead now. He had wandered most of the main streets of the city, as well as knowing many of the smaller lanes and back alleys. Familiar shortcuts saved him some time and distance as he rode toward the harbor. From time to time, he glanced up at the crescent moon and the stars, barely visible through a thin haze of clouds. It would have been the perfect night for an attack on the warehouse—had Daniel not been captured.

Quincy was making an effort not to think about Daniel's predicament. There was nothing he could do about it right now, and the job Samuel Adams had given him was important. He had to concentrate on that, he told himself, and worry about Daniel later.

But when this task was over, Quincy would turn his attention to Daniel. Something had to be done. Somehow, the committee could help him gain Daniel's freedom. Quincy was sure of that.

He was within a few blocks of the waterfront now, and he slowed his mount to a walk. The sound of a galloping horse might warn the British that something was happening. Better to approach quietly and keep his eyes and ears open, he decided.

He rode down Orange Street, which led straight to Boston Neck, until he reached a crossroad called Bonnet Street. This road came to a dead end at the harbor itself, east of the wharf. This would be a likely spot to intercept the patriots, Quincy thought.

But as he turned onto Bonnet Street and approached the waterfront, he had to suppress a groan of disappointment. Several dark shapes—which had to be small boats—were drawn up on the shore. The raiders had already landed. Quincy drew his horse to a halt and squinted into the darkness. After a moment, he made out some figures flitting from one storage shed to the next in the lot next to the warehouse.

The patriots were making their approach, and in a matter of moments, they would walk right into the trap the British had laid for them. Of course, there was no guarantee that an ambush was set up. But it was a strong enough chance that Quincy felt sick at heart for the men he had failed to warn.

But there could not be an ambush, he suddenly realized, if something happened to draw the soldiers out of hiding before the attack began. No sooner had that thought raced across his brain than he had wheeled his mount and sent the horse galloping back toward Orange Street.

He took the turn at a dangerously high speed, using all

the strength in his young body to haul the animal's head around. He raced toward Castle Street, the crossroad just west of the wharf. Heedless now of any noise he might make, he dug his heels into the flanks of the horse and urged it on to greater speed.

Another sharp turn put him on Castle Street. So far, there had been no shots, no yells of warning or alarm. He might still be in time, he thought.

What he was about to do was utterly insane, and he was well aware of that. But if there *was* a trap, his actions were the only chance his fellow patriots had of escaping. He tried not to think about the possible consequences as he sent the horse plunging toward the harbor.

The road came to an end at a low wall of timbers. On the other side of the wall, the waters of the harbor lapped at the timbers. There was no beach here. Quincy reined in sharply, bringing the horse to a halt only a few feet from the end of the road. Looking to the east, he could see the warehouse some seventy yards away, a small light burning in a window near the front, no doubt where an office was located.

The night was still silent. Quincy grasped the smooth wooden butt of the flintlock pistol and slid it from his waistband. He hooked his thumb around the hammer but did not pull it back just yet. With his other hand, he settled his tricorn hat on his head and then broke into a loping run toward the brick building.

When he was thirty yards from the warehouse, he shouted, "Ho, lobsterbacks! Come on out, you bloody British!" No sooner had his cry shattered the stillness of the night than he thumbed back the hammer of the pistol, pointed it toward the deep black sky, and pulled the trigger.

The blast of the shot rolled out across the space between Quincy and the warehouse. As its echoes died away, he howled, "At 'em, boys! Kill the damned redcoats!"

On a night as dark as this one, anyone watching from inside the building would not be able to tell how many men were charging toward the warehouse. But the pistol shot and Quincy's shouts would be clearly audible, and the muzzle flash would have been visible from inside, too, giving the soldiers a target. That thought made Quincy dart rapidly to one side while he continued running forward, shouting and whooping.

Suddenly the main door into the warehouse was thrown open and men poured out, an entire company from the look of them. In the light coming from behind them, Quincy could make out the long coats and tall black bearskin hats of British Grenadiers. With a sound like the popping of firecrackers, the redcoats loosed a ragged volley at him.

Quincy dove forward, landing hard on the pavement. He heard the whistling sound of musket balls passing close over his head and the whine as some of them struck the ground and ricocheted off into the night. He rolled over and over, looking for some sort of cover, and knew he should give some serious thought to getting out of here. The patriots on the far side of the warehouse must have heard the fusillade by now and realized that all was not going according to plan. They would be safe if they would withdraw to their boats and row away from shore as quickly as they could.

Rifles began cracking from the sides of the warehouse, however, and as Quincy came up on his hands and knees, he saw bright muzzle flashes of gunfire that sent the British troops scurrying for cover. The patriots had circled the warehouse, Quincy realized, and taken advantage of the diversion he had provided to catch the redcoats in a cross fire. Cut off from the warehouse, the Grenadiers ran toward the scant cover of two empty wagons parked nearby.

Quincy leapt to his feet. His actions had not caused the raiders to flee, as he had hoped, but at least he had ruined the trap set by the British. He wheeled around, ready to dash back to his horse and safety. As much as he would have liked to join in the battle, he had already spent the single round in his pistol.

He had taken only a couple of steps when something smashed into his right thigh. The horrible impact sent him sprawling to the ground. Curiously, although a part of his brain already grasped that he had been shot, there was no real pain. But when he tried to get to his feet, he found his right leg no longer worked. He twisted around on the ground and brought his hands to his thigh. The fingers found a hot, sticky wetness, and Quincy began to gasp as he realized it was blood—his blood.

A flare caught his eye, and he looked up to see a man running toward the warehouse, a fiercely blazing torch held high over his head. The redcoats were firing at the man from the protection of the wagons, but the musket balls all seemed miraculously to miss him, as if a divine hand were steering his course. When he was close enough to the door of the building, the man drew back his arm and then flicked it forward, sending the torch spinning into the warehouse. Then he turned on his heel and sprinted away.

Some of the British troops had stopped firing and were now shouting in alarm. There were several crates of powder stored in here, they knew, and if the flames reached them—

The redcoats broke and ran, just like the patriots. Now they had one common thought—to get away from that warehouse as quickly as possible before it was blown to kingdom come.

Quincy knew he was too close. His wounded leg was hurting like blazes. But he ignored the pain and used his arms and his good leg to lever himself to his feet. Hopping, stumbling, half falling, he windmilled his arms for balance and started moving away from the warehouse.

He had covered perhaps twenty yards that seemed like a mile when the world exploded.

At least that was what it sounded like as the powder stored inside the warehouse detonated with a fierce roar. Fire leapt from the door and window of the building as the roof was shattered and thrown high in the air, and the walls toppled outward. The night sky over Boston Harbor turned red, and a noise like a thousand thunderclaps shook the city. Quincy had his back to the blast, and it felt as if he were being buffeted forward by a giant hand striking between his shoulder blades. Pushed by the force of the blast, he rolled over and over.

He finally came to a halt, though, and felt strong hands gripping his arms. He was jerked to his feet, and although he cried out in pain as the rough handling sent jolts of agony through his leg, he could not hear himself. The noise of the explosion had deafened him, at least temporarily.

But as he blinked, he saw the red coats of the men surrounding him and holding him up. For one wild instant, he dared to hope that their coats merely looked red because of the fiery inferno lighting up the night nearby. But he saw the angry looks on their faces and knew that was a vain hope.

Just like his brother, Quincy had fallen into the hands of the British.

Chapter Fifteen

"I don't like it," said Elliot Markham. "You'll be taking too much of a chance, Roxanne."

"It doesn't matter. Daniel is my friend. We've worked together for months. I can't let him down."

Not now that she knew she loved him, Roxanne thought. But even though her feelings were crystal clear in her mind, she could not bring herself to voice them. Not yet.

Maybe if Daniel lived through this night . . .

Roxanne and Elliot were sitting at a small table tucked away in a corner of the Salutation Tavern, all but oblivious to what was going on around them as they discussed Roxanne's plan to free Daniel from the Brattle Street jail. Elliot's expression had become more and more dubious as Roxanne laid out the details of the scheme, and he said, "You should at least let me go with you."

Roxanne shook her head. "I can't do that. Everything hinges on my getting into the prison without the British suspecting anything, and it's more likely that I'll be able to talk my way past the guards if I'm alone."

"I still don't like it," Elliot said with a frown.

She leaned closer to him and said, "Besides, you have to protect your position as a Tory sympathizer. You can't go around rescuing rebel spies from a British jail and expect to do that."

"Daniel asked me months ago to help him in what he was doing, and I said I would. Since then, though, I haven't done anything other than introduce him to a few people!"

"Until tonight," Roxanne reminded him. "Don't forget it was you who brought word of Daniel's capture."

Elliot shrugged. "Anyone could have done that."

"But *you* did, Elliot."

"All right." He shook his head, giving up reluctantly. "I want you to know, though, that if anything goes wrong, if you fail in your mission . . . then I'll find a way to free both of you."

Roxanne reached across the table, took hold of his hand, and squeezed it. "Thank you, Elliot. I knew I could count on you, just as Daniel did." She stood up and brushed her hands across the front of her long skirt. "When Quincy gets back, tell him what I'm doing. But *keep him here.* That's important, Elliot. We can't have him rushing in recklessly and ruining everything."

He nodded. "I understand. If you do get Daniel out, where will you go? His apartment won't be safe anymore."

"I know. And I haven't figured out that part yet. But we'll get in touch with you and let you know where we are."

"Fair enough." Elliot caught Roxanne's hand and gave it a final squeeze. "Just be careful."

"Thank you," she said softly. She did not know Elliot all that well, only through Daniel and the Tory parties they had attended, but she sensed there was a solid core to the young man, buried beneath the façade of idleness and cynicism. Only now, in this time of trouble, was that core beginning to emerge.

Straightening her shawl around her shoulders, Roxanne went to the bar and caught the eye of Pheeters, the burly proprietor. Leaning close to him, she said, "I need a pistol, Mr. Pheeters."

He looked only mildly surprised. "Yer up to somethin', missy. I expected as much. Took some rum to the back room a few minutes ago, I did, and I heard 'em talkin' back there. You wouldn't be doin' somethin' foolish like goin' after that young man of yours, would you?"

"He's not my young man," lied Roxanne, "but I want to help him if I can."

Seeing the determination on her face and hearing it in her voice, Pheeters sighed and said, "Come with me."

He led her to the end of the bar and into a storeroom. A narrow window opened from it onto the alley that ran alongside the building.

"You can go out this way," Pheeters told her. "And I'll give you me own pistol." He lifted his soiled white apron and reached under it to draw out a flintlock pistol. "Comes from the Rappahannock Forge, down in Virginny, and you won't find a better handgun anywhere in the colonies. Have a care now, it's loaded."

"Thank you, Mr. Pheeters," Roxanne said, taking the gun. "I'll see that you get it back."

A savage grin pulled at the tavern keeper's ugly features. "Just see that you use it in a good cause, girl." He threw open the window. "Now, on yer way—and good luck to you."

Holding up her skirts and not worrying about modesty, Roxanne climbed through the window and dropped lightly to the packed dirt of the alleyway. Pheeters closed the window, cutting off the candlelight from inside the storeroom. As she stood in the darkness, Roxanne drew her shawl more tightly around her, wishing the garment could ward off not only the chill of the night but also the terrors it might contain. She hid the pistol under the wrap and started toward the street.

She had grown up in Boston, so she knew quite well how to get to Brattle Street and the grim gray stone building that was now being used as a jail. She headed for it at a brisk walk, but she had only gone a few blocks before some instinct made her steps slow. She listened intently for a moment, sped up again, then suddenly stopped short. The sound of a footstep behind her made her spin around, the Rappahannock Forge pistol emerging from under her shawl. She held the heavy weapon steady in both hands as she pointed it in front of her. The darkened street seemed to be deserted, but she knew better.

"Whoever is following me, either go away or come closer so I can see you," she said, forcing her voice to remain calm. "Otherwise I'm going to shoot."

A huge shape loomed up out of the shadows, making her gasp in fear, but before she could fire the pistol, a familiar voice said quickly, "Ye'll not be needin' that f'me, lass."

"Murdoch!" Roxanne exclaimed.

Her cousin, Murdoch Buchanan, came even closer, and now she could make out his buckskin-clad form and the coonskin cap perched on his thatch of coarse red hair.

"Why are you following me, Murdoch?" Roxanne asked, still a little shaken but greatly relieved.

The big man grimaced and rasped a thumbnail along the rugged line of his jaw. "A better question might be what ye be doing out at this time o' night, in this part o' town. 'Tis hardly the place for an innocent young girl. But then—" He gestured at the pistol she was still pointing at him. "—judging from the looks o' that, ye may not be as innocent as I'd thought!"

"Oh!" Quickly Roxanne lowered the gun. "I'm sorry, Murdoch. I wasn't thinking."

" 'Tis all right. The gun wasn't cocked, anyway."

To her chagrin, she realized he was right. She had neglected to pull back the hammer. If she was going to be a spy—if she was going to rescue Daniel—she would have to start remembering things like that.

"I've been keeping an eye on ye," Murdoch went on. "Figgered this spying of yours would get ye in trouble sooner or later."

"Is that why you've stayed in Boston, instead of going back to the frontier?"

He shrugged his massive shoulders. "Part of it, I reckon." He chuckled and added, "An' I want to be on hand when things start popping a'tween the rebels and the lobsterbacks. Also, I figgered one o' these days, I might be able t'give ye a hand. With ye carrying a pistol, I reckon the time's come."

Roxanne was very glad to see her cousin. She had refused Elliot Markham's offer of assistance, but unlike Elliot, Murdoch was a seasoned fighting man. While she still intended to try to get into the prison alone, having Murdoch on hand nearby might prove quite useful.

"Where're ye headed?"

"I'm going to Brattle Street, to the jail," Roxanne told him. "Daniel is a prisoner there."

"Dan'l a prisoner?" echoed Murdoch. "How in hell'd the British get hold o' him? Do they ken what he be doing?"

"I'm afraid so," Roxanne replied grimly. "Come with me, and I'll tell you about it along the way."

Murdoch fell in step beside her, checking his own stride to stay even with her. As long as he was with her, Roxanne knew, she did not have to worry about being bothered by anyone. Just the sight of Murdoch Buchanan would be enough to frighten off any would-be troublemakers. As they walked, she told him everything she knew about the night's events.

"The committee was certain that Daniel would be taken to the Brattle Street stockade, so that's where I'm going," she concluded.

"And what'll ye do when ye get there, lass?"

"Get inside, find Daniel, force his jailers to release him, and then get out as quick as we can."

"As simple as that, eh?"

"The more complicated the plan, the more there is to go wrong," Roxanne said.

"Aye, there's some truth to tha'. But ye'll need a whole heap o' luck on your side t'get away wi' it."

"I know," she admitted. "But there's no other way."

"We'll see," mused Murdoch. "Right now, let's just find this here jail."

It did not take long for the two of them to reach the neighborhood of Brattle Street. With the city under virtual siege due to the Intolerable Acts—unless you happened to be an influential Tory, of course—very few people were abroad this late at night. But not long before Roxanne and Murdoch reached the vicinity of the jail, an explosion sounded loudly from somewhere near the harbor. Roxanne clutched Murdoch's arm and exclaimed, "What was that?"

"A few dozen kegs o' black powder going up, from the sound of it," Murdoch said. He lifted a long arm and pointed toward the waterfront. "Ye kin see the glow in the sky from a fire."

Roxanne shivered and licked lips that had suddenly gone dry. The explosion had come from the same area where the British munitions storehouse was located. Could the patriot raiders have been successful in the mission after all, even though Quincy had gone to warn them to call it off?

But answers would have to wait. She had her own task before her now, and it was as dangerous and vital—at least to her—as anything else going on tonight.

She and Murdoch hurried on toward the prison, and a few minutes later Roxanne spotted it down the road. It was a squat, two-story stone building that took up most of a block. Originally built for government offices, it had in recent weeks been converted into a prison. The doors of its rooms had been taken down and replaced with iron bars. Part of it, Roxanne knew, was still used as offices for the British military.

"There it is," she whispered softly to Murdoch as she put a hand on his brawny arm to stop him. She pointed out the building on the other side of the street. No soldiers were on duty at the entrance, which was lit by a pair of lanterns, but there would no doubt be at least one guard inside. Roxanne was hoping the lateness of the hour would mean fewer redcoats were on duty in the building.

"D'ye still think it wise t'go through wi' this?"

"I don't have any choice," Roxanne said. "Daniel is in there. I can feel it. He may be hurt, and he's certainly in danger."

Murdoch shook his head. "I wonder if th' lad sees what's right in front o' his face."

"What do you mean by that?"

"I be talking about the way ye feel about him, lass."

Impatiently, Roxanne said, "I don't know what you're talking about. Why don't you stay here while I see if I can get inside?"

"All right, but keep ye eyes open. Ye never ken when I might be turning up."

Roxanne did not know what he meant by that, but there was no time to worry about it. She had just started forward when a quick touch on her arm stopped her.

"Somebody be coming," Murdoch warned quietly.

They hid in the shadows of a store's entranceway. The business was closed for the night, and the darkness here was deep. Roxanne stayed where she was as a wagon appeared on the street, moving toward the jail from the opposite direction. Murdoch had heard its approach before she did, a testament to the keenness of his hearing, honed by his years on the frontier.

His sharp eyes proved to be important now as the redcoat driving the wagon brought it to a stop in front of the gray building. Several soldiers riding in back hopped down from the vehicle, and they reached into the wagon bed to haul someone out of it. From the way they were acting, they had a new prisoner they were delivering to the jail.

"By the lord Harry!" exclaimed Murdoch as the light from the lanterns fell on the slender figure of the captive. "Tha's Quincy Reed! An' the lad's hurt!"

Roxanne leaned forward tensely. The figure in the grip of the redcoats was limp, probably only half-conscious. From the way he dragged his right leg, there was obviously something wrong with it. The boy's head hung down loosely on his chest.

Things had certainly not gone as the rebels had hoped, although judging by the explosion a few minutes earlier, at least one goal had been attained. The British munitions storehouse had apparently been destroyed, but Quincy had been injured, perhaps badly, in the process.

Roxanne took a deep breath and tried to calm herself. Catastrophe was piling atop catastrophe, but dwelling on the disastrous chain of events that had led her here would not accomplish anything. Instead she had to take action and try to reverse the way luck had been running tonight.

The soldiers disappeared into the building, taking their prisoner with them. Roxanne and Murdoch stayed where they were for ten minutes, safely ensconced in the darkness of the doorway, until the British troopers emerged from the jail once again. They climbed into the wagon and drove away, heading toward the harbor and the site of the explosion. Roxanne glanced in that direction and saw a red glow in the sky, which meant that the fires were still burning. The British would have their hands full tonight, coping with the damage from the blast.

Which was all to the good, Roxanne thought. The busier they were, the more likely she would be able to rescue Daniel—and now Quincy as well.

"All right," she said quietly, standing up on her toes to bring her mouth closer to Murdoch's ear. "This changes things somewhat. But first I have to get in there. That's still the most important thing."

"Aye, but now ye have two stray lambs t'bring home," Murdoch reminded her. "Are ye sure ye dinna want me t'go wi' ye, lass?"

"I'm sure," Roxanne said bravely, but in reality her heart was pounding frantically. She inhaled deeply again, willing her pulse to slow and her raging emotions to grow calm. Underneath the shawl her fingers tightened on the butt of the pistol, and the hard, cool, smooth wood seemed to give her strength.

She squared her shoulders, lifted her head, and strode out of the darkness toward the prison.

The wooden heels of her shoes made clacking noises as she walked. The sound seemed so loud that she was surprised the redcoats inside the building did not come out to see what the commotion was.

Three steps led up to the double doors of the building. She climbed the steps and reached out with her free hand for the knob of the door on the right. She took a deep breath, glanced back at the shadows where Murdoch was still concealed, then twisted the knob, pulled the door open, and stepped into the jail.

On the inside, it looked like any other building that housed government offices, at least this part of it did. There was an entranceway, then an open area separated from the rest of the front room by a low wooden railing. On the other side of the rail were several desks, only one of which was occupied at the moment. A young British trooper sat at it, his tall black hat on the floor next to his chair. His long-tailed red coat with its green lapels was unbuttoned, as was his collar. He looked up sharply and straightened in his chair as the door opened, but when he saw that the visitor was a stranger, rather than a superior officer, he relaxed again. Then a frown creased his lantern-jawed face as he realized how odd it was for a young woman to be out at this time of night, especially visiting a prison.

" 'Ere now," he said. "What are you doin' 'ere, girl?"

"This is the Brattle Street jail, isn't it?"

"Last time I checked, it was," said the trooper with a grin. His teeth were prominent and yellow.

"There was a young man brought in a few minutes ago," Roxanne said, forcing herself to go on before her courage deserted her. "I have to see him."

The guard's frown deepened. "There've been a couple of rebels brought in tonight. Some trouble down at the harbor from that damned lot, from what I understand."

Roxanne's heart leapt at the mention of two new prisoners tonight. That would be Daniel and Quincy, she thought. She tried to keep the excitement from showing on her face as she went on, "This was just a short time ago. The young man was hurt."

"Oh, right, I remember the lad now. Shot through the leg, 'e was. But you can't see 'im."

"I've got to!" Roxanne said fervently. "You see, he's my brother." She was making this up on the spot, but the lie seemed to have a good chance of working.

The guard was thinking with all his might, which was obviously an effort for him. Letting a civilian in to see a prisoner, especially this late, would be against the rules and a good way for him to get into trouble if he was caught. On the other hand, this redheaded young woman was quite attractive, and she might be grateful—and willing to show her gratitude—if he helped her.

Roxanne could almost see those thoughts going through the soldier's head, as plain as any of the books or pamphlets her father printed. He was giving her request serious consideration, and for a moment, she thought she had him convinced.

Then, just as visibly, the fear of being caught by his superiors exerted itself, and his features hardened. He shook his head and said, "Sorry, miss. I just can't do it. Would if I could."

"I'm really sorry to hear that," Roxanne replied. Clutched in her right hand, she drew the pistol from under the shawl. She pointed the gun at the guard and went on,

"You're going to take me where I want to go, or I'll kill you."

It took all of her courage and strength to maintain the hard-edged pose. And perhaps it was not really a pose, she thought. At this moment, thinking about Daniel and Quincy in the hands of the British, Quincy with a hole in his leg from a musket ball, she really might pull the trigger.

The guard gaped at her, plainly shocked by the very idea that a pretty girl would pull a gun on him like this. He began, "You can't—"

Suddenly, Roxanne noticed something the young trooper had not. Once again, she had neglected to cock the pistol. Quickly, she thumbed back the hammer, and the sound of the flintlock being cocked cut off the guard's protest and made him swallow nervously, his prominent Adam's apple bobbing up and down.

"I can and I will," Roxanne said quietly. "Now take me to the first prisoner who was brought in. His name is Daniel Reed."

"I know who'e is," the guard said as he scraped back his chair and stood up slowly. Roxanne backed off a little to put more distance between them now that he was on his feet. "You know, I ain't the only guard 'ere. I can call for 'elp."

"If you do, they'll be too late to help you," Roxanne said meaningfully.

The trooper shrugged. "All right, all right," he muttered. "I ain't in no mood to cross a crazy woman with a gun. No offense."

"No offense," Roxanne agreed with a tiny smile. She jerked the barrel of the pistol. "Now get moving."

The guard took a ring of keys from a drawer in the desk and motioned for her to pass through a gate in the railing. Roxanne did so, being careful to keep the muzzle of the gun trained on him. He led her through an open door into a long corridor that was deserted at the moment. " 'E's back 'ere," the soldier said.

Roxanne did not think he would try anything, not with her behind him and armed. Since he had his back to her, she tucked the pistol out of sight under the shawl again, just in case they ran into any more soldiers. She was still ready to fire at an instant's notice, however.

The corridor was dimly lit by candles set in niches. Some of the makeshift cells were occupied, but the prisoners within them were already asleep. Loud snoring came from several of the rooms. Roxanne felt a pang of sympathy for the men who were incarcerated here. Not that the conditions were unusually bad. If anything, Roxanne had heard, prisoners brought here might have a slightly easier lot than those taken to other jails. But they were still prisoners, their freedom stolen from them by the British.

The corridor came to an end at an intersection where another hallway crossed it. "Over 'ere," the guard said to her, gesturing to the left. She hoped he was not leading her into a trap.

That hope almost faded as they turned the corner and she saw a guard standing on duty outside one of the cells. This one was all spit and polish, as opposed to the rather slovenly trooper who was her guide. She expected the first man to call out a warning to this one, who held his Brown Bess musket ready for use at his side.

Instead, the first soldier said lightly, "Got a visitor for that prisoner of yours, Clancy."

"A visitor?" repeated the second guard with a puzzled frown. "Major Kane didn't say anything about a visitor."

"Well, maybe 'e didn't know about it. Bloomin' major don't know everything."

"Suppose not," said Clancy with a shrug. He looked past the first guard and smiled at Roxanne. "And who have we here?"

"Don't harass the lady," the first guard snapped. "Just let me open the door, all right?"

"Sure, sure. Have at it, lad." Clancy moved out of the way to let the first soldier step up to the iron-barred door.

Roxanne was standing so that she was not visible from inside the cell, and she had not heard a sound from the chamber so far. If Daniel was wondering who might have come to see him, he was not asking any questions about it yet.

The key clattered in the lock, then the door swung open, given a shove by the guard who had unlocked it. At the same instant, he twisted around quickly, hoping to take Roxanne by surprise and lunge at her, perhaps wrest the gun from her hand before she could fire.

The guard froze as he found the barrel of the pistol centered on his forehead. Roxanne had whipped it out from under the shawl with surprising speed, and it was steady in her hands as she pointed it at him. Clancy, the other guard, let out a curse when he saw the pistol, and he started to shift his grip on his musket so he could bring it up into firing position.

"Don't try it, or I'll blow your friend's brains out." Roxanne smiled coldly, thinly. "Not that that would take much doing."

At the sound of her voice, a startled exclamation came from inside the cell. "Roxanne?"

"That's right, Daniel," she said, stepping into view but keeping the two guards under the gun at the same time.

She ordered Clancy, "Put that musket down and slide it into the cell with your foot."

"And if I don't?" Clancy asked indignantly.

"Then I'll just kill you and have done with it." Roxanne's tone was calm and dangerous, and the two guards interpreted it correctly.

Clancy laid the gun on the stone floor and grimaced as he pushed it into the cell with his booted foot. Daniel snatched it up immediately and trained it on the guards. He was staring at Roxanne in surprise, but he was not going to let his shock keep him from doing what needed to be done.

A wave of relief ran through Roxanne, but she knew they would still need a great deal of luck to get out of here.

When he first heard Roxanne's voice, Daniel was barely able to credit his senses. Surely his mind was playing a trick on him. But when she spoke again, he knew he was not just imagining things, and so he sprang to his feet from the bunk, where he had been sitting and staring down disconsolately at the stone floor.

She had never looked more beautiful, he thought, even though there was something incongruous about a pistol in the hands of a lovely young woman. She should not have been here, risking her own life to save his.

But he was extremely glad to see her; there was no denying that.

He snatched up the Brown Bess and trained it on the two guards. "Back away from the door," he ordered. With both the rifle and the pistol menacing them, they had no choice. They backed to the opposite wall of the corridor, giving Daniel room to step out of the cell and still keep them covered with the long-barreled musket.

Daniel wanted to seize Roxanne and crush her in an

embrace, but there was no time for that now. Moving aside from the cell entrance, he said harshly to the guards, "Get in there."

" 'Old on there," protested the guard from the front desk. "You can't put us in our own cell."

"The hell I can't," Daniel said with a tight smile. "Move."

Clancy and the other guard exchanged a despairing glance, then reluctantly stepped into the cell. Daniel moved around as they did so, keeping the musket pointed at them.

"You," he said to the first guard. "Take your clothes off."

"Wot?" the man exclaimed.

"You heard me. You're the closest to my size. Get that uniform off, now!"

Sighing, the guard complied with the order. "There's plenty of troops around 'ere. You can't get out, you know. And you can't shoot us, 'cause that'd draw too much attention."

"Never underestimate a dangerous man," Daniel told him. "Take the boots off, too."

Roxanne, blushing furiously at the sight of the young man in his underwear, moved up beside Daniel and put her free hand on his arm, but the hand holding the pistol never wavered. The warmth of her touch made him glance over at her, just long enough for both of them to smile. Instantly they turned their attention back to their prisoners.

"Quincy's here, too," Roxanne said.

Daniel's head jerked around as he stared at her. "What?" he demanded. "Quincy?"

"And he's hurt," Roxanne went on. "Shot in the leg, that one said." With the gun barrel, she indicated the British trooper who had now stripped down to his long underwear.

"Is that true?" Daniel asked the man. From the look on his face, he was ready to pull the trigger of the musket, consequences be damned.

The guard nodded and said nervously, "I suppose so. There was a lad brought in with a wounded leg, a rebel troublemaker from the sound of it. I don't know what 'is name is, though."

"Did you hear that explosion earlier?" Roxanne asked Daniel in a voice low enough not to be overheard, and when he nodded, she went on, "I think that was the warehouse down by the harbor being blown up by our men. Quincy was supposed to warn them to call the raid off. He must not have made it in time, and in the confusion, he got hit by a stray shot."

Roxanne's theory made sense to Daniel. As soon as Major Kane had shown up at Avery Wallingford's party to arrest him, he had known that the men who planned to attack the munitions storehouse were possibly walking into a British trap. From the sound of things, that was how it had worked out, and yet the patriots had still managed to destroy the cache of powder, shot, and muskets. He wondered if Quincy had had anything to do with that. But mainly he wondered how the British had gotten the information that brought about his arrest and allowed them to plan the ambush at the warehouse. Daniel didn't want to credit the suspicion forming in his mind.

Although only a few hours had passed since the debacle at the Wallingford mansion, this had been the longest night of Daniel's life. Sitting alone in the cell, his thoughts had been dark, consumed by memories of the good times he had had with his brother and parents, plagued by the idea of what he had missed with Roxanne. Now, there was still a chance that what he had with Roxanne could grow into something good and lasting.

But first he had to make sure that Quincy was safe, too.

"Keep an eye on them," he told Roxanne. He stepped forward, careful not to get between her and the two British soldiers, and scooped up the uniform and boots that had been thrown on the floor by the first guard. While Roxanne continued to cover the men with her pistol, Daniel put on the uniform. It was not an exact fit, but close enough to fool a casual glance, certainly. As he straightened the scarlet coat across his shoulders, he asked, "Where is the infirmary? Is that where my brother would have been taken?"

"I'm through talking to you, mate," said the first guard in a surly voice. "I won't 'elp you any more."

"It's that or get shot, you fool," Clancy said. "Can't you see that these rebels have lost their minds?"

"That's right," Daniel agreed, resting the muzzle of the Brown Bess on Clancy's forehead. "You just keep thinking that we're crazy enough to do anything, friend, and you might come through this alive."

Pale and sweating, Clancy said, "Go down to the other end of this corridor. Infirmary's on the right."

"Thanks. Now tear some strips off your shirt and tie your partner to the bunk."

Once that was done, Roxanne held her pistol on Clancy while Daniel checked the bonds securing the other guard to the bunk. Satisfied that they would hold, he told Clancy, "Lie down beside him. It'll be a tight fit, but there's room."

For a second, Clancy started to protest again, but then he nodded and did as he was told. Quickly, Daniel used more strips from the trooper's shirt to restrain him. All that was left was gagging them so that they could not cry out. They cooperated, once Daniel explained that the only alternative was to knock them out with the rifle butt, which could easily crack their skulls. Both men took the gags without fighting.

Daniel shut the door and turned the key in the lock. The guards would be secure unless someone happened to come along and see them in there, and that was unlikely, considering how gloomy and shadowy these corridors and cells were. He put a hand on Roxanne's arm and said, "Come on. Let's find Quincy."

He had buttoned up the uniform coat, and he held the musket at the ready as he fell in step beside Roxanne. He hoped that if they encountered anyone before they located Quincy, he could pass as a British soldier escorting a late-night visitor. However, no one stopped them as they started toward the infirmary, and Daniel was struck by how lax the security was here. That probably had to do with the lateness of the hour, he thought. While they walked, they worked out the story they would use to gain entrance to the infirmary. They would try the same tale Roxanne had used on the guard at the front desk, perhaps with more success this time. If not, they would do whatever they had to in order to get in.

"I thought I would never see you again," Daniel whispered. "Unless it was in the crowd at my hanging."

Roxanne had hidden the pistol under her shawl again, and she had her arms folded across her breasts. She hugged herself and said, "Don't talk like that. No one is going to hang you."

"Thanks to you. But we're not out of here yet."

They reached the infirmary a moment later. The door into the room was open, and a guard stood just inside the entrance. Beyond him, the room was cramped, a narrow chamber with glass-fronted cabinets along the walls. Inside the cabinets were surgical instruments, bandages, and a bottled array of powders and potions. An examining table, its wooden top marred by old, dark stains that could only be dried blood, sat in the center of the room, and stretched out on the table was Quincy. The youth's features were pale, and his eyes were closed. For an awful moment, Daniel thought his brother was dead, but then he saw Quincy's chest rising and falling at a regular rate. Standing over Quincy was a well-built man in shirtsleeves who had just finished securing a thick bandage around the youngster's right thigh. The doctor had his back to the doorway and did not look around until Daniel, in his best British accent, said to the guard, "This is the prisoner's sister. Been sent from headquarters with her, and she's got permission to see the lad."

At the sound of Daniel's voice, the doctor's head snapped around. Their eyes met, and Daniel stared in shock into the distinguished face of Dr. Benjamin Church. Roxanne recognized him immediately, too, and gasped in surprise.

That was not the only indication that something was wrong. Quincy's eyes popped open. He lifted his head from the examining table and exclaimed, "Daniel!"

The guard at the door grimaced and started to lift his rifle. Before he could bring the weapon up, Daniel lashed out with his own musket, slamming the butt of the Brown Bess against the guard's jaw. The blow knocked the man against the wall. His tall hat fell down over his face, and he sagged to the floor, dropping his musket as he slid slowly down the wall. He slumped into an unconscious heap.

"My God!" said Dr. Church. "What's the meaning of this?"

"We could ask you the same thing," Daniel said coldly.

Church gave a short, barking laugh. "Don't jump to conclusions about things of which you know nothing, young man. I'm here for the same reason you must be—to help Quincy."

Daniel's sudden suspicions eased a little. Church was a well-known physician, one of the best in Boston, and it was only natural that the British would make use of his medical services from time to time, despite his support of the patriots. They knew him as a speechmaker, but not as a member of the inner circle of the Committee of Safety.

Quincy pushed himself into a sitting position on the table and said excitedly to his brother, "I thought you were a prisoner, too. Elliot told us the British had taken you."

"And so they did," Daniel told him. "Roxanne freed me."

"Quite a daring escapade, my dear," Church said. "And now the two of you have come for Quincy, I suppose."

"That's right. You won't interfere with us, will you?"

"I wouldn't dream of it," murmured Church. "Just don't give me away in the process." A smile suddenly appeared on his handsome face. "In fact, why don't you take me prisoner? I'll make an excellent hostage. General Gage hates me because I'm an insurrectionist, but he needs my medical skills."

While the doctor's proposal made sense to Daniel, he couldn't help wonder why Church, a known supporter of the patriot cause, was asking him to make it appear that he was assisting them against his will. The British already had him pegged as an insurrectionist and would not be surprised that he was helping two rebel prisoners escape . . . unless Church was known by different stripes to the British. Daniel looked at the doctor. *Could he be the one who had tipped off the British about the raid? Could he be the turncoat in the Committee of Safety?*

Daniel pushed these thoughts out of his head for now.

Such knowledge wouldn't change his present course of action. He stepped over to the table and hugged Quincy briefly, then pointed to the bandaged leg and asked, "Can you walk with that?"

"I'd crawl if it meant getting out of this place," Quincy replied fervently. "But I think I can walk, if someone will give me a hand."

"That'll be your job, Doctor," Daniel told Church. "Roxanne and I will hold our guns on you, to make it look as if we're forcing you to help us."

"All right," Church nodded. "Come along. We had best get this done while we can."

Without wasting any time, Daniel and Church helped Quincy down from the table while Roxanne kept an eye on the hallway. Then, with Church assisting Quincy, the group moved into the corridor and headed toward the front of the building.

Daniel intended to walk boldly out the front door, using the threat against Church to hold back the enemy if they were discovered. They had just turned into the main hallway from the rear corridor and gone a few feet when a shout went up behind them.

Tensing, Daniel guessed, "Somebody's found those tied-up guards." A second later, more shouting proved him right. Running footsteps sounded from the rear corridor.

A group of soldiers must have come in a back door of the building, Daniel thought, then spotted the guards in the cell. "Keep moving!" Church urged in a hiss. He increased the pace that he and Quincy were hobbling down the hall.

Daniel risked a glance over his shoulder as he broke into a trot with Roxanne right beside him. The soldiers had not yet appeared, but the noise of their approach was louder.

They would come into sight at the intersection of the corridors at any second.

"Go on!" Daniel ordered Roxanne, then stopped abruptly, whirled around, and raised the musket. Without really aiming, he discharged it at the far end of the corridor. The noise of the shot was deafening in the narrow, low-ceilinged passageway. The musket ball thudded into the wall at the end of the hall, knocking chips of stone from it. Maybe that would slow down the pursuit a little, Daniel thought. He turned and ran after the others.

They reached the reception area and plunged through the gate in the railing. Quincy was even more ashen now, and he bit back cries of pain as he forced his wounded leg to work. Daniel hated to put him through this, but there was no choice. They made it to the front doors of the building, and Church threw them open.

As the four fugitives emerged from the prison, more trouble was apparent right away. Less than a block down the street, a group of British Grenadiers was marching along, heading for the prison. The officer leading them called out in surprise at the sight of four people running from the jail.

There was no cover here, Daniel realized, and they had foes coming at them from two directions. Heading across the street would do no good, and if they turned to run the other way, the Grenadiers would have a clear shot at them and would be able to to cut them down before they could get out of range.

Suddenly, with a rumble of iron-rimmed wheels on cobblestones, a wagon careened around a corner behind the soldiers in the street. Murdoch Buchanan was at the reins, flapping the lines against the backs of the horses in the team and bellowing at the top of his lungs. "Out o' the way, ye bloody fools!" he shouted at the redcoats as he sent the wagon barreling straight at them.

The soldiers had only seconds to scatter and leap frantically out of the way. Any thought of trying to stop Daniel and his companions from escaping was gone now. Survival was all that counted.

Leaving the troops in disarray behind him, Murdoch hauled back on the reins, slowing the plunging horses as the wagon drew up in front of the prison. "Get Quincy in the back!" Daniel ordered Dr. Church, pitching in to help as the physician lifted the injured youth into the wagon bed. Daniel turned to help Roxanne then, but she had already scrambled into the vehicle. She lifted her pistol and fired toward the door of the jail, where the redcoats were beginning to emerge. The ball clipped the hat of a soldier and sent it spinning off, and all of them ducked back into the safety of the entrance.

"Go!" Daniel shouted to Murdoch. The big Scot whipped the team into motion again as Daniel pulled himself up beside Quincy, Roxanne, and Dr. Church. The sudden lurch made Daniel sway, and for an instant he was in danger of toppling backward out of the wagon. Then Church's hand caught his wrist, holding on with a steadying grip that pulled Daniel firmly into the wagon bed.

"Almost lost you, lad," Church said with a grin. Muskets flamed in the darkness behind them, and lead balls whined past them. Church went on, "Just keep your head down!"

More shots popped behind them, but Murdoch was handling the horses skillfully, getting all the speed out of them he possibly could. The springless wagon—Lord knew where Murdoch had stolen it, Daniel thought—bounced and jolted them roughly, which had to be quite painful for Quincy's wounded leg. The wagon skidded precariously around a corner, threatening for a second to overturn before straightening up again. That took the death-defying passengers out of the line of fire from the British.

"Keep going!" Daniel called up to Murdoch. "I want to put a lot of distance between us!"

Murdoch responded with another urgent shout of encouragement to the horses, and the wagon raced into the night, leaving the prison far behind.

Chapter Sixteen

The bandage on Quincy's leg was soaked through with blood by the time Murdoch finally slowed the wagon from its breakneck pace. The prison was many blocks behind them, and while pursuit was inevitable, it probably would not be immediate. First the redcoats would have to go through the jail and determine just how many prisoners had escaped.

"I imagine that leg's hurting quite a bit," Dr. Church said to Quincy. He turned to Roxanne and went on, "Could I trouble you to tear off some of your petticoat, Miss Darragh? I need something to tie these bindings a bit tighter."

"Of course," Roxanne said quickly. She turned away, and a second later there was the sound of fabric tearing. She handed Dr. Church several strips of fine white lawn.

Daniel borrowed some paper cartridges from Murdoch and reloaded the musket and Roxanne's flintlock pistol, tearing a corner of each packet, pouring a little powder in the flashpan, then emptying the rest of the powder down the barrel. That done, he tamped down the ball with the ramrod stored under the barrel of each gun. He felt considerably better when the weapons were reloaded. Murdoch had a brace of pistols tucked in his belt, so that gave them four shots primed and ready. Dr. Church was unarmed; Daniel had noticed that earlier in the infirmary. There was nothing unusual about a medical man's not carrying a gun, however.

While Church worked on Quincy's leg, he said to Murdoch, "I'd head for Boston Neck if I were you, sir. The British can be quite efficient when they want to be, and they'll soon think of barricading the Neck to prevent you from escaping that way."

"Aye," Murdoch agreed. "Dinna know who ye be, mister, but ye got a good head on ye shoulders."

Roxanne moved closer to Daniel and took hold of one of his hands. "Why did the British take you there to take care of Quincy, Dr. Church?" she asked the physician.

"And why not?" he said with a grin as he knotted one of the cloth strips that had come from Roxanne's petticoat. "I am one of the best doctors in Boston, if I may be so immodest as to say so. I often do work for the British, and my colleagues on the Committee of Safety are fully aware of it, if that's what's worrying you. It gives me the opportunity to sometimes garner useful information about the British plans and their troop strength. It's quite an advantageous arrangement."

"I'm surprised they trust you," Daniel said, "given your opposition to the Crown."

"I never said they trust me. But they do make use of me, and sometimes a man says things he doesn't mean to when he's in pain and under the care of a doctor."

Daniel frowned. Church's explanation had not convinced him of the man's innocence, but after considering their situation with Quincy's wounded leg and the redcoats on their trail, he decided not to say anything accusatory right now. "Then I hope that by helping us, you haven't jeopardized your position."

Church was finished with Quincy now. He waved a hand carelessly. "Don't worry about that. Those troops in the street must have seen the way you were threatening me with your guns and ordering me about. My story is that I was forced to cooperate at gunpoint, and no one can disprove it."

Daniel leaned closer to Quincy and asked, "How are you doing? Does the leg hurt too badly?"

"I'm fine," Quincy said with a smile, but his voice was shaky and revealed the pain he had to be suffering. "I knew you'd find some way to get us out of that mess, Daniel."

"Don't give me the credit," insisted Daniel. "It was all Roxanne's doing. And Murdoch's, too, of course."

"The four of you seem to make quite a good team," Dr. Church commented. "Unfortunately, the British will be hot after you now, especially you lads. You'll have to get out of Boston and stay out, perhaps for a long time."

"Until the war comes, anyway," said Quincy.

Church shrugged. "It does seem inevitable, doesn't it? At any rate, where will you go? Do you have a hiding place in mind?"

"I know a place," Roxanne said. "I'll tell you how to get there, Murdoch. First of all, we need to go to Cambridge." She turned to Daniel. "You and Quincy can pick up some things from your apartment while there's still time."

The wagon rolled unmolested across Boston Neck. There were no guards on the narrow stretch of land, but within a half hour there probably would be. Daniel felt very lucky as the wagon left the Neck and entered the township of Roxbury. Boston was behind them now, and with every mile that passed, the power of the British grew weaker.

"You can stop here and let me off," Dr. Church told Murdoch as the wagon turned onto the road that led to Cambridge. "I'll hike back across to the city and find Major Kane. I'll tell him that you let me go and that I overheard you saying you were going back to your apartment. Of course, I'll make sure that I don't pass along that knowledge until you've had plenty of time to visit the place and get away."

Daniel reached over and clasped Church's hand. "Thank you, Doctor. Thank you for taking care of Quincy and for helping us."

"Think nothing of it, my boy. Nothing's too good for our fellow patriots, you know that. I'm just glad Providence placed me in a position to help." He paused, then went on, "When you get where you're going, be sure you change the bandage on the lad's leg. Keep the wound clean, change the bandages daily, and it should be all right. But if it does start to fester, find a doctor for him right away, understand?"

"Of course. Thank you again, Doctor."

Murdoch brought the wagon to a stop, and Church hopped down lithely. He lifted a hand and waved as the fugitives drove off into the night, then turned and started to trudge toward Boston.

No matter how carefully Murdoch drove, the wagon was still jolted by its passage over the road. Quincy gasped in pain after one particularly rough bump, and Daniel put a hand on his brother's shoulder and squeezed. "Hang on," he said. "We'll soon be where it's safe."

Roxanne pushed back a lock of red hair that had strayed over her face. "I know a farming family near Concord who'll be willing to shelter us."

Daniel frowned. "Shelter Quincy and myself, don't you mean?"

Roxanne shook her head and said, "All four of us. Those British soldiers got a good look at me—good enough to recognize me later if any of them happened to see me on the street. And Murdoch's appearance is distinctive, to say the least."

Murdoch gave a hoot of laughter at that comment.

Roxanne went on, "I really think it would be better for all of us to go into hiding for a time."

Daniel could see her logic, although he hated to think of Roxanne as a fugitive. "All right," he said grudgingly.

"After things have calmed down a bit, Murdoch and I can return to Boston and see if it's safe for you and Quincy to go back as well. I wouldn't count on that, though. General Gage is going to be furious about that munitions storehouse being blown up."

"That reminds me," Daniel said, looking down at Quincy. "You're going to have to tell me all about that."

The youngster grinned through his discomfort. "I'll be glad to tell you the story, Daniel," he said. "It's a night that'll go down in history. Quincy's Raid, they'll call it."

"I don't know. It sounds to me as though you may be delirious."

Quincy ignored the comment and launched into a rambling recitation of the night's events while Murdoch headed the wagon down the road toward Cambridge. They were safe, Daniel thought, and for now, that was all that mattered.

Dr. Benjamin Church was ushered immediately into the office of Major Alistair Kane. Even though the hour was well past midnight by now, the major was still at his desk. He glanced up angrily at the interruption, then sat back in his chair when he saw the identity of his visitor.

"Well," Kane said sharply. "I know all about tonight's fiasco, here and at the warehouse. What do you have to say for yourself, Doctor?"

"Just that your men are sometimes utter incompetents," Church said as he tossed his tricorn onto Kane's desk. "I told you well in advance that the rebels were going to attack that warehouse tonight. Not only did your forces fail to trap them, but they also let the munitions be blown up. You should have moved that powder out of there."

Kane flushed angrily. "You're a spy, Doctor, not a military man," he said in tones of faint contempt. "If we had moved the munitions out, rebel agents might have seen us and realized that we were on to their little plot. Everything had to look normal in order to flush them out."

"But they still let a mere boy draw them out of hiding and ruin everything."

"It was an honest mistake," Kane snapped. "They thought the raid had begun."

Church sighed and sat down. "It's too late to do anything about it now. The munitions are gone, and so are Daniel and Quincy Reed and a giant of a man named Murdoch."

"We'll snare them, you can count on that."

"I'm not sure," Church said with a shake of his head. "They're slippery, those three."

"Who was that woman with them, the one I've heard so much about this evening?"

Church shook his head again and lied, "I have no idea. I had never seen her before. But obviously, she knew the Reeds. Probably the inamorata of the older one."

Kane glared impatiently. "I'd like to get my hands on all of them. I'd find out a great deal about those rebels, I'll wager."

"I can tell you more than a pair of couriers and eavesdroppers," Church said smugly. "But if you want to find the Reeds, I suggest you check their apartment in Cambridge."

"An excellent idea. That's why I sent a detail there half an hour ago."

Half an hour, thought Church. Well, that was cutting it rather close, but there was at least a chance Daniel and the others had gotten away from Cambridge before Kane's troops arrived there. Not that it really mattered one way or the other to him. Daniel Reed was an annoyance, as was the Darragh girl; Church had sensed that right from the first, and that was why he had hired those men to give Daniel such a severe beating that he would not be able to function as an intelligence agent. That plan had been spoiled by the unexpected appearance of that lout Murdoch, just as tonight's plans had been spoiled by unforeseen circumstances.

"At any rate, thank you for your help, Doctor, in this and other delicate matters," Major Kane went on. "As usual, a handsome payment for your services will be forthcoming."

Church nodded and got to his feet with an eager smile, quite pleased to hear the promise of payment. "Very good. I'll be taking my leave, then." He settled his hat on his head. "Good night, Major. Or rather, good morning."

Kane grunted his farewell, and Church left the office.

The physician's smile faded as he walked away from the ugly building on Brattle Street. He was walking a thin line in feeding information to the British, and he knew it.

While he was careful to give the impression that he was politically motivated, in truth he spied only for the money. He had to be cautious not to tell them too much. That was why he had withheld his knowledge of Roxanne's identity. If he told Major Kane everything he knew, he would no longer be of any value to the British officer. He had to keep them hanging; that was the only way to insure the continuous flow of money from the king's coffers.

This had been a dangerous night all the way around. Those young rebels had been suspicious of him, and he was not sure his explanations had put their doubts to rest. In the future, he was going to have to be more careful about associating with the enemy. If he could come up with another way of communicating with Major Kane . . .

Perhaps I should start using coded letters, he mused, allowing himself another faint smile. That was it. He would have to come up with a code.

The hours he had spent in jail in Boston had been one of the longest times of Daniel Reed's life, but the next month seemed to fly by. If not for the fact that Quincy's leg wound was slow to heal and the boys worried about what their parents must think of their disappearance, Daniel's existence could have almost been considered idyllic.

Daniel, Quincy, Roxanne, and Murdoch had gotten away from the apartment in Cambridge before the arrival of the British troops, and Murdoch had driven the wagon straight to the farming community of Concord, some twelve miles to the northwest. To the north of the settlement, not far past the bridge over the Concord River, was the farm of Lemuel Parsons, a faithful member of Concord's Minuteman group. This civilian militia trained nearly every day on the Concord Green, and Lemuel was only too happy to take in the four fugitives. He had known Roxanne's father for many years, and Roxanne had visited the farm before. Lemuel, his wife Lottie, and their five children made the guests welcome.

The wound in Quincy's leg had closed up and seemed to be coming along nicely, but then the skin around it turned an angry red and the area swelled. Knowing that was a sign of putrefaction, a doctor was summoned from nearby Lexington. The man was a staunch patriot and would not give away their presence on the Parsons's farm, but Lemuel warned Daniel ahead of time that he was not highly regarded as a physician. The doctor took one look at Quincy's leg and announced that it would have to be amputated.

Daniel would never forget Quincy's cry of horror when he heard that diagnosis. That was when Murdoch stepped in. "I've seen Injuns and frontiersmen hurt worse than this, and they dinna carve off their legs. Let me go out in the woods an' see wh' I kin find t'make a poultice." He poked the doctor in the chest with a blunt finger. "Stay away from the lad until I get back, sawbones."

Murdoch returned with a sticky mass of leaves, moss, mud, and God knew what else. Over the objections of the doctor, he applied it to Quincy's wound. "We'll wait and see if it does any good," Daniel told the doctor. "There won't be any amputation until then."

The physician had puffed up with offended dignity and left.

After a night of sleepless worry, Daniel found that the reddened area around Quincy's wound had gone down somewhat. Now, after a month of care from Roxanne and Murdoch, plus of a month of hearty meals prepared by Lottie Parsons, there was plenty of color in Quincy's cheeks. The wound was not yet completely healed, but it got better every day. The lad's right leg was weak, making him limp and struggle for balance when he walked, but he was exercising it as much as possible and hoped that its full strength would soon return.

Not having anything else to do, Daniel pitched in to help Lemuel Parsons with his farm chores, in exchange for sheltering them. It felt good to be behind a plow again, working in the warm spring sun.

One day, when Daniel and the others had been on the farm about two weeks, Lemuel took a wagonload of produce into Boston, and when he returned, he looked grim.

"You and your friends really raised a ruckus in town," he told Daniel. "General Gage was so mad about that warehouse being blown up that he's forbidden anybody to so much as mention it around him. I reckon he'd like everybody to forget it even happened. And he's got the city cut off more than ever before. The damned lobsterbacks built a barricade across the Neck, and nobody comes or goes through the gate without passing the guards."

Daniel shook his head, sorry that he had contributed even indirectly to the hardships being suffered by the citizens of Boston.

"Rumor has it even more troops are on their way from England," Lemuel went on. "Going to be more redcoats in town than normal folks. There's soldiers staying in nearly every house now. No room for them anywhere else."

"I wonder if my parents have been forced to quarter some of them," Roxanne said, and Daniel wondered the same thing about the Markhams. He wished he could talk to Elliot again, just to make sure his cousin was still unsuspected by the British. That would have to wait, though. By no means would it be safe for any of them to return to Boston yet.

Murdoch Buchanan, for one, was very happy to be out of the city at last. Although he could have left at any time during the last few months, he had stayed in Boston out of curiosity and a desire to help his cousin Roxanne with her espionage activities. Now that he had done so, he was as deeply involved as any of them. Hiding out on this farm gave him a chance to roam the wooded countryside, sometimes accompanied by Daniel. The young man from Virginia was no stranger to the woodlands, but he learned a great deal in a short time from the big frontiersman. Murdoch had a genius for reading sign, and every time they went out hunting, they brought back a pair of turkeys or a bait of plump squirrels and rabbits. Murdoch's own long rifle had been left behind at the Darragh house, but he borrowed a musket from Lemuel, as did Daniel, and demonstrated some of the most superior marksmanship the younger man had ever seen. Although the usual range of a musket was no more than fifty yards, in the hands of an expert like Murdoch, it was accurate up to sixty or seventy yards.

Their jaunts through the forest solidified their friendship as they got to know each other better. Murdoch told Daniel about many of the things he had seen and done in the wilderness, awakening a desire in Daniel to see the frontier himself. When the coming war was over—if he survived—he might even go west, down the Ohio River valley to the great vistas of forests and grasslands, the rolling hills and the breathtaking valleys that Murdoch described with such longing. If the frontier was anything like what Murdoch was saying, then Daniel could understand how it could get into a man's blood and refuse to relinquish its hold on his dreams.

Not all his time was spent with Murdoch, however. Forced by circumstances to distance themselves from the day-to-day details of the growing rebellion, Daniel and Roxanne had more time for themselves. Daniel's capture by the British and the desperate rescue attempt orchestrated by Roxanne had left both of them changed. They talked together more easily now, and even the silences between them were more comfortable.

Still, Daniel had not brought himself to tell her how he really felt, and she had not said anything to him, either.

On a sunny April afternoon, as Daniel was plowing by himself in one of Lemuel Parsons's fields, Roxanne appeared at the edge of the woods bordering the clearing. She held up a clay pitcher and called to him, "I've brought you some water."

Daniel pulled the mule to a halt and left the plow there in the field. His linsey-woolsey shirt was wet with sweat and clinging to his body in places. He wiped moisture from his brow as he walked gratefully into the shade at the edge of the trees. Roxanne handed him the pitcher, and he drank deeply.

"That's wonderful," he said as he lowered the pitcher. "How did you know I was thirsty?"

Roxanne shrugged and smiled. "I just knew."

Daniel understood. They both seemed more in tune with each other's feelings now. And Roxanne looked lovely. She wore a plain woven kerchief tied over her hair, but the red curls still spilled out around the cloth and sparkled brightly even here in the shade. Daniel wished he could find the words to tell her how pretty she was.

But as usual, the words would not come. Frustration finally grew in him to an unbearable point, and he leaned over, placed the water pitcher on the ground, and reached out for her. If he could not tell her how he felt, he could at least show her.

Roxanne did not look surprised as his hands rested

on her shoulders and gently urged her toward him. She did not resist. Daniel kissed her, not pulling her into a tight embrace but rather just holding her close to him as his lips found hers. Roxanne was the one who slid her arms around his waist and let her body press against his.

Daniel ended the kiss, looked into her green eyes, and whispered, "I love you." He expected to hear the same words back from her. He thought he could read them in her eyes.

But before she could say anything, there was a crashing of brush nearby. Roxanne stepped back quickly, putting some distance between them. Murdoch emerged from the woods, and his lean cheeks had deep trenches of emotion in them as he regarded the two younger people.

"There's trouble coming," he said. "Bad trouble."

Daniel stiffened, his passion forgotten. "What is it?" he asked tautly.

"Lemuel was in Concord a while ago, and he heard a rumor tha's come up from Boston Town. Seems tha' General Gage be thinking about marching up here wi' his army t'capture or destroy all the powder and cannon he kin find." Daniel and Roxanne exchanged a grim glance.

As opposition to the British grew throughout the countryside, the colonists had begun to gather up their arms and cache them for the coming conflict. A large amount of munitions was stored in the area of Concord and Lexington. Cannon, cannon balls, kegs of powder, crates of musket balls—all these were hidden near here. Considering what had happened to the British munitions in Boston, General Gage would probably deem it entirely fitting and proper to strike a similar blow against the colonists.

"This is just a rumor, you said?" Roxanne asked.

"Aye, but a strong one. Lemuel said it came direct from the Committee o' Safety."

"That is bad," Daniel said. "But did you ever consider how Gage found out about the guns stored around here?"

"The answer to that is simple," Roxanne said in a cold, angry voice. "The British have their spies, just as we have ours. Remember, they knew you were working for the patriots."

Daniel had not forgotten, nor was he likely to. Somewhere in the inner circle of rebel leaders, there had to be a traitor. Nothing had happened to change his mind about Benjamin Church. He still seemed the most likely suspect. But Daniel had no proof of Church's complicity. The good doctor had covered his trail well.

Murdoch was not finished with his news. "Lem said a fella named Colonel Barrett wants all the Minutemen t' go into Concord and get ready t' turn the British back if they get this far. They'll be doing the same over in Lexington, Lem says." The frontiersman grinned. "Dinna know about ye, Dan'l, but I be itching for some action again. I be no Minuteman, but I figgered I'd go on into the village anyway, just t' see what happens."

Without hesitation, Daniel nodded. "I'm with you," he declared. "Lemuel has another extra musket he'll loan me. If he doesn't mind me using it to pot at squirrels, I wager he'll let me have it to shoot redcoats."

Roxanne laid a hand on his arm and began, "Are you sure—"

Daniel turned to face her, and she stopped in midsentence, reading the answer to her unasked question on his face. "We knew this day was coming," he said quietly. "We've known it for a long time."

"Yes. You're right. But . . . please be careful, Daniel."

Murdoch grinned and slapped Daniel on the back, staggering the smaller man a bit. "Faith, lass! Once the tea-swilling, red-coated dandies see a rugged bunch of us bold colonial boys, they'll turn tail and run. Ye wait and see."

Daniel hoped Murdoch's cocksure prediction turned out to be true. He had a feeling it was not going to be that easy, though.

Before this conflict was over, a lot of men would bleed and die—on both sides.

Chapter Seventeen

Daniel and Murdoch walked along the road to Concord with Lemuel Parsons. All three men carried muskets and had cartridge boxes slung over their shoulders. The tall, thin Lemuel looked uneasy but determined. Daniel had an anxious frown on his face, and Murdoch was wearing his predictable grin. If there was to be fighting, it could not come too soon for the big redhead.

"I hope Roxanne is able to keep Quincy from following us," Daniel said. "He was certainly upset when I said he couldn't come along."

"His leg's still too weak to be runnin' around with a bunch of Minutemen," Lemuel said. "My Lottie will help Roxanne if she needs it. I don't reckon we need to worry about the boy taggin' along."

"There'll be fighting aplenty for all of us a'fore this is over," Murdoch put in. His stride was eager, almost jaunty.

"That's not what you said back at the farm," Daniel reminded him. "You said the British would turn tail and run."

"I said tha' for the sake of the lass. I saw the redcoats fight the French and Injuns a few years back. There was a heap they did'na ken about fighting a bunch o' skulking savages, but ye could'na fault their grit. They will'na give up easy."

Daniel nodded gloomily. "That's exactly what I thought."

It was late afternoon, and as the shadows grew longer and the light took on the faint red haziness of approaching dusk, Daniel saw other men coming across the fields and down the lanes on both sides of the road. The word had gone out, and all over this part of the colony the Minutemen were turning out.

The three patriots crossed the bridge over the Concord River, and then the village itself came into sight, its white-washed houses and church steeple looking picturesquely beautiful in the midst of the woods and fields. The only thing that ruined the scene were the armed men streaming into Concord from all directions.

Daniel, Murdoch, and Lemuel walked up to the green in the center of the village, and Lemuel called out to a well-dressed man who appeared to Daniel to be a successful farmer. "Colonel Barrett!" Lemuel said. "Got some more men for you."

"We're liable to need every man we can get," the leader of the militia said as he turned to face the three new-comers. He shook hands with Daniel and Murdoch and went on, "I'm Colonel James Barrett. I own the farm right next to Lem's place."

Daniel had noticed the well-kept farm, and he knew his initial estimate of Colonel Barrett was correct. "We'll do anything we can to help, Colonel," he said. "Just let us know what you want done, and we'll do our best."

"For now, all any of us can do is wait," Barrett replied. "We have people keeping an eye on the situation in Boston, and as soon as the troops move out, riders will let us know if the British are marching by land over the Neck or crossing the Charles in boats."

"We've heard they're after the munitions stored around here," Daniel said.

"That's what we think," Barrett agreed. "There's a sizable cache on my farm, if that's what they're after. But we'll stop 'em before they get there, I'm thinking."

Daniel hoped so. If the patriots were to become badly outgunned, there would be no way they could ever stand up to the British.

That was the beginning of a long night. Several hundred members of the militia had gathered in town, and many of them sat or lay on the green, conserving their energy for the battle they knew was coming. Others visited the tavern adjacent to the large clearing. As Colonel Barrett had said, there was nothing to do but wait.

Daniel, Murdoch, and Lemuel settled down with their backs against the thick trunk of a large tree. Lemuel dozed off as night settled over the village, but Daniel felt as if he might never sleep again. His eyes were wide open, and his heart was thudding. He knew in his bones that the showdown between the British and the colonials had finally come.

"I've been thinking about something," he said suddenly to Murdoch, keeping his voice down so as not to disturb Lemuel. "This afternoon, when you came looking for me, you made an awful lot of noise for someone who moves as silently through the woods as you usually do."

Murdoch chuckled. "I saw Roxanne taking some water to ye, an' I thought it might be a good idea not t'come up on the two o' ye unannounced, as it were."

"You saw us kissing, didn't you?"

"What does it matter if I did?" Murdoch asked with a shrug of his massive shoulders. "I think ye be a fine man, Daniel Reed, and th' cousin o' mine be a right smart lass. I dinna think either one o' ye could do a bit better."

"Thanks, Murdoch," Daniel said softly. "I just hope I get back to her all right."

"Ye will. I'll see t'tha'."

Daniel had to laugh at the frontiersman's confidence, which was every bit as big as his powerful frame.

To Daniel's surprise, he did nod off after a time. A sound sleep stole over him, and when he woke again, he was alone. His muscles were stiff from sleeping on the hard-packed earth under the tree, but he forced himself to sit up, open his eyes, and look around.

There was a glow in the sky to the east, the light of an approaching dawn. It was the morning of April 19, 1775.

The lamps were all lit in the nearby tavern, which had remained open all night. Men still wandered in and out of the place, and as Daniel climbed to his feet, he saw Murdoch and Lemuel emerge from the building. Murdoch was chewing on a turkey leg and held a tankard of ale in his other hand. Lemuel sipped from a cup of hot buttered rum. Despite the early hour, it did not strike Daniel as incongruous that the men were drinking; many of these patriots had been up all night and needed something to fortify them.

"Mornin', lad," Murdoch called to Daniel. "We dinna want t'wake ye up when we went t'get a bite to eat. Be ye hungry?"

Daniel nodded, realizing that he was more than hungry. He was ravenous.

"C'mon inside," said Murdoch, holding up the turkey leg. "We'll get ye one o' these."

"I'm going to take a look around," Lemuel said. "I'll see the two of you later."

Daniel nodded to the farmer and followed Murdoch into the tavern. The owner and his family looked haggard and exhausted, having been up all night serving the Minutemen, but he refused to take any payment for the turkey leg he handed to Daniel. "I'm a patriot, same as th' rest o' ye," he insisted. "Got to do me part."

Daniel thanked him, accepted some hot buttered rum as well, and then strolled back outside with Murdoch. The sky was much lighter now, and the sun would be up soon. An early morning chill was in the air, but that would fade away quickly once the sun rose. They walked across the green, the dew on the grass wetting their boots.

Colonel Barrett was sending out patrols to check the surrounding area. Nothing had been heard from Lexington or Boston, and the look on the colonel's face was a mixture of worry and hope. Perhaps the British army had not marched after all.

With a full belly and the stiffness worked out of his muscles, Daniel felt considerably better. His nerves were still on edge from waiting, but he could cope with that. Murdoch was getting impatient, however. He leaned his musket against a tree, doubled up one knobby fist, and smacked it into the palm of his other hand.

"If they be coming, why dinna they come on?" he growled.

As if in answer to his words, the sound of a horse's hooves drumming on the Lexington road came to their ears. Like everyone else on the green, Daniel and Murdoch swung around sharply to see what was about to happen. A lone rider came into view, galloping toward the village.

"That's Doctor Prescott, from Lexington," someone cried, recognizing the horseman. Colonel Barrett led the move forward to greet the new arrival.

Prescott reined in his horse, which was lathered from a long hard ride. "What is it, Samuel?" Barrett asked as he reached up to help the doctor down from the saddle. The young physician looked almost as tired as his horse.

"The regulars are out, just as we thought they'd be," Prescott replied. Daniel and Murdoch were close enough in the crowd to hear every word, especially since the Minutemen had fallen silent in anxious anticipation of the doctor's report. "Paul Revere and Billy Dawes came out from Boston to warn us. Colonel Revere rowed across the Charles right under the nose of the *Somerset*!"

Daniel knew from what he had heard in recent days that the British warship was patrolling the Charles River basin regularly to keep Boston cut off. He could easily imagine Paul Revere being daring enough to slip past the vessel, though.

Prescott gulped down a couple of breaths, then went on, "The troops came across the river, too, then started marching toward Lexington. They didn't get there until a little while ago."

"What happened?" Barrett snapped.

"Colonel Parker and a couple of hundred Minutemen met them on the green. The British came up and just looked at them, and I . . . I thought for a moment they might pull back." The doctor took another deep breath and a shudder ran through him. "Then someone fired a shot. I don't know who. Maybe one of us, maybe one of the soldiers. But the British opened up on our boys. They fired two volleys."

A rumble of anger ran through the crowd. All of them had been expecting armed warfare to erupt sooner or later, but knowing something would happen was different from hearing an eyewitness describe it.

"Eight of our men were killed," Prescott said solemnly. "Another dozen or so were wounded. I have no idea what the British losses are. We were forced to pull back and let them through. There was no other choice. The only good news is that Adams and Hancock got out of town before the British arrived. I'd been spreading the word with Revere and Dawes earlier, so when it was over, I grabbed my horse and came here to warn you. There's eight hundred or a thousand of them, Colonel. You can't stand up to them."

"There's that many of us," Barrett said stubbornly. "And I don't like the idea of backing down from a bunch of tyrants."

A cheer of agreement went up from the assembled men.

"Well, you can't meet them here," Prescott insisted. "Out in the open like this, the fire of the regulars would cut your men to ribbons."

Barrett nodded, a frown of deep thought on his face.

"If my memory be sound," Murdoch spoke up, "the British had a hell of a time fighting the savages during tha' French an' Injun war a few years back. Seems to me we could—"

"Of course we could!" Barrett exclaimed, his mind leaping ahead to Murdoch's idea. He began to nod, as did all the men within hearing of the big frontiersman.

Barrett lifted his voice to address the whole gathering

and went on, "We'll pull back, men! Form up into your companies, and head for the north bridge!"

Quickly, the Minutemen positioned themselves in ragged lines. Daniel and Murdoch found Lemuel again and joined the same group. A couple of mounted officers whom Lemuel identified as Dave Brown and Amos Barrett, the commander's cousin, got the men into some semblance of order and then sent them marching out of town on the road that led over the Concord River.

Daniel's heart was pounding in his chest. He had struck blows against the British before this morning, and he had risked his life in doing so. But something about this business of battle was especially nerve-racking. In the things he had done before, there had been the chance of death, yes, but there had also been the chance that he would succeed without anyone's losing his life. Today, that was not true. Today, men would die. It was as certain as the rising of the sun.

As the patriots pulled out of Concord, the sound of church bells ringing came faintly to their ears. That would be their friends and brothers in Lexington, warning them that the British were on the way.

It did not take long to reach the river bridge and march over its arched wooden span. The Concord was not a large river; in fact, it was little more than a brook at this point. When the colonial forces were all north of the stream, Captain Barrett and the other officers gave them the order to spread out into the gently rolling hills on either side of the road. The hills were dotted with clumps of trees and criss-crossed by low stone walls. As Daniel watched the patriots concealing themselves in those trees and behind those walls, he thought that an army *could* hide itself here. Then he caught himself and realized how foolish that thought was. An army *was* hiding itself here.

"I want you men to stay on the road," Captain Barrett called, pointing at the group that included Daniel and Murdoch. "I need you for a job."

One of the farmers doffed his floppy-brimmed hat and shook it in the air. "Whatever 'tis ye want, Cap'n, we're the boys t'do it for ya!" His companions shouted out their agreement.

Barrett grinned a little as he regarded the grim-faced men, most of whom had been planters and harvesters all their lives. Now, for the first time, many were about to take up arms to oppose the might of the strongest military nation in the world. No one could have blamed them for wishing they were somewhere else. But if that thought was going through anyone's head, he never voiced it.

"The British will come through the village," Barrett said quietly to them. There was no need for shouting or blustering now. "They won't find what they want there, because most of the munitions have been cached on my farm. So they'll head for there, too, considering they've got better information about us than we sometimes do. I reckon we can stop 'em right here."

That sounded good to Daniel. No use letting the redcoats advance any farther than was necessary—or unavoidable.

"I want you to march back toward Concord," Barrett went on. "We have to give the British a show of force to draw them on. If they think there's only a handful of us, they'll get overconfident."

Looking around at the men remaining in the road, Daniel could follow the colonel's logic. Scarcely a hundred men were left here; the rest were out of sight, hidden in the hills above the road. For a change, it would be the British walking into a snare.

Daniel felt a strange calm stealing over him. His heart-beat slowed to its normal rate, and the fear that had been lurking in the back of his mind went away. What he felt now was a sense of relief that the worst—whatever it might be—would soon be over. When he glanced at Murdoch, he could tell the big man felt the same way.

The Minutemen turned toward Concord and straightened up their ranks. Even though all of them were volunteers, when they met the British, they wanted to look like real soldiers. A young fifer and a drummer boy, sons no doubt of one of the men in the group, took their places at the forefront. They began playing a martial air Daniel recognized as "The White Cockade," and marching raggedly to its tune, the men started toward Concord.

As they topped a hill, they could see down across the river into the village, and for an instant, the blood froze in the veins of every man there, even big Murdoch's. The British troops had reached Concord and swept on through the nearly deserted settlement. The road was like a sea of red from the coats of the soldiers. The route of march extended almost all the way to the bridge.

The fifer and the drummer boy stepped up the pace of their music. As he marched near the head of the rebel column, Daniel looked down at the enemy and sensed somehow what they should do. The bridge—that was the place to meet the British! On the narrow, arching span, they would be unable to advance in full force. They could be stopped at the bridge.

The colonists marched on, quicker now but still under control. As the road neared the bridge, it flattened out on both sides of the stream. Over the planks of the bridge, Daniel could see the tall black hats of the soldiers drawing near.

Suddenly, Murdoch Buchanan let out a whoop that shattered the tension in the air. He surged forward, lifting the musket in his hands. The British troops were just as tense, and they fired the first shots as they, too, charged toward the bridge.

The fifer and the drummer boy got out of the way in a hurry as the Minutemen attacked. All the rage and frustration of the past few years came out of their throats in a hoarse shout that seemed to shake the earth. Suicidally, they charged into the teeth of the British.

The redcoats reached the bridge first, their boots thudding hollowly against its surface. There had been some scattered firing on both sides, but now the first real damage of the battle was done. Muskets blasted from the hills overlooking the stream, and suddenly several men in the front of the British charge staggered and went down, tripping up some of their fellows.

Daniel threw his musket to his shoulder, sighted on the mass of red clogging the bridge, and fired. No sooner had the butt of the weapon kicked against his shoulder than he began shouting, "Peel off! Peel off!"

Some of the men heard him and veered away from the road, and others followed their lead. The trap had been sprung when the British surged onto the bridge, and now Daniel and his companions had to get out of the line of fire.

As Daniel angled off the road to the right, out of the corner of his eye, he saw that Murdoch was still heading straight toward the redcoats. Daniel slid to a halt and cried, "Murdoch! No!"

The frontiersman ignored him. Murdoch fired his musket from the hip, then tossed it aside and yanked the brace of pistols from his belt. He stopped, raised the guns, and triggered both of them. Smoke and flame erupted from their barrels.

Daniel started toward him but stopped as Murdoch wheeled away from the British. The battle frenzy had gotten the best of him for a moment, but now he was doing the smart thing.

Lead continued to rain down on the British. Several of them had toppled off the bridge to land in the stream below, their blood mixing with the waters of the Concord. This army of Grenadiers, Fusilliers, and Light Infantrymen had no way of striking back at their enemy this time. The shots seemed to come from everywhere, and all the British could do in response was fire blindly into the hills.

This was a new kind of warfare, a style of fighting these troops had encountered only once before, and their commanders had obviously learned little from the French and Indian War. The British stood their ground for long moments, staying in the open where the colonists could take potshots at will.

In the meantime, Daniel raced toward one of the low stone walls that lined the fields. When he reached it, he vaulted over the barrier and threw himself full-length behind its shelter. It was awkward reloading in such a position, but he reached for his cartridge box and began the process.

A few moments later, another body sailed over the wall, and Murdoch dropped to the ground beside Daniel, a huge grin on his face. "Did ye see me, lad?" he asked. "The lobsterbacks must've thought me a madman!"

"They weren't the only ones," Daniel muttered, concentrating on tamping down the ball and wadding in the musket's barrel. Satisfied that the load was seated well enough, he asked Murdoch, "What were you trying to do?"

"Keep 'em busy until our boys had a chance t'get a couple'o more volleys in them," replied the Scot.

"Well, you did that." Daniel lifted himself on his knees, poked the barrel of the musket over the wall, and sighted hurriedly on the British column that was still bottlenecked at the bridge. He fired and then ducked down without waiting to see if his shot had struck home. With the haze of smoke and dust that now filled the air, he probably could not have seen the results anyway, he thought.

Besides the powder smoke, the air was thick with the sound of gunshots and the awful cries of dying men. The patriot attack was taking a fearsome toll on the British, and as Daniel reloaded again, a triumphant cry rose from the hills, issuing from the throats of hundreds of men. Daniel lifted his head and looked over the wall just in time to see the redcoats break ranks and flee wildly back toward Concord.

"They're on the run!" Daniel shouted.

Murdoch had his pistols reloaded. "I'll be speeding them up a mite," he said, then sprang to his feet, leapt over the wall, and set off in pursuit of the British.

"Dammit, Murdoch—" Daniel bit off the exclamation and vaulted over the wall to run after him. There was nothing else he could do. Besides, with the British retreating toward the village, men were appearing from their cover all over the hills and racing after the redcoats.

The British soldiers had been pulling cannon with them, and while some of the heavy guns had been abandoned, others were still being wrestled along by the men in charge of them. Murdoch sprinted toward one such group of redcoats, and when they saw him coming, they dropped the small wheeled cart that held the cannon and grabbed for their muskets. Murdoch was on them like a whirlwind, firing both pistols and dropping two of the soldiers. He tucked the guns away, ducked aside from a musket blast, and wrenched the empty weapon out of its owner's hands. Flailing around him with the Brown Bess, Murdoch splintered its butt on the head of one man, crushing the soldier's skull in the process, then smashed the breech of the weapon across the face of another man. That redcoat went down with a broken nose and jaw, a flood of crimson covering the lower half of his face. Wielding the shattered musket in one hand now, Murdoch used it to knock aside the Brown Bess held by his remaining opponent. Then he jerked his hunting knife from its sheath and plunged the blade into the soldier's chest. Ripping free the bloodstained knife, Murdoch whirled around looking for someone else to fight.

The battle was moving back toward the village of Concord, though, and as Daniel passed Murdoch, he shouted, "Come on!"

That was the beginning of the bloodiest, most brutal fighting any of the men on either side had seen. For the next several hours, as the British officers tried to rally their troops and form them into an orderly retreat toward Boston, they were harried every step of the way by colonists firing on them from behind trees, rocks, buildings, and any other bit of cover they could find. It was a wholesale slaughter, with the British losing five men for every one of the patriots they managed to down. Concord and then Lexington were left behind as the rout continued. Their spirits broken, the British now wanted only to get back to Boston.

Daniel and Murdoch were in the thick of the melee, firing, reloading, dashing from one tree or rock to the next. Daniel had forgotten what peace and quiet were like. It was as if his ears had been assaulted by the crash of musket fire all his life, and the stench of burned powder had replaced the sweet smell of clean air. There was nothing left of life now except killing and trying to keep from being killed. Somewhere in the back of his mind still rested the reason for this fighting, but he could no longer think of anything but survival.

Murdoch was right beside him, firing his pistols again and again, seemingly unaware of the burn on the back of his right hand where a musket ball had grazed him or the trickle of blood on his cheek where a stone splinter from one of the walls had gashed him after being knocked loose by a shot. So far, Daniel was unscathed, although he had heard the noise of countless balls passing close to his ears. If he considered it a miracle that he was unharmed, he gave no sign of it. There was no time for thoughts like that, either.

The men who had stood up to the British in Lexington early that morning had reformed after being driven off, and they joined in harassing the frantic retreat of the soldiers. Others who had turned out too late to confront the British when they marched through on their way to Lexington had a chance now to strike a blow of their own. The road to Cambridge was lined with Minutemen, all of them armed. If the British had expected things to get any easier once they left Lexington behind, they were sadly mistaken.

Finally, Daniel could go on no longer. He dropped to the ground, exhausted, and leaned against the trunk of a tree. Laying the borrowed musket beside him, he let his head droop loosely onto his chest and dragged great breaths of air deeply into his lungs. He became aware that his heart was racing. His eyes stung and watered from the smoke, and his throat was raw from breathing it.

Noticing that Daniel was no longer with him, Murdoch turned and ran back to him, kneeling beside the younger man. "Daniel!" he said urgently. "Are ye all right?"

Wearily, Daniel raised his head and looked up at him. "I'm not hurt," he said hoarsely. "I just can't go on anymore."

Murdoch sat cross-legged beside the tree. "Aye," he agreed, lifting a big hand to wipe sweat from his brow and leaving streaks on his powder-grimed skin. "The battle be moving on, but I reckon it can move on without us. We've done our share, lad."

Daniel knew that Murdoch would prefer to keep going, to continue harrying the British, but out of a sense of friendship and duty, the frontiersman was going to stay with him. For a second, Daniel thought about telling him to go on, then decided against it. As Murdoch had said, they had done their share, both of them. And there would be plenty of fighting in the future, that was certain. The British had lost dozens, perhaps hundreds of men, and they would never forgive that. Nor would the patriots forget the friends and relatives killed by the British. The effects of this day's fighting would ripple through the colonies like waves on a pond. The war was no longer coming—it was here.

The war for American independence had finally begun.

Chapter Eighteen

It was late afternoon when Daniel and Murdoch trudged up to the farm of Lemuel Parsons. Someone inside must have been watching for them, because the door of the farmhouse opened with a bang and Roxanne raced out, her long red hair streaming behind her. She ran into Daniel's arms and buried her face against his chest. She was not crying, but he could feel great shudders of emotion running through her body as he tightened his embrace around her and buried his head in the soft curve of her neck.

Quincy limped out onto the porch, followed by Lemuel, Lottie, and the Parsons children. Lemuel had a bloodstained bandage wrapped around his upper right arm. A wave of relief went through Daniel at the sight of the farmer. He and Murdoch had lost track of Lemuel, then searched for him with no success after leaving the battle. Lemuel had become a friend, and Daniel was glad to know he was not lying dead somewhere in a ditch on the road between Lexington and Concord.

"Daniel! Murdoch!" cried Quincy. He stepped down from the porch and hurried toward them. He hugged the big Scot, then traded places with Roxanne as brother embraced brother and cousin embraced cousin.

Lemuel walked up and shook hands with Daniel. "Glad to see you're back, son," he said fervently. "I was afraid the British had done in both of you."

"Not hardly," grunted Murdoch.

"How goes the battle?" Lemuel gestured at his wounded arm. "I took a ball from a Brown Bess and couldn't keep fightin', more's the pity."

"The battle's probably over," Daniel said. "When we saw them last, the British were still pulling back toward Boston, and they should be there by now. What's left of them, anyway."

"It was bad, wasn't it?" Roxanne said. "From what Lemuel told us, a lot of men were killed."

"Over two hundred of the British. That's what we've heard from men while we were walking back here," Daniel replied. He shook his head. "I don't know about our side."

Roxanne looked up at Murdoch's face and saw the blood still oozing from the cut on his cheek. "That wound needs to be cleaned," she said firmly. "Come inside, both of you."

Murdoch started to protest that it was only a scratch, but Daniel caught his eye and nodded. It would probably make Roxanne feel better to be doing something right now, he thought. Murdoch grinned a little sheepishly and said, "Aye, lagss, that'd be fine."

Quincy fell in step beside Murdoch as Roxanne led him into the house. "You've got to tell me about it," the youngster said eagerly. "I want to hear all about the fighting."

"It was a savage encounter, lad, full o' blood and sudden death. Ye've never seen the likes of it, and ye can be thankful for that. It started wi' us charging the bloody lobster-backs . . ."

Daniel let his thoughts drift away as Murdoch was taken into the house by Quincy and Roxanne, colorfully relating the details of the battle as he went. Murdoch had been in his element there, but it had not been the same for Daniel. He believed in the cause for which he had fought, believed in it passionately.

But he had seen carnage today unlike anything he had ever imagined. It was going to take some time before he could put everything into perspective.

"Bad, wasn't it?" Lemuel said quietly, when only he and Daniel were left outside.

Daniel nodded. "Bad enough."

"It'll get worse, you know."

"That's what I'm afraid of." Daniel took a deep breath. "But we have to believe the goal is worth the struggle, don't we? Otherwise, we couldn't carry on."

"It is worth it," Lemuel said, his voice tired but confident. "You're a young man, Daniel, and there's a lot you don't know about the world yet. No offense meant by that, either. But when you get older, you'll understand. Freedom for you and the folks you love . . . Hell, that's worth nearly any price in the world, son."

Daniel managed a weary grin. "I think you're right, Lemuel," he said, feeling a little better now. "Let's go inside."

As they entered the house, Daniel heard Quincy saying

excitedly, "I'll be there next time. When the next battle comes, I'm going to be right in the thick of it!"

Those words shattered what little good mood Daniel had built up. The fervor in Quincy's voice was obvious, and Daniel knew there was no way he could keep his brother away from the fighting. As Lemuel had said, the battle with the British was worth the price, but Daniel had seen enough bloodshed and death today to wish with all his heart that there was some other way to secure liberty for the colonies.

Roxanne glanced up from the table, where she was sitting on a bench next to Murdoch and cleaning the deep cut on his cheek. In her eyes, Daniel read the same wish. Both of them were all too aware that along with love and hope, the days to come could also bring suffering and death. . . .

The sound of hoofbeats on the path outside brought Daniel to the open doorway of the Parsons house, musket held ready in his hands. Two days had passed since the battles of Lexington and Concord, and during that time, everyone on the farm had remained alert for more trouble.

Astride a fine chestnut mare, Elliot Markham rode up to the farmhouse and grinned at his surprised cousin.

"Good morning," Elliot said as he swung down from the saddle. He stepped up onto the porch and tightly gripped Daniel's hand. "I heard that you were alive, but I had to see for myself."

"I wasn't hurt in the battle, if that's what you mean," Daniel told him. "Lord, it's good to see you, Elliot! But how did you know we were here?"

"Dr. Warren told me. He knew because of the messages Roxanne has passed back to the Committee of Safety."

That surprised Daniel even more. "You've been in touch with the committee?"

Elliot's grin widened, and he said, "Meet the patriots' newest full-fledged spy."

Roxanne stepped out of the house in time to hear his statement, and she exclaimed, "Elliot! What are you doing here?"

The young man's eyes had been twinkling, an indication that he still regarded this whole thing as something of an adventure, but his expression and demeanor became more solemn as he said, "I've come to take you back to Boston, Roxanne. And to tell you, Daniel, that you and Quincy and that big redheaded brawler had best leave this part of the country behind you."

"What are you talking about?" Daniel demanded, but before Elliot could answer, Quincy stepped out of the house and there was another round of enthusiastic greetings. Murdoch was right behind him.

After Elliot and Murdoch had been properly introduced, Elliot went on, "Boston is closed up tighter than a drum after what happened the other day. General Gage is furious, and he won't rest until he's smashed this rebellion. The only reason I was able to get out of the city today is that I'm the son of one of Gage's strongest supporters." Elliot's mouth twisted a little, as if the words held a bitter taste.

"You said you're working with the committee now?" Daniel asked.

Elliot nodded. "That's right. I wanted to get out of town and join a Minuteman company, but I talked to the committee first, and they persuaded me otherwise. They knew of my connection with the four of you, of course, and I suppose they decided to trust me—for a while, anyway. According to them, my access to the Tories is going to be indispensible. I don't like it, but I see their point. Roxanne, you'll be my contact, just as you were for Daniel."

Sliding an arm around Roxanne's shoulders, Daniel said quickly, "Are you sure it's safe for Roxanne to go back to Boston? After all, she helped Quincy and me escape from prison."

With a humorless chuckle, Elliot replied, "The British have more important things on their minds now than some jailbreak, boys. They took a bad beating, and they don't like it. Mind you, I'm not saying that you and Quincy can go back. You can't; it would be much too dangerous for both of you. I'm afraid Harvard and the Latin School will have to wait until this war is over before resuming the education of the Reed brothers. And, Daniel, I took the liberty of writing to your parents and explaining what happened. I was afraid to put too many details in the letter, lest it be intercepted by the British. I said you were both well and would contact them when you were able to."

"Thank you, Elliot. And what about Quincy and me?" he asked. "Does the committee have anything in mind for us?"

Crossing his arms on his chest and leaning casually against the railing along the front of the porch, Elliot said, "As a matter of fact, they do have an assignment for you." He glanced at Murdoch. "I think this job will interest you, too, Mr. Buchanan." Turning his gaze back to Daniel, Elliot continued, "The committee wants you to go to New York."

"New York?" echoed Daniel, surprised.

"That's right. Colonel Ethan Allen of the Vermont militia is preparing to march on the British fort at Lake Champlain. Ticonderoga, I think it's called. The committee members want you to accompany Allen and report back to them once the campaign is over."

Daniel nodded slowly, trying to digest this news. Murdoch and Quincy were more enthusiastic. The big frontiersman said, "Ethan Allen, eh? I've heard o' him and his militia. Calls them the Green Mountain Boys. Supposed to be a rugged bunch o' lads. Wouldn't mind seeing how they handle themselves."

"It sounds like a good idea to me, too," Quincy added. "My leg is in good enough shape to ride now, even if you wouldn't let me go to Concord the other day, Daniel."

They could not turn down the assignment, Daniel knew. Quietly, he said to Elliot, "Tell the committee we'll leave as soon as possible. But be careful, Elliot. I am convinced one of the members is a traitor to our cause. I will not name him until I can prove my suspicions."

"I agree," Elliot said. "And you can be sure I'll step lightly around them and keep my eyes open." He rubbed his hands together. "Now, it's a long and dusty ride from Boston. Would there happen to be any ale or rum around here to quench a man's thirst before he starts back?"

Murdoch laughed boomingly and looped an arm around Elliot's shoulders. "For a city boy, ye ain't too bad a sort, Elliot," he said, leading the young man into the house. Quincy went with them.

That left Daniel and Roxanne alone on the porch. Facing her, he murmured, "I don't like leaving you. And I don't like your going back to Boston, either."

"Neither of us has a choice," Roxanne told him quietly. "We have to go where we can do the most good for the cause of liberty."

"In other words . . . love has to wait."

She smiled sadly. "I'm afraid so."

Daniel drew her into his arms, then felt the wet warmth of her tears falling on his shirt as she rested her head on his shoulder. He stroked the long red hair and whispered,

"Someday this will all be over, and then we can have time for ourselves. I pray to God it's someday soon."

But until then, he knew, other things had to come first. First, the sons and daughters of liberty—young and old, rich and poor, frontiersmen and city dwellers alike—all of them had to see to building a new nation.

A new nation and a better life for themselves . . . and for all the generations to come.

Author's Note

Any novelist who writes a book mixing fictional characters and situations with the actual details of history is of necessity writing what has come to be known as "alternate history." *PATRIOTS* is an example of this, and while a great effort has been made to insure that the background of this novel is accurate, mistakes are always possible. In addition, certain minor details of history have been altered slightly for dramatic purposes. And history itself is full of inconsistencies, even events as written about and important as the beginnings of the American Revolution.

The author would like to thank Greg Tobin of Bantam Books and the people of Book Creations Inc.—Marla Engel and George Engel, Paul Block, Judy Stockmayer, and Pamela Lappies—for making this novel not only a possibility but a reality. Thanks also to Harold Reasoner, whose technical assistance made it possible to finish the manuscript on time. The biggest thank-you of all goes to L.J. Washburn, whose inspiration and assistance is unending and greatly appreciated.

And thanks to you, too, Skeeter—even though you'll never read this book.

ABOUT THE AUTHOR

"ADAM RUTLEDGE" is one of the pseudonyms of veteran author James M. Reasoner, who has written over sixty books ranging from historical sagas and Westerns to mysteries and adventure novels. Reasoner considers himself first and foremost a storyteller and enjoys spinning yarns based on the history of the United States, from colonial days to the passing of the era known as the Old West. He lives in Azle, Texas, with his wife, Livia, and daughters Shayna and Joanna.

PATRIOTS Volume II:

REBEL GUNS

by Adam Rutledge

"The shot heard 'round the world" has been fired. England and her colonies stand poised on the brink of a bloody war that will bring change to the four corners of the earth.

Caught up in the drama of this historical conflagration, brothers Daniel and Quincy Reed, along with their frontiersman friend Murdoch Buchanan, find themselves allied with Colonel Ethan Allen and his Green Mountain Boys. Their mission, vital to the rebel cause—the capture of Fort Ticonderoga, the British stronghold on Lake Champlain.

In Boston, patriot spies Roxanne Darragh and Elliot Markham become embroiled in a plot to capture a shipment of British munitions and place them in the hands of the insurrectionists. But will an unexpected passion jeopardize not only their mission but also their lives?

Meanwhile, England's most highly placed secret agent continues his shadowy double dealings that may spell defeat for the young revolution.

As the confrontation at Fort Ticonderoga looms, Daniel, Quincy, and Murdoch are caught up in a scheme involving murder, deceit, stolen guns, and a lovely, mysterious blonde. Will they survive this labyrinth of passion and betrayal, or for them will the war be over almost before it begins?

For more of this exciting adventure turn the page for a sample of REBEL GUNS, Volume II of the PATRIOTS Series, on sale September 1992 wherever Bantam paperbacks are sold.

Daniel Reed took his time checking the cinches on his saddle. His younger brother, Quincy, might be in a hurry to leave the Parsons's farm, but Daniel was not, even though their saddlebags were well stocked with provisions and their long rifles and flintlock pistols were loaded. There was nothing left to do now but ride away.

"Are we going or not?" Quincy asked impatiently.

"We're going," Daniel said heavily. "Come on. Mount up."

Gripping the reins too tightly, he swung up into the saddle. If nobody else was going to say anything about Roxanne, he would be damned if he was going to. He had thought she would come out to say good-bye to them . . . to him . . . but if she didn't want to, that was fine. He wasn't going to wait around all day.

There had been no argument between them about Daniel's going; he had direct orders from the Committee of Safety to meet up with Ethan Allen's Green Mountain Boys and join in the expedition to take Fort Ticonderoga, on the southern shore of Lake Champlain. And Roxanne Darragh understood because she was as passionately devoted as Daniel to the cause of liberty and had risked her life more than once in pursuit of freedom for the colonies. But this morning the young man she loved was leaving, and the future was too uncertain.

With bittersweet melancholy flooding through him, Daniel heeled his big bay into motion and slowly rode away from the barn and around the farmhouse toward the lane that led to Concord. Quincy and Roxanne's cousin, Murdoch Buchanan, rode right behind him.

Daniel was less than ten yards past the house when the front door banged open and a voice called, "Wait!"

Reining in sharply, Daniel turned in the saddle to watch Roxanne hesitantly walk out onto the porch and come down the steps to the ground. She stood there, her beautiful green eyes leveled at Daniel. The morning breeze plucked idly at the long red hair framing her face.

Daniel slid down from his horse and walked toward Roxanne. He looked deep into her eyes before he reached up and gently rested his hands on her shoulders. She leaned into him, and his mouth came down on hers, their lips brushing in a soft, warm kiss that quickly became more demanding. Daniel dropped his arms around her waist as their mouths expressed their passion. Their bodies came together with a wanting that so far had been denied.

Breaking the kiss, Roxanne rested her head on Daniel's chest. He stroked her hair, his senses full of its fragrance and feel. The warmth of her breath in the open throat of his shirt made him shiver.

"I'll be back," he whispered in her ear.

"I know." Her voice was husky but still strong and firm.

"Will you be here?"

"I don't know, Daniel. I'll be wherever the revolution needs me."

"I was afraid you weren't going to say good-bye," he said quietly.

Her tongue moistened her lips. "I didn't know whether to say anything or not. I didn't . . . didn't want to make things more difficult for you."

He bent his head and kissed her again.

She broke the kiss and trembled in his embrace. "It's

not fair!" she whispered angrily. "I never expected to fall in love!"

"Goin' t' be gettin' warm in a bit, once th' sun's up good an' high," Murdoch said, hinting that they needed to get started.

Fearing he would never be able to leave her, Daniel embraced Roxanne fiercely one more time, released her, turned, and without looking behind him, strode back to his horse. He took the reins from Quincy, stepped up into the saddle, and urged the animal into a trot. Quincy matched the pace. Only Murdoch hung back a little to turn and wave a big hand at those who were left behind.

Roxanne stood in the farmyard, watching until they had disappeared down the lane.

Five days had passed since the three riders had left the farm near Concord. They had ridden nearly the length of Massachusetts Colony and were now angling northwest toward Vermont. This was a rugged, isolated area, and settlement was sparse. The road that Daniel, Quincy, and Murdoch followed was little more than a trail through the woods. The thick forest of pine, ash, and birch reminded Daniel of the Virginia woods he had played in as a boy, and Murdoch was plainly happy to be away from civilization.

"I be tellin' ye, there were times I thought I was goin' t' suffocate in Boston," he said. "I needed t' get back in th' wild, t' breathe some fresh air again."

Daniel admitted that the wooded hills were pretty, and from the heights he could gaze west, across the valley of the Connecticut River, and see the rounded gray upthrust of the Berkshire Mountains.

As he rode, Daniel wondered what it would be like if this war were over and he and Roxanne were together. He could see the two of them coming to a place like this to begin a life of their own: clearing the land, building a cabin, tilling the soil, raising a family. . . . An ironic smile plucked at his mouth. Roxanne would never be happy to be a simple farmer's wife.

"What the devil!" he exclaimed when the sound of gunshots suddenly yanked his thoughts back to the present.

The men reined in, and Murdoch lifted an arm and pointed. "Comin' from over there. Are we goin' t' see what's up?"

"Come on, Daniel," Quincy urged. "Somebody's in trouble!"

"Wha' do we do, Dan'l?"

Damn it, why are they asking me? Daniel thought. I'm no leader.

The decision was taken out of his hands when a rider rounded the bend and came thundering toward them. A dark cloak flowed out behind the figure that bent far forward in the saddle.

"Get out of the way!" Daniel snapped to his companions when the rider urged the horse to greater speed.

Suddenly the advancing horse stumbled. Its front legs tangled with each other and the animal went down hard. As it fell, the rider was thrown from the saddle and landed heavily in the road. The cloaked figure rolled over several times, came to a stop, and lay limply at the feet of Daniel's horse.

The rider's tricorn hat had been knocked off in the fall, and blond curls tumbled around the pale face. Daniel, Quincy, and Murdoch gaped as Quincy exclaimed, "It's a girl!"

And a beautiful one at that, Daniel thought as he stared

down at her. But someone was chasing her, as the sound of rapidly approaching hoofbeats proved.

Daniel darted a glance at the young woman's mount and saw that it was on its feet, moving around skittishly.

"Get rid of her horse, Quincy," Daniel rapped, sliding off his big bay. "Murdoch, give me a hand with her." As he bent to grasp the woman's shoulders he saw the rise and fall of her breasts underneath her white shirt and knew she was still alive.

Murdoch lifted a leg over the back of his horse and jumped quickly to the ground. Two long strides brought him to Daniel's side.

"I'll take her," he said. One arm went under the woman's shoulders, the other under her knees, and he lifted her as if she weighed no more than a kitten. "Ye can get her hat."

"All right," Daniel said. "Hide her in the thicket over there."

The sound of hoofbeats was louder now, although the gunshots had stopped. Down the road, Quincy caught the reins of the woman's horse, pulled it into a fast trot, then slapped his hat against the animal's rump, and the riderless horse leapt forward and galloped out of sight along the trail.

Murdoch emerged from the thicket where he had deposited the woman, then turned to make sure there were no signs remaining of his passage through the brush. Satisfied, he hurried to join Daniel and Quincy. The younger Reed was still mounted, and Daniel and Murdoch hurriedly got up into their saddles and rode leisurely toward the ridge.

Out of the corner of his mouth, Murdoch growled, "I hope ye ken wha' ye be doin'."

"Me, too," said Daniel.

Less than thirty seconds later eight men came riding around the bend in the trail. All of them were brandishing pistols. One man waved the others forward, and they surrounded Daniel, Quincy, and Murdoch.

"Take it easy, Murdoch. We don't know what's going on here yet," Daniel said quietly.

They were rough-looking, burly men with beard stubble on their faces and patches on their clothes. Their weapons appeared well cared for, however.

The leader was dressed in expensive though dust covered clothes. He was well built and handsome, but Daniel did not like the gun in his hand, held with such casual ease.

"Have you seen anything of a blond wench on a chestnut pony?" the leader asked.

Daniel pointed to the south, the direction in which Quincy had chased off the young woman's horse, and said, "Aye. She gave us quite a start, racing past us that way. Nearly trampled right over us. She's going to break her fool neck if she keeps on riding that fast. Who is she?"

The stranger laughed, but it was a harsh, humorless sound. "Fool neck is right, my friend. A fool is exactly what the lady is. As for her identity . . . she is my wife."

As Daniel tried to decide if the man was telling the truth, one of the other pistol-wielding riders sullenly asked the leader, "You believe 'im, guv'nor?"

"No reason not to," the man said. He smiled thinly at Daniel. "You are telling the truth, aren't you?"

"You can look at the tracks in the road if you don't believe me," Daniel said, silently praying his bluff would work. "They'll show that a single horse rode off southeast."

The man gestured sharply with his pistol and said, "Let's go. We've wasted enough time here." He kicked his horse into a run and headed down the road; the others followed closely at his heels.

Daniel heaved a deep sigh of relief, echoed by Quincy. "I thought sure he wasn't going to believe you," the lad said.

"Wha' do ye suppose tha' was all aboot?"

"I don't know," Daniel said, shaking his head and hoping that his impulsive actions had not gotten them in trouble. "But I intend to find out right now."

He turned his horse around, rode a few yards down the trail, dismounted, and stalked over to the thicket where the young woman was hidden. Murdoch and Quincy hung back until they saw what Daniel planned to do.

After that hard fall the girl is probably still unconscious, Daniel thought. Thrusting the underbrush aside, he found himself staring down the barrel of a small but deadly flintlock pistol.

The weapon was held unwaveringly in the hands of the woman, who said sharply, "I don't know who you are, sir, but if you come one step closer, I'll blow your bloody head off!"

For a long moment, Daniel did not say anything as he looked at the gun pointed so steadily at him. His right hand was hanging at his side, and with his leg concealing the movement, he gestured to Murdoch, hoping the frontiersman would catch his meaning. Daniel slowly straightened and said, "You have nothing to fear from me, miss. I mean you no harm."

She watched him intently with the pistol still menacing him. "You're working for him, aren't you?" she demanded.

"Working for whom?"

"For Perry." Her voice caught slightly, as if the name choked her. "For Perry Faulkner."

"I've never even heard of Perry Faulkner," Daniel replied honestly.

His heart gave a little leap when her finger twitched on the trigger, but she eased the pressure before the weapon fired. "Prove it," she snapped.

Daniel had no idea how he could prove he was not working for Perry Faulkner. But the need for proof suddenly vanished when Murdoch Buchanan lunged into the thicket, quickly reached out and closed his fingers over the flintlock of the pistol, and wrenched it away from her, unfired.

Abruptly unarmed, the young woman let out a frightened cry and flung herself away from Murdoch's looming figure. She rolled over agilely, sprang to her feet, and plunged into the brush.

Daniel went after her. Branches tore at his clothes and clawed at his hands and face. Finally he caught her arm, and they jerked to a stumbling stop.

With an angry cry, the woman twisted around and struck at him with her free hand, but Daniel grabbed her wrist and held on tightly, pulling her against him. "Stop it!" he said.

"Let me go, damn you! You've no right—"

"We're the ones who saved you from those men, young woman," Daniel grated, well aware of the warmth of her body as she squirmed in his grasp. "I think that gives us the right to an explanation."

She struggled for a few seconds, then looked at him in bewilderment and asked, "You . . . saved me?"

"That's right. Don't you remember falling off your horse?"

"I . . . I remember the horse stumbling . . . . But after that . . . I don't know."

"There were three riders in the road ahead of you. That was us. Your horse fell and threw you. You were knocked out."

"I was?"

Daniel led her out of the brush, encountering Murdoch and Quincy on the way. The young woman cast a dubious, frightened glance at big Murdoch and looked curiously at Quincy. The four emerged from the bushes and stood in a clearing beside the road.

Letting go of her wrists, he said, "I'm Daniel Reed. This is my brother, Quincy, and this big fellow is Murdoch Buchanan."

"Hello," Quincy said shyly, keeping his eyes on the ground. He was almost overwhelmed by the young woman's beauty.

" 'Tis pleased I be t' meet ye, missy," Murdoch greeted her in his booming voice. "Even if ye did go wavin' a gun aboot."

"I . . . I was afraid," she said, her chin lifting defiantly. "I didn't know who you were. I still don't, for that matter. For all I know, you intended to harm me and perhaps still do."

"If we had meant you any harm, we would have turned you over to that bunch of roughnecks who were chasing you," Daniel pointed out. "The one leading them was the man you mentioned, wasn't he? Perry Faulkner?"

A shudder ran through her. "I don't even like to hear his name. But yes, that was Faulkner. He's been after me for several days now, and he almost caught me."

"Why is he pursuing you?"

She shook her head stubbornly. "That's none of your business. It's enough for you to know that he's an evil man and wants to hurt me. If the three of you are gentlemen, you won't press me for details."

"I would appreciate it if you would at least tell us your name."

For a moment, she did not answer, and Daniel thought she was going to be stubborn about that, too. But then she said quietly, "Cordelia Howard."

"Well, Miss Cordelia Howard . . . It is Miss Howard, isn't it?"

"Of course!" she exclaimed.

"I'm wondering what we're going to do with you."

"Why should you have to do anything with me?" she sniffed. "Just let me get on my horse, and I'll be on my way and no more trouble to you." She looked around, dismayed. "My horse! Where is my horse?"

Quincy answered her. "We . . . ran it off."

"Ran it off! For God's sake, why?"

"As a decoy to throw Faulkner and his men off your trail," Daniel said. "And it worked, too."

"I thought you said you didn't know Faulkner."

"We didn't—then. But I don't think any of us liked him, even without knowing his name or what he was up to. And we certainly didn't want him getting his hands on you until we found out what this was all about." Daniel sighed. "Something we still don't seem to have accomplished."

"But my horse is gone, that's the important thing."

"Your horse is gone," Daniel agreed. "Although we might be able to locate him again with some searching."

Her bottom lip quivered. "How will I get to Saratoga now?"

"Saratoga? That's where you're going?"

She nodded, and her eyes shone with moisture.

"You don't have to cry," he said to her. "We'll take you with us."

Quincy grinned when Daniel announced his decision, but Murdoch just threw his big hands in the air and turned away, muttering to himself.

"Get the horses, Murdoch," Daniel said. "We've already lost enough time." He turned to the young woman and went on, "We're going to Bennington, Miss Howard. That's in Vermont."

"I know where it is," she said petulantly.

"There'll be plenty of people around once we get there, and I'm sure you'll be safe. You can make arrangements to travel from there to Saratoga."

"Thank you, I suppose."

"You're welcome," Daniel said curtly. She would slow them down, but there was nothing else they could do but take her with them.

"You'll ride with Quincy," Daniel decided. "We don't have time to go looking for your horse."

"What?" The exclamation came from Quincy, who immediately blushed crimson.

"All right," Cordelia said brusquely. She looked at Quincy. "Go ahead, mount up."

As his features flushed even more, Quincy swung up into his saddle, then took his left foot out of the stirrup. Cordelia placed her foot in it, grasped Quincy's arm, and lifted herself up behind him, swinging her right leg over the horse's back. Under her long cloak, she wore boots, gray twill pants, and a man's white shirt—efficient riding attire, even if the outfit was a bit scandalous.

Cordelia slipped her arms around Quincy's waist. Her body was pressed against his, and he gulped as he felt the softness of her breasts against his back. The look he shot Daniel was a mixture of fear, excitement, and desperation.

Murdoch mounted up and took the lead. Quincy and Cordelia followed him, and Daniel brought up the rear. He kept an eye on the trail behind them, just in case Perry Faulkner and his men had doubled back.

As night fell the travelers made camp in a clearing screened from the main trail by a thick stand of pine. Murdoch made a small fire, and Quincy heated salt pork and cooked corn cakes over its flame.

Cordelia ate in silence, not looking at her three companions. Finally, once Murdoch had put the fire out, she said angrily, "I'd roll up in my blankets and go to sleep—if I still had any blankets. But they were on my horse, along with everything else I had."

Daniel smiled wearily as he stood up and went to his horse. "I'll give you a blanket."

"Don't trouble yourself, sir. I shall be fine."

Ignoring her caustic tone, Daniel bent to take a blanket from his pack. The three horses had been unsaddled and staked out to graze for the night, and the gear had been piled on the ground on a bed of pine needles fallen the previous winter.

"Here," Daniel said, tossing a rolled-up blanket to Cordelia. The moonlight was bright enough for him to see that she caught it easily. However, in the shadows under the trees on the other side of the camp, Murdoch and Quincy were merely dark shapes in the gloom. The rays of moonlight seemed to find their way through the trees just to illuminate Cordelia.

"Thank you," the young woman said, the words mumbled so softly that Daniel could barely make them out.

Something prodded him to settle himself on the ground beside her. She still did not look at him.

"It seems to me that since you're under our protection, we have a right to know what kind of trouble you're in," Daniel began, determined to get some information from her. "Otherwise we won't know how to help you."

Haughtily, she said, "I'm hardly under your protection. We simply happen to be traveling together because of an unfortunate turn of events."

"Unfortunate?" repeated Daniel. "I'd call it very fortunate, if I were you. If we hadn't been there, Faulkner would have found you unconscious in the road. You'd be in his hands now, instead of sitting here safely with us."

"And you call being in the middle of the wilderness safe? Why, there could be a hundred Indians out there in the darkness, just waiting to murder us!"

"No hostiles 'round here, lass," Murdoch rumbled. " 'Tis farther west they are."

"Well . . . there could be a few of them around," Cordelia insisted.

"That's not the point," Daniel said. "You've admitted that Faulkner is after you. Were his men shooting at you, or merely trying to frighten you?"

"I'm sure I wouldn't know. I had my back turned and was riding away from them, after all."

"Is Faulkner a constable, or some other sort of authority?" he asked abruptly.

"What?" Cordelia sounded shocked. "A constable? You think I'm a criminal, is that it? That's the farthest thing from the truth!"

"Then Faulkner is a criminal."

"I didn't say that, either."

"Ye'll no' be gettin' a straight answer from this one, Dan'l."

"You claim you want to go to Saratoga," Daniel exclaimed, "yet you were riding in the opposite direction."

"I was riding in any direction I could to get away from those men," Cordelia snapped. "If I had escaped from them, I could have circled around and gone back toward Saratoga."

Daniel frowned. He found himself believing Cordelia, even though she had not told him very much.

He sighed and said, "I'm getting tired of arguing with you."

"You're the one who is arguing, Mr. Reed. All I wanted to do was get some sleep. It's been a dreadful day."

"Yes, it certainly has."

Daniel rolled up in his own blankets, but he did not settle down quickly. While Quincy, on guard, rested against a tree trunk, Daniel shifted around restlessly and felt a stirring deep within.

Cordelia was beautiful, but he had left behind an equally beautiful young woman who was intelligent, passionate, and in love with him.

Tonight, more than ever, he missed Roxanne.